THE RAY HUNTERS

Andy Jarvis

Copyright © 2016 Andrew Jarvis
'The Ray Hunters'
First published in 2016 via Lulu Publishing (www.lulu.com)
Andrew Jarvis asserts his moral right to be identified as the author.
No part of this publication may be reproduced, stored in a retrieval system, or transmitted in any form or by any means, electronic, mechanical, photocopying, recording or otherwise without prior written permission from the author.

The following work is fiction, set in the past. Some of the place names are fictional. The name of the fictional market of 'Ancen Medina' is not meant to be confused with the modern day area of Casablanca known as Ancienne Medina. All characters portrayed in this publication are fictional. The two tribal villages in the story are not authentic names of any people of West Africa; these are also fictional so as not to be mistaken for settlements that exist today or in the past. Some of the ethnic names of characters are authentic, others are not. The actions and dialogue of the characters are not meant to be representative of particular persons living today or in the past or generally representative of any individuals or cultures in any locality in the world. All reasonable efforts have been made to ensure that the characters do not resemble actual persons, living or dead. Any similarity is entirely coincidental.

My first thanks go to Vanessa, for her unbiased advice and valuable critique.

Cover image from Fotolia.com. Cover text layout by Sam Jarvis.

With special thanks to Katie, for the surname of the character I have enjoyed creating more than any other: 'Barclay Billington.'

ISBN: 978-1-326-59232-5
9000

He who does not travel does not know the value of men.

-old Moorish proverb

Circa 1830

'What do you see, child?' the old man asked.

The boy knelt down, peering over the edge of the raft into the depths, his eyes strained hard against the sparkle of the setting sun on the ripple of the sea's surface. 'I can see the ray,' said the boy.

'You lie,' said the old man. 'No one can see the ray; he is wise and disguises himself like the sand. But there are still many ways to catch it, child. You can fish and wait all day for nothing, because the ray's wisdom tells him not to take the bait set by the fisher. And you can sink a net early in the morning and lay down to sleep in the sun as I do,' said the old man laughing. 'And as you sleep, you hope for the ray to settle on the net by dusk and then scoop him up quickly before he swims away. But you may end up with nothing, and a young fisher coming back to the tribe after a whole day with nothing will be scorned. So child, how do you choose to catch the ray?'

'I will hunt him,' said the child.

'Good,' said the old man. 'To hunt him is the best way, even though you may never see him on the ocean floor. So look again, child. See the sand rising like dust on the seabed? Very little and faint, the dusting of the sand is not the ray, but it says where it is.'

The boy looked again. 'Yes!' he said excitedly. 'I understand. The dusting of sand is the tail of the ray. So the ray is in front,' He raised his spear but the old man grabbed the hilt as the boy was about to thrust it into the sea.

'No, child,' said the old man. 'You still do not understand. My eyes are not what they have been. Yours are still young and see well, but you still do not see the ray. Look for the sand dust, yes. You see the sand dust, but which way is the ray? Where is the head, in front or back? Or is it left? Perhaps it is anywhere around the sand dust you can see. Wait until the ray moves and watch the trail of sand dust. When it stops then you will know where the ray is. You cannot know now, child. If you throw now you will almost certainly miss. Watch the dusting very carefully and do not let it out of your sight.'

The old man gently flicked the surface of the water with his hand as the boy fixed his eyes on the tell-tale brush of the ray's tail. The ray glided forward at the old man's disturbance above, silently and unseen, its tail flicking the sand as it swam until it stopped, settling nearby once it felt it was away from the splash of the surface water.

'Now, child,' whispered the old man. 'You still cannot see the ray, but you know where it is. Now is the time to hunt.'

The boy knelt upright on the raft, aiming the spear, his concentration on the position of the ray unbent, he poised for a long while, the spear raised above his head, considering his shot. He did not want to disappoint the old man. He held his breath and launched his spear hard into the sea. The spear-end thrashed and spun quivering in the water, the attached line whistling as it lashed the air back and forth before the boy pulled it taut and excitedly dragged the writhing and whipping fish onto the raft.

'Excellent, child,' said the old man. 'But beware of the tail of the ray. Never approach it from behind, even when the ray is not moving. It will sometimes lie still and pretend to be dead, but the ray will know you are there and will flay and sting when you least expect.'

Cautiously the boy approached the fish and clubbed it several times before he dare place his foot upon its head to pull the spear.

'Now tell me, child,' said the old man, pointing out across the water. 'What else do you see?'

The boy again strained his eyes out towards the horizon, shading them with his hand against the low sun. 'There are sails!' he said excitedly.

'How many?' the old man asked.

'Many,' said the boy. 'Many tall sails!'

'Come, child, we must make haste.' The old man stood and began poling the raft hard towards shore until it ground up onto the sandy beach.

'Do not wait,' said the old man. 'They will not be interested in a withered one such as me.

'Now run, child! Run like the wind!'

1.

The moon floated its gentle rays to Earth, bathing the beach in silver light, casting ghosts between the palms and tipping the cresting waves with diamonds. Two figures silently ran the shore, stopping occasionally and listening intently.

'We must be very quiet,' whispered the boy.

'But why must we do this thing tonight?' replied the friend. 'You can see that the moon is full, it is like daylight. We will be seen for certain.'

'We should not delay. Trader leaves soon for the north lands. He will not see us. He drinks the rum and sleeps deeply, and in the morning will not remember.'

Along the beach the two could see the trader's boat anchored into the sands below a copse of palms swaying softly in a warm night breeze that hissed through their branches. The boat, marooned as the receding tide had left it, glowed with an unearthly pallor under the moon's spell. Spread across its white painted side was a large net that had been drying in the sun that day. Quickly the two boys cut the net free and hastened their way back along the shore to their village.

The following day the people of the tribe emerged stretching and yawning from their huts dotted between palms. In a clearing among the trees the trader stood above them upon the trunk of a large fallen palm. Many of the people had already gathered and there was much chatter between neighbour and friend. It was always an important day whenever the trader spoke. The trader removed his straw hat revealing his sandy blond hair which looked very bright under the morning sun, and to the villagers much like gold against his handsome tanned face.

When the trader had first come to the village, many years before, the tribe were afraid as he descended from his boat. Never before had they seen a man with such light skin and hair the colour of the sandy beach upon which he had stood and were unsure, believing that he might be a spirit. But the kindness in the man's eyes calmed them and they overcame their fear. They were both puzzled and amused at the trader's strange hat gesture, until over time, as they learned each other's tongue, the trader explained that in his land it meant he was a humble man and at their service. From then the tribe always laughed, clapped and cheered loudly at his hat greetings.

'My good friends of the Mjumbi,' called the trader. 'Today is always a day of sadness for me, departing for the north as I must. However, I am much pleased that once again we have had good trade. The people of the markets of the north will be most pleased with the medicine herbs of the forest, the soft skins, and most of all they will be pleased with your beautiful craft.'

Again there was huge applause, jumping and chanting at the trader's words.

'I also trust that you are pleased with the spices, the tools and the colours from the cities of the great civilisation.'

On that note there was an almighty cheer. Tribesmen danced and sang and beat drums, some holding aloft the axes or machetes that had become so much a part of their way of life.

A young woman wearing a bright orange and purple dress coloured with dyes from the trader's previous visit sang as she danced her way forward. 'See the brightness of the sun and the darkness of the forest in my clothes, Trader!'

The trader smiled and applauded the woman.

Another man came forward holding an axe and a section of palm. 'See Trader, watch the craft of the north in the hands of Jaji!' whereupon Jaji stood the section on its end and split it in two with one blow.

The crowd erupted in cheers. 'The north!' they cried, 'the north and Jaji. We are the rulers of our world! Jaji, Jaji, north, north, north!'

The trader smiled then held up his hand, another gesture the tribe had learned when the trader wished for silence. 'It is also a day of sadness for another reason,' he said.

There was a hush among the tribe followed by whispering and looks of puzzlement at one another.

'For many years I have brought you these wonderful things and done much good trade,' continued the trader. 'You have come to trust me, and I to trust you in our great partnership. Is this not a wonderful thing?'

'Yes Trader!' many of the tribe cried joyfully.

'But alas, I am sad that the trust is in doubt.'

The tribe fell silent. They could see the seriousness in the trader's face. A young boy who was still dancing and singing to himself was slapped abruptly by his mother and shushed.

'In the night there was a thief,' said the trader. 'A thief who stole something I had done good trade with one of you for. Yesterday, I traded with the old man Injua a leather sheath and a good knife made by the Bedouin craftsmen of Marrakesh for a net so that I might catch fish to eat at sea on my voyages. Last night that net was taken from my boat.'

There was a gasp from the tribe. 'Who has done this thing?' many of them cried, and 'There cannot be a thief in the Mjumbi; tell us his name, Trader! Tell us, tell us!' became the chant. 'We will drive him into the sea, into the forest! This man is not a man among us!'

'Alas, I do not know who this man was. Now I must leave.' And on that note the trader jumped from his place upon the fallen tree and marched down to the shore.

The tribe followed, some running ahead and begging forgiveness on behalf of the unknown thief, some imploring the trader to stay at least until they could find the thief. Many were tearful and shocked at the trader's abrupt departure. In years past there had been celebration, and the trader had stayed long days telling the tribe of the outside world and teaching the children of his language. And always there had been feasting and much ritual and thanks at the end of the trader's visits.

The trader released his anchor from the shore, slung it aboard and clambered into his boat. Men and women waded into the sea as they always had done before to push him out to the deeper waters, all the while chanting his name, asking him to promise to return. The tribe watched tearfully as the trader lifted sail and turned into the northern current under a good breeze from the ocean winds until he was out of sight around the coast.

Mila stood silently for a long while after the trader's boat laden with the art of his people had disappeared sailing to a place he had never seen but often visited in his dreams from the trader's tales. As he stared out to sea a sense of deep disquiet overcame him, and a feeling that somehow his foolishness had forever changed the destiny of his people.

That evening there was a mood of apprehension and fretfulness among the tribe. Families argued between themselves. Friends and relatives eyed one another with suspicion. Late into the night the tribal Elders sat talking and arguing among themselves in a circle around a fire in the great meeting hut.

The Head of the tribe stood up and the Elders fell silent. 'You know what this means. Trader brings us the things we need to survive. Think how much richer our lives have been because of Trader.'

The Elders mumbled among themselves nodding in agreement.

Then the Head of the tribe's tone changed and darkness came to his voice. 'But you know also what Trader brings. He brings us *news*. Each time he visits he tells us the plans of the slavers. Even though it is long between Trader's visits, he tells us how many sunrises and how many full moons before the slavers are coming. He teaches us the slaver's language, the *miles* as is the slaver's means of measuring, so that we understand how far they are from us. He is wise and knows these things and he knows when the slavers are going to be near to us and many times we have taken refuge knowing that the slavers are coming many days before they arrive on our shore. But we cannot live forever in the forests; we need to have our village near to the sea. The sea is our life. Trader's tools have helped us lift the creatures of the sea in a time when we were hungry for more than root and leaf. So for our gifts of carvings and medicine Trader has given us life itself. Trader has been good to us and we have been a good partnership with the *great civilisation*. But if Trader cannot trust us, we do not know if he will return. And if he does not then we are at the mercy of the gods and the slavers.'

There was a burst of discussion among the Elders. Some insisted that the trader would surely return; that the north must love the goods of the tribe as much as the tribe depended upon the tools of the north. Others were uncertain and frightened and said that the tribe was doomed. A quarrel broke out at which the Head cast a stone into the fire causing a shower of sparks that leapt into the air.

'This fighting is not helping!' the Head bellowed. 'Trader is gone! Whatever our fate is to be it is already sealed. We must find the thief and decide what we must do with him.'

'Death,' said one. The others nodded in agreement.

'Death is the only punishment,' said another. 'We may all have been condemned to death as it is, if Trader does not return.'

'And if by the grace of the gods,' said yet another, 'he does return, we must show him that the tribe will not tolerate thieves and that this thing will never happen again. We must cut off the thief's head with Trader's axes – to show him that the tools of the north also have justice in them – and the carcass must be thrown to the sharks. And when Trader returns we must show him the head of the thief as proof of our honesty.'

They all agreed one by one casting a *fate* stone to the ground and repeating 'death.' The Head picked up each of the stones in his hand. 'It is decided...death,' and cast them into the fire.

They had begun to discuss how they might find the thief when there was a commotion outside the meeting hut. A woman's angry voice and a child's squeals of protest could be heard approaching.

The Head threw back the hide flap of the entrance and mother Hadiya entered dragging her son by the ear.

'Here is your thief!' she scolded, pushing the boy to the ground.

'Obi! Is this true?' said the Head.

'Injua found the net back in his hut,' said Hadiya, 'like he had never sold it to Trader, only Trader has gone already. But Injua found the footprints in the sand and he knows. He came to see me and I know this is Obi's doing. I look at the footprint and I know. Foolish boy! Do you understand what you have done?'

'Speak, Obi!' demanded the Head.

Obi sat shivering and tearful on the ground looking terrified at the Elders stood around him.

'And I see another footprint,' said Hadiya, 'a different print.

Someone else helped him, I think.'

'Obi,' said the Head, 'you must speak now. Why have you done such a foolish thing?'

'We did not want to stop fishing with Injua,' Obi mumbled.

'We?' said the Head. 'Who is this other person?'

'He doesn't need to answer,' said Hadiya. 'You know the two boys already. They both helped Injua with his catch for a long time before he stopped fishing. Injua teaches them how to spear the ray. It can only be the other one who has helped him.'

The Head nodded to two of the warrior Elders. 'Go bring the boy to me.'

'Tell me,' asked Hadiya, 'have the Elders decided the price of this boy's foolishness?'

'Death,' whispered one of the Elders solemnly, and he cast his gaze to the ground.

Hadiya looked at the Head in disbelief. The Head stood stern and straight-faced at Hadiya and then slowly nodded his admittance. Hadiya collapsed to the ground in tears begging mercy at the feet of the Head and Obi let out a wail of despair.

The two warriors burst through the door of Mila's hut. 'The boy is to come with us!' they demanded to Mila's stunned family.

'What is the meaning of this?' said Mila's father.

'The boy has been summoned to the council of Elders.'

Mila's father turned to his son in astonishment. 'You? You are the thief? Mila, what have you done?'

Before Mila could answer the warriors had lifted him from the ground and carried him through the door, his father protesting, his mother and sister crying in disbelief.

Mila was dragged into the meeting hut followed by his family and cast roughly to the ground at the feet of the Head.

'Tell me Mila,' said the Head coldly, 'what possessed you to act so unwisely?'

Mila glanced nervously at his friend Obi shivering in a corner. 'We wanted Injua to keep his net. For a long time since we were small, old man Injua has shown us how to hunt the ray. Then he can no longer hunt, his eyes are not good, he can no longer see the fish as they disappear into the sand under the raft. So Injua made a good net for catching as he sleeps on the raft. But we still go out on the sea with Injua, he wants us to be the ray hunters now and he teaches us well. But now Injua has stopped fishing, he has no net. I can still fish with Obi, but we feel sad for Injua and wanted to return the net.'

'Injua was paid a good price for his net,' said the Head. 'And he is old. He cannot fish anymore with or without net, he is too tired. The knife Trader has given him he will use to spend his days making carvings for the north, and the tribe will care for him now. The net is no good to him, so the gesture was in good heart but a foolish one.'

The Head paused for a long while and the meeting hut fell into silence awaiting his words. 'The vote cannot be undone,' he said at last. 'The tribe will not see thieves.'

'The vote?' said Mila's father. 'There has been a vote?'

The Head nodded to the first of the Elders. 'Death,' whispered the Elder and there was a gasp of disbelief from Mila's family. 'Death.' said the next Elder. 'Death,' they all said grimly.

The Head turned to Mila's family. 'The tribe will survive. In order to do so we must show Trader our honesty. The fire has accepted the vote and does not change. The boys will also accept the will of the gods. They will be taken away and sacrificed as prayer in turn that Trader will come back to us again.'

An argument had broken out between the Elders and Mila's family and mother Hadiya just as Injua appeared at the entrance.

'The vote is not worthy without the Elders,' said Injua, and all eyes turned to the old man.

'What is this nonsense, old one?' said the Head. 'The Elders' vote has been cast. This is justice on your behalf. You have been made to look a thief by these bad children.'

'But the Elders were not all present,' said Injua. 'You forget, Akua the Head, that I too am an Elder. For long sunrises past my presence has been accepted in the meeting hut, but now I am not called, yet you cast the vote in my absence. What worth is this? You know I am old, I cannot fish, but I am not forgetful. I am not yet in my grave. Perhaps you think judgement is unworthy from a frail that walks in the shadow of his life? Does this make me ignorant? You call for death to young men, but what worth is this? Have we no future such that we butcher our own children? Are we like the tribes that Trader has told us about far into the east forests that kill and eat their own kind? Trader has told us of these *savages*. We are not that kind. But what will Trader think of us if he sees the heads of children impaled upon spears? Will he still see us as the *civilised ones* that he calls us? As my presence here has not been granted I will go now, but consider my words before you act upon your vote.'

Injua walked away into the darkness leaving the rest of the meeting hut silent for a long while before arguments broke out that lasted most of the night. In the end the Elders descended upon Injua's hut, awakening him and asking what the justice should be.

Injua arose from his slumber and asked for water. The Elders stood around him in anticipation as he sat up and slowly drank. 'You consider me an old fool, yet you spend all the night arguing and cannot see what is already in front of you. You know that Trader sails north. Yet you forget that Trader visits the Baja tribe and does *business* with them. Unless there is also a thief in the Bajas, Trader will stop for one night, maybe more if dealings go well and the Baja are pleased with their trades.'

'What are you suggesting?' said the Head impatiently.

'You know Mila is the runner. He is fast and does not tire. For the last *five of Mila's fourteen years*, as Trader would say, you have sent him running the coast when we know that the slavers are due, to see if the ships are near. When Trader has given us the days you have sent Mila out to run north looking for the tall sails. Mila speaks and understands the tongue of Trader better than most of us. Trader has taught him well and Mila has learned of the *great civilisation* over Trader's many years of visiting our shores. The boy speaks the *English* tongue of Trader. He should ask Trader for forgiveness. Give the net to Mila and tell him to return it to Trader.'

The Head was astounded at Injua's words. 'You are going to ask a boy to run as far as the Baja tribe? And to carry a net with him? How far is the Baja? How long will it take him?'

'You can still cut off his head,' said Injua, 'if that is your wisdom.'

The Elders argued among themselves about whether the boy could manage such a task carrying a large net that would normally take a grown man's strength to haul it from the sea, with or without fish and whether the vote could be undone and whether it would displease the gods to do so.

Injua held up his hand and silenced the disorderly conference. 'It is as Trader would say, *fifty miles*, to the Baja village. And remember, there were *two* thieves. Obi can help to carry the net. If Trader stays another night with the Baja the two can make it in time. If the task fails, then you must carry out the justice.'

'*Fifty miles*,' the Head muttered. 'By my understanding that is indeed a great task for a man, even.'

'That is my wisdom,' said Injua, and he lay back down to sleep.

The Elders argued for the briefest of times then marched quickly back to the meeting hut where the two boys were being held. They put Injua's proposition to Mila and Obi and the boy's family who were stunned at the idea.

'How far can you run?' the Head asked Mila.

'I think I run *twenty miles* once, when Trader said the slavers were one day away.'

'How long did this task take?'

'Sun to Moon,' said Mila proudly.

'Sun to Moon! That is too long! Why so long?'

'There were no tall sails,' said Mila. 'So I rest and stop to pick dika fruit on way home.'

'So how long to get to Baja village?'

'I don't know.'

'But you will go?'

'I will go.'

'Then you will take Obi and go now. There will be no dika fruit. Go take the net to Trader.'

Mila and Obi set out straight away as the first light touched the shore on as fine a morning as ever. With the net strung between them and a stiff breeze from behind, they set a good pace. They ran chattering and laughing, for the time being happy at their lucky escape from the Elders vote.

After a while they stopped to take some water. 'Not too much, Obi,' said Mila as he watched Obi gulping from the hide bottle. 'You will slow down if your belly is full.'

'How long to the Baja village now, Mila?' Obi wiped his mouth and handed Mila the bottle.

'Look at the sun, Obi, it has not moved. We will reach the village before the sun is high. We are fast today. Trader will be pleased with us when he sees how far we come so soon.'

Time passed but there was less talking. The day quickly warmed as they darted along the surf edge, sometimes running into the groves avoiding palms that had bent low in storms or fallen across the beach, where the tides and wind had strewn them across their path. They stopped, ate a little food, took some water and soon set off again. As the sun rose higher, Obi struggled, often falling back and letting Mila wait while he took up the slack of the net between them.

'Come Obi, we must hurry,' Mila urged.

'I must stop, Mila,' Obi protested. 'I have no strength. The net is too heavy.'

'But we must run. If Trader decides to leave today he will go before the sun has peaked.'

They drank a little more water and Obi reluctantly took up his half of the net. Before long Obi collapsed to the sand, crying. 'We are doomed, Mila. We cannot do it. It is too far.'

'Then you choose death, Obi. Come, we try again.'

Each time they took up the net Obi would run a little and fall, his legs betraying him. In the end he lay in the sand, the net spread out in a line where Mila had been trying to pull Obi along.

Mila stood over Obi as he gasped and cried. 'I will take the net myself then, Obi. But you must follow when you can. I will tell Akua we both carried it to the Baja when we return. I do not know how far the Baja are now, but I think I remember the groves on this beach from Injua's fishing trips and I think the ray are near this shore. We cannot be far away.'

Mila bundled the net up as best as he could, draping it around his shoulders and set off again, slower but with much determination. The sun crept up the sky and the heat bore down upon him. He stopped very briefly to cool in the sea and continued but his feet sank into the wet sand and his legs wandered under the weight of the net. He tried running further from the water's edge where the sand was still wet but firm. But the waves had picked up, hindering him as they swept in long swathes across the beach and lashed at his legs making him zigzag and the breeze had changed direction, now hitting him sideways straight off the whitecaps. He sang to the sun spirit, begging her to pity him and cover her face with cooling cloud.

The wind picked up and a tall cresting wave sent its fine spray across Mila's back. And as a vigorous gust from behind swept him, easing his effort and lifting his spirit, he ran with renewed strength, believing his prayer had been answered.

Soon Mila came to the edge of a cove where, on the inland beach, a trail of smoke rose from the Baja village and his heart leapt. Trader was casting his lines aboard his boat. He dashed round the cove edge, stumbling and staggering with the net, shouting and desperately hoping to catch the tribe's or Trader's attention. Fallen palms hampered his way along the shore and he cut into the groves, catching the net onto tree root and brushwood. Fighting and dragging to untangle the net, he abandoned it, eventually emerging from the woods onto the beach at the edge of the village. Some of the Baja people who saw him shouted to the others and ran over to the desperate looking boy who collapsed in despair at the sight before him.

Just beyond the cove mouth and out onto the open sea, Trader's white sail bobbed upon the cresting waves.

2.

'Trader did not even stay one day,' said Nnamdi the wise. 'We did the good trade as always, but there was a sadness in Trader's eye that he would not speak of.'

'I am the cause of that sadness,' said Mila, then he told the story of his theft along with Obi and the judgement of the Elders.

'This is most unfortunate news,' said Nnamdi, inspecting the net which Mila had laid before him. 'It would be too much of a task to take it back again, Mila. Why not leave it here until Trader returns? That is, if he decides to return. It is still uncertain that Trader will come back to us again, but there was no theft in the Baja village, so perhaps he shall.'

'But what am I to do?' said Mila. 'To go back is certain death, yet I am a coward if I stay here. And what about Obi? I do not know if he is following or if he has returned to face his death like a brave warrior.'

'Come, Mila. We will walk a while.' Nnamdi stood and they walked through the Baja village as the people went about their daily tasks of washing clothes, grinding, cutting, or cooking things with Trader's new tools. With sadness in his heart, Mila watched as some young boys helped a fisherman with his raft just setting out for the day's catch.

After a while, away from the shore, they came upon a stream in a shady part of the forest. Nnamdi sat upon the bank beckoning Mila to join him. Nnamdi closed his eyes and chanted quietly to himself then became silent again. Mila waited and waited for words from the wise man but none came.

Eventually Mila became impatient, believing that Nnamdi had fallen asleep. 'Wise man,' he sighed. 'Why are we sat here doing nothing? I must know what I am to do.'

'Shhh,' Nnamdi whispered, his eyes still shut. 'We must wait for guidance.'

From a nearby tree overhanging the stream a leaf detached and floated gently in the air. Nnamdi opened his eyes. 'Watch Mila, watch the leaf on its journey.' Nnamdi pointed and his finger followed the leaf as it spun and fluttered like an insect in the warm breeze before alighting into the stream where it swirled briefly in an eddy before flowing away.

'So what happens to the leaf, Mila?' said Nnamdi.

'It dies,' said Mila. 'It has left the tree and will be no more.'

'It has left the tree; that is for certain. But it is still there.'

'But the leaf rots once it leaves the tree. It becomes nothing, it is dead.'

'Oh no, no,' said Nnamdi. 'The leaf has simply changed. It rots as you say, but then what happens? The fragments of leaf sink to the bottom of the stream or are washed out to sea. They become food for the creatures there. So the leaf has not died, it has simply changed its form. The leaf thinks it is dead, as *we* do, when the time comes. It does not know that it is only changing. It becomes something else which was once a leaf.'

'I don't understand,' said Mila.

'Look at me, Mila. I was once you. A boy. Now I am me. I no longer look anything like the boy. I have changed but I am still me, you cannot deny that? Everything in life changes. I become old and wither like the leaf. And when death comes to greet me and the tribe send me on my journey, I am as the leaf. I change yet again. It is the journey we all take. And who knows, perhaps the leaf will come back again as a leaf? You know that the bare branch shoots the leaf always, but ask yourself, Mila...where does the branch get the leaf? The root digs down deep into the earth where many leaves have passed. And you say that they are all dead? But always the leaf is born again from the dead.'

'But, wise man,' said Mila, 'what is the meaning of the sign?'

'You are merely starting another journey, Mila. A journey that will see you change.'

'But where does it all end?'

'The journey never ends.'

'So, what must I do, wise man?'

'For tonight you must rest, Mila. I will have a conference with the Elders over this new turn of events. My advice to them will be that you must leave the net here. And in the morning you must set out to find the *great civilisation* and Trader to tell him the good news that he can come back for his net and resume the good trade.'

The next morning Mila was given a small raft with sail and a few supplies for his journey: some food, water carriers, a blanket, some fishing line and a knife. These and the rest of Mila's provisions were packed into a basket tied securely at the base of the mast. The Baja people gathered at the water's edge chanting a tale about Trader's visits they had made into song as Mila pushed his raft out. Nnamdi waded out to steady the raft as Mila hoisted the sail. And with final blessings from the Elders, Mila set out on his journey to find Trader.

As the days passed Mila's heart lifted and the dread of his own tribe's judgement went to the back of his mind. The sun shone each day and the oar work was easily keeping the raft within sight of the shoreline as a good wind carried him steadily north. In the evenings he would beach the raft and collect nuts and fruits to eat with dried salt-fish the Baja had provided him with, and drift to sleep wrapped in his blanket listening to the swaying palms and lap of surf.

But one day, still early in the afternoon as he was daydreaming about the *great civilisation* and what a fine place it must be, Mila noticed that the breeze had very quickly become cold and had an intensity that had not been there before. It would whip and then suddenly drop as if to say: *I'm not going to bother you any more*, before blasting his sail with renewed ferocity. Although the sailing was still forward, it was awkward and Mila decided that he'd had enough for that day and turned in towards the shore. Only then did he notice the reason for the teasing winds. From the south a great black cloud that reached down from the heavens, obliterating the horizon, was rolling fast across the sea towards him. A flash of lightning seared across the cloud to the beach followed closely by a huge *boom* as Mila struggled desperately with the oar. He pulled the sail down which seemed suddenly to have a mind of its own, dragging him further out to sea, but hard as he worked, Mila would get somewhere near the shore, only to get dragged back out again. The surf began to rise and each time he tried to catch it on the curl, paddling quickly with it, hoping it would roll him onto the beach. But the tide was at ebb and no sooner had he got somewhere near the shore than the swell would suddenly drop and the sea would suck him out again. The cloud engulfed him; lightning crackled and thunder rolled from all sides. There was nothing he could do but hang onto the mast and hope. The storm seemed to last for an eternity as the sea lifted, pounded and threw the raft in all directions.

When at last it finished, darkness had fallen and Mila could no longer see the shore. He looked up for the bright light of *Yoonir* as direction, but ragged clouds drifted across the night sky disorienting him. He wrapped himself in the sodden blanket and spent the night shivering and dozing fitfully upon a rolling sea.

In the morning, as the sun rose the sea was calm once more,

and although the shore was gone, Mila was glad to have at least survived the storm. From the sun's position he found his direction and raised the sail. All that day he carefully tacked with the sun as it rose and set again, but still the shore was not in sight. In the evening *Yoonir* rose in the east and he carried on certain of his course and that the shore would be visible by the light of day. As the first light tipped the sea crests his hopes were dashed. He had not rested for two nights; the last remnants of food were gone and the leather water carriers were fouled with seawater. The sun coursed its way through the morning beating down hard upon Mila. At the sun's zenith Mila stopped, exhausted, and with all the intention of having a short slumber before resuming his course, he fell into a deep sleep.

When he awoke the raft was in shadow and rocking with a deep green and foaming sea. He raised his head, blinking and confused. Beyond the shadow the sun shone and sparkled upon a sea blue and calm. Gulls hovered, cawed and skimmed the waves. And on the horizon the dark blue-green outline of coast stood out stark against the ocean. He jumped up with joy, steadying himself on the mast, the turbulent and thrashing water that he couldn't understand nearly knocking him off the raft. A voice called from somewhere and he turned to face a black wall moving slowly before him. A voice again and he looked up.

Men were watching him.

And Mila felt as though the blood had drained from his body.

3.

The slave ship *Belladonna* loomed high and dark above Mila's raft. Men were shouting and pointing. Mila panicked and grabbed the oar paddling swiftly away as far as he could before raising his sail. A good breeze picked him up and with fortune was taking him towards shore. He looked back. The slave ship appeared to have stopped, and Mila breathed a sigh of relief as it receded into the distance. Picking the wind was easy and Mila's hopes soared as the raft glided upon the gentle swell.

At first Mila thought he'd imagined it. There were voices again. Across the water, faint and softened by the wind, men were shouting. He looked back and a boat with many oars was gaining on him. Soon they were near, crying out and swearing and threatening. He could see their faces, their eyes filled with hatred. A gaff was reached onto the rope bindings of Mila's raft and he was pulled alongside and a man jumped aboard grabbing him around the neck with a curse and dragging him into the boat.

'Haul him up lads!' a man cried and as Mila was hoisted spinning and turning on a rope sling in the hands of his captors he cried out in despair. Across the fair ocean the distinct blue outline of the shore he nearly made could still be seen on the horizon. He was dragged roughly onto the ship at the hands of several men who now gathered around him as he sprawled out on the deck. Two more lifted him under the arms and shoved him frightened and shivering before another man.

At first glance Mila was almost relieved. The smiling man was different from the others. His dress was colourful and bright, like some of his own people at ceremonies. His gold decorated blue jacket, white blouse and leggings and strange hat suggested to Mila that he must surely be the Head of his captor's tribe. All he need do was explain who he was to the Elder and he might be released.

'Well, what have we here?' said the man. 'Escaped slave, I suspect, probably managed to jump ship somehow. Well, this is a spot of bad luck for you, isn't it? Straight out of the pan and into the fire, eh?'

'I am Mila,' Mila mumbled. 'I am Mjumbi people and lost. Please let me go.'

The gathered men gasped and the finely dressed one grabbed Mila roughly by the neck. 'You speak English?' he growled, shaking Mila. 'Where did you learn it, boy? I always suspected there was some renegade mingling with your kind. Speak up boy!'

But Mila was too frightened to speak again and instinctively felt that it might be wrong to tell his captor's about Trader.

'He's been taught by some interfering nigger lover,' said the finely dressed man, who shoved Mila roughly to the deck.

'Too right, Captain,' said one of the men. 'He's no slave, not aboard a raft with sail like he were, a proper little black sailor. Reckon he's got lost out fishing like he says. Probably swept away by that storm we had.'

'Well it makes no difference how he got here,' said the Captain. 'Still, a windfall for us, an English speaking nigger should fetch a very good price at market. Driver Briggs! Throw the boy below and slap him in irons with the rest of them. I'll question the boy further later. One way or another I'll find out who this interferer is.'

'Can't do it, Captain,' said the slave driver. 'We're full down there. Neither inch nor shackle to spare.'

'Well take him down and stay with him!' the Captain bellowed. 'An extra rum ration for your misery, if you must. Feed him up along with the rest and keep an eye on him. I don't want any free wanderer getting up to any tricks. No doubt there'll be a space soon, one or two of the weaklings will give way long before we berth, I reckon. Shackle him up with the rest of this shitty cargo when you get chance. Come on, come on, look alive the rest of you! There's a fair wind coming and we lag behind schedule already!'

Slave driver Briggs grabbed Mila roughly by the arm. 'Right, you little bugger! You heard the Captain; you're mine now and you better do as I say or you'll get plenty of this!' and Briggs shook his *scourge*, a whip of many twisted leather tongs at Mila. He dragged him across deck and stopped at the ship's hatch, grinning and laughing at him. 'You have no idea, do you boy? What's down there, eh? What you reckon, eh? Little sailor boy...or is it little lost fisherman? Go on, lift it up boy.'

Terrified, Mila was unable to speak to the repulsive looking man with black teeth and bloodshot eyes that glared inanely at him.

'Oh, a bit shy are we?' said Briggs, raising the scourge. 'Perhaps this will help!' And he lashed Mila hard across the legs.

Mila cried out and fell to his knees, nearly fainting with the shock. His eyes rolled in agony until the searing pain abated, then stared wildly at the other crew members who'd gathered around to laugh at him.

Briggs pulled up the hatch and a burst of hot air plumed out along with an unearthly stench. Mila thought for a moment that the slave driver had unleashed an evil spirit that now whipped around him, tormenting his nostrils and trying to penetrate his soul. Moans and cries of despair and hopelessness that Mila imagined were souls of the departed floated up with the spirit.

'Get your worthless ass down!' cried Briggs, raising the scourge and Mila stared down into the darkness. The slave driver brought his boot across Mila's face and lashed him a second time across the back before dragging him and bundling him over. Mila grasped at the ladder rungs, slipping and tumbling into the darkness. As his eyes adjusted he recalled a scene that Trader had described to him and his people many times on his visits. But the vision was beyond even Trader's descriptions of the slavers and their cruelty. He peered into the dimness and a thick, vaporous stench that seemed to suck the light away with it. He walked the aisle slowly between the berths looking at the dark, melancholy faces that gazed back at him. They were shackled at their ankles and a long thick chain that seemed to run the length of the ship through loops was holding each slave in place. Many, whose feet overhung into the aisle, had cuts and bruises to the legs. Some seemed stunned at Mila's sudden presence and sat up pleading. Some began to shout and clap their hands. A woman cried out joyously at the sight of Mila wandering between them unshackled and reached out to kiss his hand. Many thought that Mila was one of them and had been freed and that it was now the turn of the rest of them. They held up their arms begging him for release. He came closer to the woman reaching for him and froze. To his horror he now realised the source of the stench, but was quickly brought back by another lash from Briggs who then pushed and kicked him into a corner. The slave driver cracked the whip again and a silence fell, the slaves hung down their heads in hopelessness and understood that Mila had not come to liberate them.

Slave driver Briggs carried out his orders, delivering hard bread and slops of rice and beans ladled out onto the boarding between the slaves, swearing as he went, sometimes cracking the scourge as a threat to maintain silence. Some ate willingly, others didn't and Briggs thrashed them into feeding as ordered.

Some were sick and vomited and Briggs relented when the whip couldn't induce them. He cursed these with threats: 'You'll be next for the sharks,' he'd bellow, then he'd take particular delight in tormenting these, ladling beans onto their privates and beating the soles of their feet with the ladle.

Briggs slopped a plateful out for Mila. 'Go on, eat it up boy, Captain's orders, reckons you'll fetch a pretty price in Virginia…yes, no doubt some filthy rich, pretty-boy queers will take a shine to you. Your fault I have to stay down in this stinking hole, so don't you be giving me any grief. Get that crud down you boy! You want to live out this voyage then you'll eat the lot!'

Mila fingered the food cautiously then put some to his mouth and ate, his hunger overcoming the unpleasant taste. The bread was no better, but Mila ate as much as he could stomach.

As the day wore on and evening eventually fell, Briggs disappeared up the ladder leaving Mila with a warning shake of the scourge to stay sat exactly where he was. He returned shortly with a lamp and a jug and tin cup. 'Now I can see you, you little piece of vermin,' he growled, hanging the lamp to a rafter. 'Don't you be wandering where I can't see you or you'll be for the lash, I say. He sat on a barrel by Mila and poured himself a drink. 'A nice bit of rum as the Captain promised. But you wouldn't know anything about that, would you?' he sneered at Mila. 'You and your kind, bloody savages…only good for a beating, I say.'

Night rolled on and Briggs drank and sang to himself, sometimes cracking the scourge to silence the moans and sometimes nodding and slipping off the barrel. As the ship pitched gently over the waves, Briggs slumped to the floor and began to snore. Mila lay down on the hard deck, sobbing silently to himself. As he closed his eyes hoping to catch a vision of his people and home in his sleep a voice whispered nearby.

'Boy? Boy?' A man's voice was hissing in urgency and Mila shot up. 'Over here boy, come here quickly.'

Mila peered into the dim light and wandered cautiously between the berths.

'I am here boy,' said the man when Mila reached him. 'Who are you, boy? Where have you come from?'

'I am Mila. My people are Mjumbi, we live south of the Baja. I was lost at sea and was found by this ship.'

Mila could see the man now, muscular and proud, his eyes flashed in the lamplight and the intricate white decoration of tattoo down his face, arms and chest shone out from his large frame denoting a warrior of high esteem in all the tribes of Mila's world.

'Yes,' said the man. 'I have heard of the Baja people and Nnamdi the wise. His wisdom is highly praised by many. I am Kobina of the Mensu tribe. We live in the forests away from the sea which is dangerous. But the slavers are sending their kind in deeper all the time looking for more slaves. We were captured three days ago as we slept thinking we were safe. They torched the forest behind us, throwing us into light and driving us into their trap of nets.'

'That is most unfortunate,' said Mila.

'Yes,' said Kobina. 'And it is unfortunate that you were taken also, but it is fortunate for us.'

'What do you mean?' said Mila.

'You can help us, Mila. You must free us. Can you tell me, Mila, is it a clear night?'

'I think so. I could see the stars when the slave driver went above.'

'Then you must free us or we are doomed to die. You heard the slave driver? Some will not live out this journey, many are sick already. You have seen and tasted the putrid slop they feed us? And I will not live as a slave in chains. I would rather die like the warrior I was born to be.'

'I cannot get you free,' said Mila. 'You are in steel. Even the tools of Trader could not break it.'

'The slave driver carries the keys,' said Kobina. 'It hangs from his belt always. The lock is at the end of each row of us. You must get the key and set us free. If you don't then you too will be shackled like the rest of us before the next night. One of us will surely die by then and your last chance of ever returning to your home will be gone. You must get the key from the slave driver.'

'I can't,' said Mila. 'He will surely awaken if I try.'

'He will not wake so easily,' said Kobina. 'He drinks the *water of no dreams* and is gone from this world tonight.'

'But he will wake as we step over him trying to leave. Many people moving in the darkness and someone will trip or fall on him for certain.'

'Then Mila...you must kill him first.'

'But I have never killed a man,' Mila fretted. 'It is wrong. I have no weapon and I am not strong enough to overpower a grown man.'

'Here, Mila, come closer,' said Kobina. He revealed a small knife he had hidden in his loincloth. 'Think of the people that will die on this journey. Do you think the slavers care? Think of the people of my tribe, the men, the women and even the children who were slaughtered trying to defend our village. Think of the burning whip and lying in your own filth for how long? This will happen. Think of these things and it will give you strength. You are nearly a man who will grow to stand tall and be proud one day, but only if you can do this thing.'

'I am afraid,' said Mila.

'I have something else for you, Mila,' said Kobina. He reached again into his loincloth and handed Mila a skin bag. 'It is the *Yoonir* stone, from the star of our people. It has been in the tribe for many generations. My people believe that it once fell from the heavens, a piece of the very star of Yoonir itself and carries magic and fortune in it. So far I have hidden it from the slavers, but they will find it before long.'

Mila opened the bag to reveal something he had never seen before. A large pearl resting comfortably in the palm of his hand seemed to glow with a violet and green lustre in the lamplight. He closed his hand but his fingers could not fit around it. 'It is very beautiful,' he said. 'I have heard of such beautiful things from Trader, that they are very valuable. I should not take it from you.'

'It is yours, Mila,' said Kobina. 'I only ask that when you come to part with it, to do so with wisdom. It only brings fortune to those that use it wisely and use it for good. The time has come for my people to part with it and my wisdom tells me that you are here by the magic of the *Yoonir*. Take it, Mila, you will know when the time comes to part with it. Promise that you will part with it wisely, and free us.'

'I promise,' said Mila after a long silence. He placed the pearl back into the skin and tucked it into his loincloth. Silently Kobina handed him the knife and nodded.

Mila silently crept towards Briggs, now laid on his side snoring loudly. He straddled Brigg's body, trying to control his fear which made him shake from head to foot. He bent down staring at Briggs' head trying to determine where the neck was, which seemed to be non-existent in Brigg's burly frame. Suddenly Briggs snorted and spluttered and mumbled incoherently. Mila froze and prayed silently that Briggs didn't roll over or unexpectedly reach out. Briggs groaned and lapsed back into his rhythmical snore once again. Mila bent down close and raised the knife. He poised in silent concentration without breathing as Injua had taught him when spearing rays.

Briggs opened his eyes, suddenly aware that a shadow loomed over him and cried out, spinning onto his back and grabbing at Mila's legs. Desperately Mila tried to pull free and lost his balance. He dropped heavily onto his knees and wildly plunged the knife down, unsure exactly where he'd stabbed the slave driver. Briggs released his grip and Mila jumped back. Briggs struggled to his feet, thrashing about frantically and in his death dance Mila caught sight of the knife handle protruding from Briggs' mouth. Blood rushed down the front of Briggs' tunic onto the decking in drips and splashes as he struggled to find the ladder. Desperately, Briggs pulled the knife from his mouth, sending a plume of blood spurting from his throat onto deck. He tried to cry out but all that came was a gurgling squeak. Grasping the ladder, he climbed two rungs, arched his back and dropped to the deck with a thud, the blood still pumping from his throat.

Mila stood shocked and gasping for breath. Slaves that had awoken during the unfolding drama now cried out, but Kobina silenced them with stern words.

'You must be quick now, Mila!' urged Kobina. 'Free us now!'

Mila unfastened the keys from Briggs' belt. There were several of them. He tried one in the lock at the end of the berths without luck. Two more and the lock sprung open. Cautiously and as silently as he could he pulled the chain through the steel rings securing each slave along the berths. As the chain got longer and heavier the further he went, the freed slaves helped until the chain row was done. Another key, another row of berths, and one by one each slave that still had strength and the will to live stood and either helped Mila or helped the sick and the women and the children to their feet. Another key slipped the shackles at the ankles. It was a long and painstaking task and the night wore on as each passed the key to free themselves

Kobina was the first to climb the ladder and partially lifted the hatch, peering cautiously around the deck. Others gathered around the ladder or clambered near his feet, whispering and anxious. Kobina lowered the hatch and whispered: 'Come, Mila. You must be the first to be free. Show us the way to land.'

Mila climbed up and slipped out through the hatch. The moon had set and the sky was filled with stars. He could see nothing around other than the motionless silhouette of the deck cabins and the billowing of sails in the starlight above. Silently he raised the hatch fully over and beckoned Kobina who was the first to emerge.

'Where is the land?' said Kobina.

Mila looked to the sky for the Yoonir star then pointed across the starboard deck. 'It is that way.'

'How far?' said Kobina.

'I was very near to the shore when I was captured,' said Mila. 'I was tacking west of Yoonir all that day until I fell asleep. When I awoke it was there. I was so close I could smell the forest even, but it was too late. It cannot be far.'

'Then we put our trust in Yoonir and you, Mila, and swim for our freedom. Yoonir will guide my people back to our home.'

Kobina signaled the others to emerge and one by one the slaves slipped silently along the deck and over the side. Mila pointed the direction and Kobina assured the doubtful and afraid. With no more than the sound of wind through sail and rolling wave to be heard on board, the slaves dropped into the sea. A child cried and was silenced by its mother, who muffled its mouth and stood nervously over the edge of the ship. Other slaves emerged and gathered at the ship's rail.

'Do not be afraid,' Kobina assured the mother. 'The choice is clear. A shameful death in chains and wallowing in filth at the hands of the slavers, or we let the light of our spirit god guide us home.'

An emerging slave stumbled awkwardly on a barrel and fell

heavily to the deck with a loud thud and a man cried out from the rigging above: 'Slaves out! Slaves out!'

'Go now!' cried Kobina, pushing and shoving the slaves to the edge.

'Slaves overboard!' cried the watchman above and men suddenly emerged from out of nowhere. Lamps lit up and muskets fired. The still emerging slaves scrambled across the deck and dived into the sea. Some were shot before reaching the edge, others unable to pass the swarming crew chose to stand and fight, lashing out at their tormentors with a strength driven by fury. Crewmen whose guns had discharged and missed their target ran in panic. A slave chased one to the rail and dived into him wrapping his arms around the neck and tumbling over with him into the water. More muskets cracked. One of the crew with a discharged musket spotted Mila. He picked up a barrel and ran towards him with a roar of anger and fire in his eye. He slung the barrel hard at Mila and Mila ducked as the barrel flew over his head and into the sea. As the man pounced Mila jumped to the rail and dived over.

He swam hard away as men fired into the water at the swimming slaves. As he swam frantically and blindly in the dark his face thudded into the barrel that had narrowly missed him. Gasping for breath he flung his arms around it kicking and drifting away with the ocean current.

As the day broke and the slave ship *Belladonna* receded into the distance the sounds of angry men and guns disappeared to be replaced with the despairing cries of drowning slaves.

4.

Mila floated in a netherworld filled with spirits. The sea, calm and silent raised the voices of ghosts. Mila clung to his barrel going nowhere, slipping in and out of consciousness, but all around, in sleep or dream, he imagined and heard the desolate sound of people, forsaken and lost. Faces appeared, rising up from the water and hands reached out for him. The wind echoed in his ear like the whispering of departed souls in sorrow. Now the hands felt to be touching and nudging him from beneath and all around. He awoke with a start as he slipped from the barrel and realized that the nudging was real. But even the curious sharks, circling and looking for sea turtles soon abandoned him as nothing more than a piece of wreckage, and in his despair Mila begged them to return and devour him, that his wretched life might serve some purpose.

Night came and went again and Mila drifted in both the sea and in his consciousness. Hands touched him again, this time hard, grasping and clawing at his belly. Kobina's angry face stared up from the depths, furious and roaring. His giant frame rose up from the ocean like a monolith above Mila screaming vengeance at him: *Mila, what have you done!* And Kobina's body crashed down upon Mila. Claws dug deep into him, dragging their talons down from his chest across his belly, loins, buttocks and thighs, thrashing his back like the slaver's scourge, and across his skull and every single part of his helpless body as he twisted and churned in the pounding surf.

Then, having thrown him away in bitterness and resentment, the angry sea of *Kobina* receded, ignoring him, leaving him as a piece of useless debris, utterly alone on a far away shore.

In the early light Mila surveyed his new world. The shingle and shale beach was broken by a rocky outcrop and Mila wondered how the angry sea had chosen him to miss these and his certain death, or why it had decided not to snatch him back into its depths as he slept on its shore in a fathomless world of exhaustion. Above the beach the gnarled trunks and twisted branches of the shore trees, stripped of leaf, bleached and sculpted by the ocean wind, stood like pale spirit guardians before a forest, lush but dense and menacing in the morning twilight. And across the ocean there was nothing, no sign of other land or sails, and he wondered if the sea that had chosen not to end his life had taken him to a shore somewhere near to his home, or even near the *great civilisation* and that he might yet find Trader.

He drank from a stream of bitter tasting water and spent the morning sorrowfully wading and searching the rock pools for sea creatures, molluscs and mussels which he cracked with stones and gathering what small berries, shoots and edible roots he could find in the forest, he ate hungrily. He lay down a while, and under the warming sun and lull of the calming surf, fell into a troubled dream disturbed by the desolate cries of slaves. He awoke mid-afternoon and felt his strength returning along with the memory of what he'd done and sorrow threatened to overcome him. He considered for a long while the fact that he was alive and believed that if the tides had drifted him towards the land then other slaves must surely have survived. And as he remembered Kobina's promise that the Yoonir pearl brought luck to those that held it and parted with it wisely, his spirits and hope lifted and he resolved that he would still try, at least, to complete his mission. He looked up for the position of the sun and set out walking the coast in what he thought would be the direction of the *civilisation*. If by chance he found his home first, he would deservedly face the justice of the Elders, and if his home was somewhere behind him, he would either come to the Baja village again, or the *civilisation* and fulfil his promise and beg the forgiveness of Trader.

The sun was descending towards the horizon and still the shore looked unfamiliar. In all the *miles* of his running to search for the tall sails, and the days spent out fishing for rays with Injua, Mila had learned every little cove and copse of his world. But the shore was strange. And there was no one. He walked on trying to imagine his own people and how they would react to seeing him again if he happened to arrive there. Or how, if he came to the Baja village, Nnamdi the wise would greet him; disappointed and with sadness in his eyes that Mila had failed, but with a tale of life that would explain the meaning of his failure, and how he should proceed with the next stage of his life. In his heart, Mila hoped that either this or finding the *civilisation* would be the outcome of his walk. And in his heart he hoped that Yoonir, the brightest star in the sky the previous night, had also guided the slaves safely to shore as it had chosen to leave him alive. And he thought about food and wondered about catching rays to eat, should his journey be many more days.

And as the light of the Earth faded in the late afternoon, the fish eagle swept low across the flat water of a sea calming in the red glow of the dying sun, skimming and pecking at silhouettes that bobbed below the surf. There must be fish. Excitedly Mila ran along the beach to where the fish eagle fed. Only when the great shoals swarmed near the coast would the fish eagle be seen. It would be easy gathering them for his supper. On these rare occasions the whole tribe would wade into the sea with baskets, scooping and gathering the sardines as they whipped and thrashed about them. And then there was such a feast in the evening! But he must be wary. Often the sharks would follow the sardines and in their feeding frenzy would bite and slash indiscriminately at anything in the water. And although the shark did not care for the taste of his people, some still carried the reminder of the encounter. And he wondered if these were the silhouettes. But they were too still, not thrashing and rolling in the joy of eating like shark. But still Mila waded out cautiously.

As the gentle surf rolled across him the fish eagle circled above cawing then gently landed upon the surface nearby pecking at the sea. There was no thrashing of fish.

And no rolling of feeding shark.

And the fish eagle that pecked out strips of flesh was not an eagle.

Mila stepped upon something soft and spongy beneath him and he jumped back. Gas bubbles rose from his feet gurgling and popping at the surface with a fetid stink. And slowly it rose from the sands below, the dark mask and grinning white sea-scoured teeth and eyes of the death-head. Gleaming bright in the sunset, it seemed to draw the rest of the body to the surface as though the departed soul had wanted Mila to see its earthly flesh whole before the creatures of the ocean devoured it or the waves washed it away forever. And as the vulture hopped from one dead slave to another, others gathered in the sky. It flew up high, cackling and circling with its friends above him, then landed upon the head of the body floating before Mila. It squawked and cawed mockingly at him, cocked its head and proceeded to pluck at the eyeballs as the others descended.

Mila scrambled blindly to shore where he ran and ran as far away as he could, stumbling and crying out in panic and despair until he finally collapsed in exhaustion face down in the shale weeping. When at last he looked up he realized that he was at the same beach with its familiar rocky outcrop and twisted trees that the sea had chosen to throw him onto. He was marooned, lost on an island somewhere far away from home and the realization that he was the only survivor of the slave ship hit him.

Mila ran as far as he could away from the hateful shore and into the forest, uncaring about any creatures that might reside there and crept under a bush. He drifted in and out of sleep and nightmares. In the darkest dream he floated in a chasm where from the depths the face of Kobina rose up, his pattern tattooing glowing bright as white stars then turning blood red as dying embers. But there was no anger in Kobina, only a deep sadness and Kobina shook his head and wrung his hands and cried in grief for his people. And Mila wrung his hands and cried also as Kobina sunk back into the depths.

And when Mila awoke in the faint light of dawn he wrung his hands, bowing his head grovelling in the soil of the forest beneath him and cried and cried, begging the soul of Kobina to forgive him.

5.

In the early days that passed Mila grew accustomed to his world but not the sorrow he felt for Kobina and the lost slaves. If he'd had the strength he would have dragged as many of the bodies that had found their way to his island ashore and buried them with the prayers and ritual of his tribe. But as many also seemed to have disappeared; either carried back out by the tide or devoured by the sea creatures and vultures. Or perhaps they were just resting at the bottom of the sea, awaiting some disturbance to refloat them to the surface in the death masks that still invaded his dreams, or just decaying away, feeding the seabed and reforming into another life as Nnamdi the wise had taught him happens to every living thing. Sometimes he was comforted by that thought, that life never truly dies and the journey continues. And at other times he despaired, knowing that his own journey had come to an end and he had failed to fulfill his promise either to his own people or the promise to Kobina. And on these days he would stand at the edge of the tide holding the Yoonir pearl out in his hand about to throw it as far into the sea as he could. 'You have brought me bad luck,' he would say. But just as he was about to depart with it he would recall the promise, to part with it wisely and he would think of the barrel that had allowed him to survive the ocean and to drift to land alive. And then he was confused, and wondered if this was good or bad luck or just the spirit of *Yoonir* testing him. And then he would remember Kobina's other words, saying that he would know *when* to part with the Yoonir pearl. And each time he would say: 'But now I am alone. How can I part with it wisely with no one to give it to?'

He was hungry always, and as Mila struggled with the simple act of survival, finding enough to eat consumed his entire day, and he all but forgot his past. It could have been very different if it wasn't for water. Inland there was a rocky formation where the trees would not take root, standing towards the centre of which was a natural dip that trapped water and occasionally trickled out as a stream in heavier rainfalls. In his journeys about the island foraging he soon came to realize that he was utterly alone, but there had been someone before. Near the water rocks stood the remains of a cabin of hewn logs, its one remaining wall charred and stark, like the blackened ribs of a long dead giant beast stood in the sun in a woodland clearing. A few remaining clues lay scattered about suggesting that people like Trader's had once been there. Some tin cups and a jug, a couple of spoons and a few rags of cloth. Mila made the most of these, gathering forest branches and tying them together with strips of cloth creating a lean-to against the standing wall. In the coming days he added what branches and bracken he could to the shelter until it was dense and heavy enough to repel the wind and rainfall and inside he laid more bracken and leaf across a bed of branches until he had a sleeping place that was not too uncomfortable. A metal spoon he pounded with a stone until the bowl end fell away leaving a good taper of steel which he carefully stroked, sharpened and polished on the rocky ground until he had a fine point. Thin strips of cloth bound the spearhead to the split end of a long straight branch. When he had finished Mila stood up proudly with his creation and declared aloud: 'Now I am master of my island! I am the Head!' And he strutted about proudly like one of the warriors of his tribe, dancing and pointing the spear at every little bird or creature that twittered or squeaked in the woods, laughing and chasing them. And for the briefest of times, Mila was elated. And with his new tool he found ease in spearing the fish that gathered near the tidal rocks.

One night many months from when Mila was cast upon his strange new world, a huge storm blew up testing his art of shelter making to the limit. And as he lay shivering with cold and fear the lightning grounded somewhere in the woods bursting the forest open with light as the ground beneath him shook and groaned with anger. It was the longest of terrifying nights Mila could ever remember. But as dawn light broke and the storm rolled on, he had survived; his shelter and life intact.

He walked up to the water rocks for his morning drink. As usual his first thoughts were for food and whether he might first forage from the woods or pick from the shore rocks. Then maybe later towards dusk when the rays gathered near the beach he might use the spear. His stomach growled with the thought of strips of nice juicy ray roasting on the hot stones of an open fire. But this was merely a daydream. Mila had never mastered the art of fire-making and had survived solely on raw fish, forest roots and berries and shellfish. Once he had speared a stork that he found drinking from the water rocks, but the taste of this raw was so disgusting he spat it out and instead used strips of the flesh thrown into the water by the sea rocks to attract the fish. Another time he managed to spear a rabbit, a creature that seemed to abound on the island and although the meat was a little sweeter it left a strange aftertaste that Mila was not too fond of.

He drank his thirst away and stood high upon the rocks and closing his eyes, imagined his people at feast. A fine fat forest boar roasted upon a spit along with pots of spiced ray fish and there were yams roasting in the embers. He could taste the boar, succulent strips of meat with crisp blackened skin seasoned with Trader's spices crunching in his mouth and the delicious smell of warming fish stews. As his mouth watered he spread his arms out wide and called out: 'Oh, love of Yoonir, please give me a beautiful roast boar. I am so hungry!' And as Mila opened his eyes a fleeting glimpse of white appeared to move through the foliage beyond the trees as though a cloud had dropped into the forest and quickly disappeared again. He dashed into the woods and carefully climbed the tallest tree he could find as high as he dare. From his position beyond the tree line, across the ocean where the sea and sky are the same colour, a vessel seemed to float on neither. He strained his eyes trying to judge the size of it and how many sails. In his heart of hearts he prayed that it might be Trader and that the boat would come his way. But still he could not tell and there was nothing he could do. And the memory of Briggs and the slave ship still burnt bright in his mind. And so he sat among the branches watching until the sail became smaller. And for a long time he still watched, saddened that the boat was going away.

But now his attention was focused on the forest and he realized what must have been the white cloud. Through the treetops smoke was rising. Somewhere a lightning tree still smouldered. He carefully shinnied down the tree, and dashed through the woods. What was once a solid and beautiful stem of life now lay split and crackled with char wood, its fire that had illuminated the previous night about to die. Mila grabbed a charred smoking branch carefully blowing and fanning it with a broad leaf until the end glowed with a faint red ember. Holding it high towards the heavens he whispered, 'Oh Yoonir, perhaps you now look upon me as Kobina has said and you bring me luck at last.'

The forest ground leaves were still wet from the night's rainfall, so using the spearhead he stripped dry splinters from the tree where the warm char met the good wood. He fed these to the ember which started to smoke heavily under the little pile he'd created and he wondered if he might have killed the fire. Suddenly, with a sound like a faint puff of wind, the smoke burst into a small flame that quickly gathered pace as it consumed the wood flakes. Excitedly Mila gathered more flakes of tinder as the fire grew. Before long he had laid branches and bracken across until a good fire crackled. Now he had to make a decision. He knew he must keep the fire going. And he knew if it was to be any good at all, he must hunt. Would he have time to spear rays at the shore rocks? He pushed fire embers up to the rest of the smouldering tree in the hope that it would catch and burn as bright as the feast fires of his tribe, or that at least something still remained when he returned.

He took the Yoonir pearl from his loincloth and held it up as he had done with the glowing branch. 'Thank you Yoonir, you have blessed me at last...' And at that moment, before Mila could finish his thanks, a rabbit darted between the trees nearby. Mila tucked the pearl away and picked up his spear. 'Truly blessed,' he whispered as he set off after the rabbit.

But the rabbit seemed to be more clever than most and was leading Mila on a frustrating chase. It darted from one tree to another and just as Mila thought he had it tracked, he would leap around the tree to find the rabbit had disappeared only to dart from another tree behind him or some way off in the woods. He was getting angry and worried that the fire might go out before he had chance to cook it. It led him to the edge of the woods near the shore where the ground was neither all shale nor forest earth but a combination of both and only grasses of fern and glasswort grew. It stopped and began to nibble the tasty little new shoots. Mila was too far off to get a decent shot at the rabbit. But as it was facing away and the sea breeze floated inshore he realized that he was upwind of the creature. Carefully he crept up to within a few yards and still the rabbit nibbled away either uncaring in the joy of eating or even unaware of Mila's close proximity. Mila took another step.

He raised the spear. He would get a good shot from here, as easy as spearing the floundering ray. A bird squawked and flapped, flying up through the branches startling the rabbit, which shot out into the open and onto the beach. Mila cursed as he gave chase and dashed after it into the sunlight. The rabbit veered right and then right again back towards the woods as it realized that Mila was in pursuit. Mila had only one chance left before the rabbit disappeared into the undergrowth. He launched his spear in an arc as he ran, trying to judge the rabbit's pace and zigzag sprint, before skidding and tumbling onto his side in the shale. The spear flew high, the tail-end quivering and humming like a trapped bird as it flew and descended and Mila watched as spear and prey drew closer.

The rabbit tumbled head over heel with a shrill squeal as the spear caught its hindquarter and Mila leapt to his feet running for joy and sliding to retrieve his prize. He lay in the shale for a while, holding the spear end, gasping and laughing as the rabbit kicked and struggled. He rolled onto his side facing the sea, and squinted and blinked into the morning sun's sparkling waves in disbelief. A ship was not far from shore. And men on a boat were swiftly rowing their way towards him. He didn't understand. The ship on the horizon? It couldn't be here so soon, it was going away and disappeared. The white in the forest? It was smoke? Sail? It must have been sail, so near to the shore. His mind had deceived him through hunger. He'd fleetingly seen the sails of a ship that must have disappeared around the island's curved shore, and not realized. And as luck would have it, he'd dashed out from the woods at the point where it had decided to drop anchor.

Their backs were to him as they fiercely rowed, but had they seen him? They would be on the beach soon. Seen or not, he had to move. He grabbed the spear and barely made the nearest sparse undergrowth as the boat hull ripped and ground shale and sand with a roar of booming surf and shouting men.

They were facing him now as he lay frightened and watching from the forest edge. They ran the boat up the beach to dry shale away from the edge where the tidal drag churned and dug the beach like teeth. He wanted to move, but they were close and he could hear their voices, close enough to see him should he try to move away from his barely concealed position. He was in the undergrowth and the trees were several yards further away. He dare not move.

There were four of them and he could see their faces and their strange clothes. Mila had imagined such things from Trader's tales. But these were different. The faces of three of them were dark but not like his own, but the fourth was white like a slaver and he dressed like the driver Briggs. The others looked equally as menacing in dark pantaloons with sashes of different colours, and strange jackets with wide lapels and wounds of cloth around their heads. All had high boots and strange looking curved knives unlike the type Trader had dealt with his people.

The ship was smaller but like that of the slavers and he had the sudden urge to run away. Even if they were not Briggs' men, perhaps they were other slavers that had heard that this was the island where the slaves had come and that they had survived and now they were here to capture them into chains again? And maybe they knew that Mila had helped them escape and where he was hiding and now they were about to find him and hand him over to the slavers? And then he remembered what he had done to Briggs and imagined that they would inflict a terrible revenge. Or maybe they were just like some of the people in Trader's tales? Trading people. Not all ships carried slaves, Trader had once said. So many thoughts ran through his mind.

'That was too close, far too close,' said one of the men in a language Mila did not understand.

'Do not worry about it, Anas,' another answered. 'They are

no match for a Xebec. We will outrun them every time.'

'Perhaps, Brahim,' said Anas. 'But they were military, French I think. And one day there may be a vessel quicker than ours, with many guns. And they have seen us approach the island. What if they had decided to follow us here? And what if they suspect our actions?'

'Bah!' said a third man. 'Let them think what they want. We are not at war with the French, they were merely curious. As long as we're not seen to be impeding the American trades they will not care about us. And they will never find our bounty once it's hidden.'

'All the more reason to get it done,' Brahim unexpectedly spoke in the English tongue of Trader. 'Isaac, you and Mehdi go find out what that smoke is all about first. If there are others about be prepared to fight or leave very quickly. We cannot risk discovery of our secret. Stow the bounty in the usual place as quickly as possible, and be vigilant lest there be others about. Anas and I will keep lookout, should the French dogs decide to get curious again.'

The fire! Mila had completely forgotten about it. And now the men would find it and surely find his encampment not far from the lightning tree. They would see his shelter, the bones and skins of his kills and small tools. And they would know that he was here somewhere on the island. And they were hiding something. They would hunt for him. His mind raced and the overwhelming temptation was to just sprint into the forest as quickly as possible and hide. And perhaps if he was clever enough they would tire of seeking him? But he was hungry and weak. The months had taken their toll on his body and mind. He could not hide forever and hunt to feed himself as well. And if the men were determined they would catch him eventually.

But then he had an idea. What if the men believed him to be dead? On another part of the coast not far from his camp there might still be a few of the dead slaves that he hadn't the strength to bury. Their emaciated bodies could still be there and would be light in weight by now. If he could only drag one to his camp before the men found it they would think the island's last inhabitant was long gone. It might be his only chance.

Isaac and Mehdi had only just dragged the chest from the boat when at that moment the rabbit jerked and with one final breath of life, let out a shrill squeal and all eyes looked towards the bush where Mila lay terrified.

'What was that?' cried Brahim.

'Just a bird, I think,' said Isaac.

'Yes, just a bird.' Brahim walked down the beach towards the shore. 'Here,' he said. 'I've something to show you.'

The others followed as Brahim talked about something he'd noticed near the shore until Mila could no longer hear them. When they returned to the boat, Brahim repeated his instruction for Isaac and Mehdi to look for the source of smoke. The two ran past Mila and into the forest as Brahim and Anas walked back towards the shore until they could no longer be heard.

Mila decided that this would be his one and only chance. He slowly backed up on all fours towards the forest all the while watching Brahim and Anas as they talked. They were facing away from him. Brahim was pointing out to sea. As soon as he reached the first trees and out of sight, Mila would run, but not straight towards camp. He would use the forest concealment and follow the shore to where he'd left the rotting slaves. He was out of the undergrowth now and past the first trees. Brahim and Anas were still looking the other way. He leapt up and spun around to run.

A blinding flash of light sprang before Mila's eyes. Pain stunned him to his toes and his legs paralyzed as Mila collapsed onto his back in a fainting shock. Stars burst around him as the cold water doused his face. Warm blood trickled from his mouth along with salt water that stung his eyes. Isaac stood over him grinning with an empty pitcher in one hand and a flintlock pistol in the other which he pointed close to Mila's head. Medhi stood to one side. Brahim and Anas stood to the other with swords drawn.

'Well, well,' said Isaac. 'What have we got here? Looks like the rabbit catcher has been caught, me thinks.'

'You didn't have to nearly kill him, Isaac!' said Brahim. 'He's only a boy; you could have caught him with one hand nearly.'

'Taking no risks, begging your pardon, Brahim,' said Isaac. 'Looks like a little spy among us.'

'If he's a spy, then indeed we must kill him now,' said Mehdi. 'He has seen our bounty and knows what we are doing.'

'I doubt that,' replied Anas. 'He has no more flesh than the rabbit. Look at him. He's shipwrecked. Escaped slave, I think.'

'Is that it?' said Brahim, poking Mila with his sword. 'You are a runaway? You have somehow managed to jump ship? Come, boy, what is your explanation?'

'Shouldn't bother asking him nothing,' said Isaac. 'He'll only speak the tongue of savages.'

Mila groaned and rolled onto his side. 'I am lost,' he whispered.

'Aha, how wrong you are, Isaac!' Brahim declared. 'It even speaks your very own language! But still a spy nonetheless. What were you doing spying on us? Thinking that you might help yourself to gold when we were gone?'

'That would be ridiculous,' said Anas. 'What would a shipwreck do with gold? Spend it on the trees and birds?'

The others laughed, all but Mehdi who was worried. 'But he knows of us now,' he said. 'It is too risky to leave him here. Others may come and he will tell them there is gold on the island and if they know even that much, they may find it. We must kill him now!'

'I agree,' said Isaac, cocking his flintlock and Mehdi nodded.

Brahim reached out and steadied Isaac's hand. 'I believe this one would be dead before long anyway,' he said. 'Pity the poor wretch! We might even be doing him a favour. But I see no slave markings upon him. A virgin piece of stock. Starving or not, I think Youssef may be interested in this one. Get him up and bring him aboard the Seyaad.'

6.

Isaac and Mehdi finished carrying out Brahim's order and the chest was dragged somewhere into the forest out of Mila's sight and out of mind. Mila lay for a long time still in pain and shock as the other two men questioned him further, but Mila said little, denying that he was an escaped slave, should the men want to return him to Briggs' ship. Eventually, he gathered his senses as Isaac and Mehdi returned and he struggled pitifully in his weakness for a while as they dragged him to the boat where they bound him hand and foot. Anas sat upon him as the others rowed, should he attempt to jump into the sea or upset the boat.

And once again Mila was hoisted and dumped sprawling like a floundering fish onto the deck of an unknown ship.

Men quickly gathered around him in their curiosity. Men of all colours. Men of all sizes and shapes with many different types of dress. Some with tattooed faces. Others wore fine looking jackets and leggings that appeared to shine in the sunlight. Others wore head cloths; turbans of white or black with blouses of blue or purple and strange footwear with curved ends and many wore swords or curved daggers tucked into sashes. Mila sensed a feeling of relief as he realized that these were very different looking people from the slave ship. Some were grinning and laughing at his bound body as he struggled and thrashed like a fish against the bindings.

'Well, Brahim,' said one, 'what manner of sea creature have you caught today!'

'An eel!' another man laughed. 'He has no meat, so skinny. Throw him back immediately! Even the sharks wouldn't bother with this one!'

'He is no fish,' declared Brahim. 'Skinny he may be but here he is. It was either kill or leave him on the island. We caught him spying on us.'

'Then kill him now,' said yet another man drawing his sword. 'Why have you brought him to us?'

'That's what I said,' said Mehdi. 'We should have slaughtered him ashore and have done. What use is he to us?'

'I agree,' said Isaac. 'But Brahim insisted.'

'Perhaps we should just slit his throat and have done then?' said the man with the drawn sword.

'Just because of who we are does not make us merciless butchers of children!' argued Brahim, cutting the bonds from Mila's hands and feet. 'Look at him! He hasn't the strength to make the shore even should he try to jump!'

'Well then,' said Isaac, 'why don't we just have a little fun with him then, before we throw him back? Let's show him the girl!'

'Yes, yes!' some of the men cried eagerly. 'Bring out the girl! Let the little Spanish maiden have a look!'

Mila was hauled to his feet and a young girl about Mila's age was dragged kicking and struggling against her handlers through the crowd and pushed towards him. 'Here, have a look at this, Julieta,' Isaac laughed. 'It even understands the *common speech*. A skinny little black English speaking eel Brahim has fished out of the sea for you!'

Her skin was fair, like a few of the men on the ship, and Mila stared back in nervous fascination at the pretty, but angry looking girl, strangely dressed with flowing white pantaloons, blue blouse and red sash. A wide red bandana around her head held her long, shiny, straight black hair. She stumbled forward as she was shoved and stood scowling at Mila. She looked around at the men questioningly, then back at Mila, her dark eyes flashing with contempt before marching swiftly forward and sharply kicking him in the shin.

Mila cried out in pain and stood hopping on one leg, clutching his shin. The rest of the crew burst out in howls of laughter.

'What you doing, foolish savage-boy?' the girl cried. 'What you doing on ship?'

'Shipwrecked, he was!' Isaac laughed. 'Must have jumped some slave ship and got washed up ashore!'

'Oh, so you float about in ocean?' said Julieta, placing her hands on her hips and glaring scornfully at Mila. 'What, you jump ship in middle of ocean and think you float about like boat without drowning? You foolish child, you think you floaty floaty like a boaty boy?' And with her hands Julieta mimicked a boat bobbing on the ocean at which some of the crew erupted in fits of hysterical laughter.

A rapid exchange of conversations, chattered and hand-gestured translations between the English speaking and the rest of the crew spread until all understood the joke Julieta had made.

'Floaty boaty, floaty boaty boy!' they all cried, some bending over in their merriment or slapping each other across their backs and making floating gestures or walking back and forth bobbing up and down miming the rolling of boats at sail.

Suddenly all fell silent. A proud and noble looking man with long black and silver-streaked hair and long silver goatee beard approached pushing the others aside as he strode purposefully through the crowd. He stood in the middle looking round at the rest of the crew. He was thinner and taller than the others, darker of skin but not as dark as Mila's and his long dark pantaloons and blouse matched his knee length black-laced boots. He held one hand on the hilt of a sheathed sword as he glared irately at the rest of the men.

'*Ma hatha?* What is the meaning of this disturbance!' he bellowed. 'Can a man not have some peace after so many days of sail followed by a night of storm?'

'We found this boy on the island, Captain Youssef,' explained Brahim. 'We decided it was too much of a risk leaving him, he was watching us from the woods and knows too much. And he speaks the *common tongue*. Others arriving at the island might understand him.'

Captain Youssef looked Mila up and down then clutched his jaw in one hand turning Mila's head back and forth examining the swelling of his face. 'Interesting. And so you decided that this mere skinny runt was such a threat that you had to nearly beat him to death? Is that it?'

'Had to stop him, begging your pardon, Captain,' said Isaac. 'But the lad were about to bolt into the forest where we might lose him for good.'

'Are there any more of your kind on the island, boy?' demanded Youssef.

'We had a scout round, Captain,' said Mehdi. 'We found the boy's encampment but there was no sign of others. Perhaps if he's jumped a slave ship he's the lucky one. It's likely most would drown in these waters.'

'Perhaps,' said Youssef. 'All the same we'll navigate the coast before our journey, look out for any sign of life. We take no chances with the bounty. A sail round and a good scouting party across the island. Capture any living person that might still remain, we shall take them as our own slaves to market. As for the boy,' continued Youssef, stroking Mila's swollen chin, 'We'll feed him up and let him rest a while. He should fetch a decent price in Tunis with a little more meat and muscle on his bones. Julieta, bring the boy to my quarters!'

Julieta shoved Mila roughly across the deck and through the

door into Captain Youssef's cabin. Mila looked around the strange room in amazement. Rolls of maps and shiny instruments lay sprawled across a table in the middle. Other strange objects hung from the ceiling and small casks stood in the corners. Oil lamps and candles in bright brass holders hung among the tapestries along with fine wood and mineral carvings and intricately engraved copperware adorning the shelves all around. A fine patterned weave rug covered the middle, running under the table. A brass telescope stood on a tripod and a pewter mug and fine cut-glass decanter filled with amber liquor glinted in the light from the cabin window. Mila had never seen glass and in his fascination reached out to touch the decanter.

Julieta prodded him sharply in the back. 'Don't touch anything!' she hissed.

'Come here, boy,' said Youssef beckoning Mila to sit at the table. He cleared maps and documents away placing them on side shelves and pouring a small drink from the decanter into a mug he sat on the bench opposite Mila. 'You must have a name, boy?'

'I am Mila.'

'And you jumped ship…a slave ship, I understand?'

Mila hesitated before answering. 'No, I am not a slave. I am lost. A storm blew me away when I was fishing.'

'Hmm,' said Youssef, stroking his beard. 'Perhaps you are telling the truth. You have no slave markings, I noticed. But I also think the wind and prevailing tide have blown you a long way from home, and in the wrong direction. I'm not so sure you could be so far off course and still survive. Gambia coast I think you're from. Indeed, a very long way off course. However, perhaps some food and drink might loosen your tongue. He slid the mug of liquor to Mila. 'Drink boy,' finest Douro Port,' he said. 'Unfortunately, Allah forbids me from joining you.'

Mila sniffed and took a small sip, immediately choking and coughing on the liquor and frowning with his tongue out. 'Water of sleep,' he grunted placing the mug back down.

'Indeed it is,' said Youssef, smiling. 'I have no need of it, and the Seyaad never sleeps. We are vigilant always. And I imagine your people have no taste for it either.'

Julieta snatched the mug away from Mila. 'Not for small children!' she snapped.

'The boy is starving, Julieta,' said Youssef. 'Fetch us some food now and some water for the boy.'

Julieta disappeared from the cabin, returning shortly with a basket that she set on the table. Then she fetched pewter plates and mugs from a cupboard. Youssef placed chunks of salt beef and bread onto plates, handing them to Mila and Julieta before helping himself, tearing bread and meat together and stuffing them into his mouth.

'Come, boy Mila,' he muffled with a full mouth. 'Eat! We are not trying to poison you. Only fatten you up a bit.'

'Eat, stupid child,' mumbled Julieta. 'Do as Captain say. You rather be skinny eel and die on island?'

Mila picked up the meat smelling it cautiously and tore a piece off, before taking a huge bite and chewing ravenously. He picked up the bread stuffing his mouth. It was good bread, hard but not tasteless like the slave bread and the meat although salty was unspoiled and flavoursome and he sighed with contentment at the joy of eating. Julieta then brought a jug of water and bowl of fruit to the table at which Mila stopped chewing in his amazement.

'What's the matter, boy Mila?' said Youssef. 'Surely you have fruit where you come from?'

Mila reached out and picked up a shiny red and green apple, turning it over in his hands inquisitively. He sniffed at it suspiciously.

'Apple,' said Julieta. 'You never see one before?'

Mila shook his head.

'We have lots of fruits,' said Julieta. 'We take them from many places. Is very good taste, you see. Go on foolish child, take bite like this!' And Julieta snatched the apple away from Mila and took a large bite. 'See? Is no poison. You eat now. Eat plenty as Captain says!'

Mila took the apple and bit a small piece off. The flesh and juice was sweet and the taste was unlike anything Mila had eaten before. His face lit up as he chewed and Youssef laughed aloud as Mila ravenously finished the fruit and the rest of his meal and felt replete for the first time in many months.

'Julieta, sort out some decent clothes for the boy,' said Youssef when they had finished eating. 'We can't have him roaming the deck like a savage. And string a hammock up for him in your quarter.'

Julieta followed out the Captain's orders, finding some black pantaloons and sash and white shirt, then fixing a hammock up from the rafters in a small side-quarter next to Captain Youssef's cabin.

'Here boy,' said Julieta throwing the clothes onto the hammock. 'Put these on as Captain says. You can't go walky walky about deck like savage-boy. Get dressed now!'

Mila picked up the pantaloons and laid them back again. Julieta frowned. 'What, you shy like little child? You frightened of what Julieta see under stupid savage-boy loincloth? Come, get dressed now!'

But Mila wasn't shy. The Yoonir pearl was still concealed in its leather bag beneath his loincloth. He gestured with his hand for her to turn around.

'Very well,' said Julieta. 'I leave stupid shy child to learn to dress himself.'

She left the cabin and Mila quickly changed, tucking away the pearl bag tying it by the inside cord of his new pantaloons.

Youssef appeared shortly after, admiring the new smartly

attired Mila. 'Rest now, boy Mila,' he said. 'We have a long sail ahead of us.'

Mila climbed into the hammock staring through the wooden fretwork of the cabin window at the coastline. At the hum of men on deck preparing the ship, he fell into an exhausted fitful sleep awakening a short time later as the roll of sea and passing landscape showed that the Seyaad had set sail. Eventually, the ship stopped and dropped anchor and Mila listened as he dozed at the sound of men running or walking and calling out orders and the squeal of winches as boats were lowered into the water. By evening the ship was moving again and Mila fell fast asleep with the gentle roll and sway of his hammock as he watched the stars rising outside.

Some while later, Mila awoke and sat up alarmed as the darkness was pierced. Julieta appeared before him with an oil lamp that she hung from a rafter and turned down low before climbing into her hammock. 'Oh, did poor little boy have bad dream and Julieta frighten him?' she whispered sarcastically. 'Go back to sleep now.'

Mila lay back down but could no longer sleep. He still felt the pain of Isaac's fist and couldn't sleep the dead sleep of exhaustion as he had been. And now he was curious about his new captors. 'Why do you hate me?' he whispered.

'Who say I hate you?' replied Julieta, her dark eyes glinted back at Mila in the lamplight. 'I just think you stupid for getting lost. You wash out to sea in big storm you say? Why you go fishy fishy in sea with big storm coming?'

Mila didn't really have an answer. He was still reluctant and untrusting of anyone to mention the slave ship. And the reason he did get washed out to sea before was because of his own foolishness for not noticing the approaching storm.

'And you kicked me,' Mila said. 'I am only like you, not even a man yet, but you kick me as if I was a slave? Are we slaves? Are you a slave? Why are we not in chains?'

'I am no slave!' Julieta snapped. 'I kick you because you savage-man like slave, wear only stupid cloth, wander in forest nearly naked. Julieta is civilised woman from civilised land.'

'Oh yes, I have heard of the *great civilisation*,' said Mila. 'Trader has told me all about this place. I would like to see it.'

'Who this Trader person? He man who come to savage-land and tell you big stories? And so you want to get in boat in big storm and find it?'

Mila realized that Julieta had somehow guessed the truth of his journey and was careful what to say to her next. 'No I was fishing, not looking for *civilisation*. If we are not slaves...who are we?'

'I said *Julieta* is not slave, not you. Captain say he sell you in Tunis.' Julieta quickly realized the carelessness of her words. If the boy thought he might be a slave again he might also jump ship. 'But I think Captain has other plan for you. You be deck hand and boy-servant like Julieta. And you very lucky. Mehdi say all your people die on island, only skeleton left for vulture.'

'They were not my people,' said Mila sadly. 'And I was not a slave.'

'So you say. Men still think you slave-boy. But Captain treat you like Julieta.'

'But who are you?' Mila insisted. 'What is this ship if not a slave ship? Are you like Trader?'

'Yes, yes!' Julieta sat upright in her hammock and waved her arms about. 'Just like traders,' she said sarcastically. 'Only we don't trade, we just take! Foolish child, you really know nothing, do you? We are *Barbaries*. Barbaries are pirates, help themselves to anything they want. This very fast ship. Captain Youssef say this is *polacre xebec* ship, many sails and many guns and very clever men. We see big ship fat and slow with gold and Seyaad catch them very quickly – we take some gold from them. We see trader ship heavy with fine cloth and wines – we take some from them. We not take all, enough for us and men on ship so we not kill them. There, you understand now?'

'Yes...I think?' replied Mila. 'But why do you steal? It is wrong, my people have very bad punishment for stealing and Trader says...'

'Never mind what stupid traders say!' Julieta retorted. 'Go sleep now, boy. Tomorrow they make you work very hard. Need sleep.'

7.

The following day was true to Julieta's words. In the early light, she stirred Mila with a shake before turning his hammock over and dumping him to the floor, leaving him sprawled and disoriented in his grogginess. Youssef had left corn bread and fruit for the two at his table which Mila gulped down greedily as Julieta watched him, shaking her head in disdain as she had her fill.

At first, Mila was given simple tasks such as mending the coiled riggings which he seemed to be good at much to Youssef's pleasure, or helping the ship's galley hand to prepare the crew's meals. But eventually he was made to work hard, scrubbing the galley floors, winching sails and mending and filling shiplap with hot pitch, the bubbling black tar filling his nostrils and taking his breath away in fits of coughing. But always he was well fed and slept well and over the days he grew strong and confident in his work and pleased when Youssef complimented him.

And although Youssef and some of the others spoke the language of Trader, it was usually Julieta who gave him orders or translated the words of others to him. But steadily, over time, Mila learnt a little of their language, enough to carry out orders from those that understood neither of his own.

Youssef was a towering and stern presence always, barking orders and making threats of physical punishment at the men. Often, when the sea was high with white peaks and the Seyaad was at full sail he would appear from his quarters in turban and *thobe*, a long flowing blue robe, and stand on the foredeck, perfectly balancing through the rolling waves with scimitar drawn, dancing and waving and swinging the curved sword as though in combat with an invisible enemy. Mila would stop and watch in fascination, and wonder if this was some ritual dance such as those of his own tribe. But the rest of the crew largely ignored Youssef, all but Brahim, the Seyaad's navigator who would carefully guide the ship over the breakers smiling and complimenting Youssef on his prowess in the rough sea. Youssef seemed fair to Mila, allowing him to recover from his injury inflicted by Isaac. And in the evening the two children would dine at his table, occasionally on fresh line-caught fish and vegetables or salt-fish soup with bread, and taking it in turn to fetch the Captain food and drink from the main galley. Youssef rarely spoke during these meals other than to ask if certain chores had been completed or to outline the following day's duties.

Most of the men ignored Mila, but others were resentful of his quartering with the Captain and muttered under their breath words of resentment at his being aboard. The worst of these was Isaac himself who would often taunt him as he worked and make threats of throwing him over or slitting his throat in the night. One day as Julieta was showing Mila how to remove lichen and plug small cracks and gaps in the main deck, Mila asked about the flintlock that Isaac carried tucked into his sash. Julieta explained about guns as Mila remembered the musket fire on the slave ship. In the meantime, Isaac had caught the two looking at him and talking. He dropped the rigging he was coiling and swaggered over. Julieta hushed immediately and averted her eyes and carried on scraping the deck.

'So, little ones,' said Isaac grinning broadly. 'You have something you want to say to me?'

Mila stood up. 'Gun,' he said pointing at Isaac's sash.

'Oh, foolish child,' Julieta muttered.

'So, you want to have a little look at Isaac's gun, do you?' said Isaac drawing the flintlock.

'There is no blade,' said Mila. 'How can that work? It makes a big noise and flashes like the lightning, this I know. Then what happens?'

'Well,' said Isaac smiling with a wicked glint in his eye. 'Perhaps a little demonstration should quell your curiosity.' He grabbed Mila by the arm, dragging him to the starboard rail and sat him upon a tied barrel, placing a tin mug on his head. 'Now, there's a clever boy. Just you see how long you can balance that cup. You're a good little black savage-lad, I know, I've seen your kind prancing about all over the place balancing their filthy ware on their heads. You can sit still for a moment or two without dropping it, surely?'

'Oh yes,' said Mila nervously.

'No, Isaac!' Julieta protested grasping at Isaac's gun as he stepped back several paces.

'Shut it, wench!' said Isaac, pushing Julieta to the deck. 'Now just hold very still, boy' He cocked the flintlock and raised it pointing it at Mila who now began to tremble with fear.

The blade of a sword appeared from behind Isaac resting upon the wrist of his gun hand. Brahim stepped forward, slowly but firmly pressing the blade of his scimitar down until Isaac's hand was at his side, then flicked it up suddenly pressing the blade-point under Isaac's chin forcing him to look upwards as Brahim spoke. 'Idle hands make foolish decisions!' he barked. 'Have you nothing better to do than play games with children, Isaac?'

'Just a bit of fun,' muttered Isaac, gurgling with the pressure of the blade on his throat. 'Lad wanted to know how the flintlock works.'

'So you thought you might just use the opportunity to blow his brains out? I've had my eye on you, Isaac. I know you resent the boy, but he is now Youssef's property, do you understand? And don't forget, Isaac, you're not really one of us despite your so-called 'conversion.' We suffer you only for your skills as a seaman. But as Allah is my witness I will not hesitate to expend you should you attempt such idiocy again!'

'You're not the Captain of this ship!' Isaac protested. 'Who gives you the right to say this!'

'I do!' Captain Youssef bellowed from behind. He marched up to Isaac. 'Brahim is my trusted man and if I see any more such foolishness from you Isaac, I'll not only let Brahim cut you, but I will personally feed your filthy remains to the sharks!'

'Nothing but a runaway slave-boy, Captain,' muttered Isaac. 'Not to be trusted his kind aren't, begging your pardon. Should have left him to rot with the other skeletons on the island.'

'But he's *my* slave-boy! Do you understand?' said Youssef, as Brahim pressed the blade harder.

'Understood, Captain Youssef,' Isaac coughed as Brahim snatched the blade away.

'Back to work all of you!' Youssef bellowed out to the rest of the crew who had stopped in their duties to witness the unfolding drama.

Isaac and the others left Mila alone as the days and nights passed. Other than Brahim, who looked kindly upon him, Captain Youssef and Julieta were the only ones who held conversation other than to shout an order or scold him for making mistakes. Brahim spoke to him often in English when he was within hearing distance from his station at the ship's helm and although Brahim was one of his captors on the island, Mila became trusting of him. As his confidence in Brahim grew, Mila became curious about how Brahim knew where they were going even in the day when the clouds covered the sun.

'Instruments,' Brahim would laugh as the ship rolled. 'The wonders of science and Allah combined! Come, boy Mila, and see.' And Brahim would produce an ivory case from his tunic. And flipping the hinged lid there was a brass housed compass. 'You see the point Mila? It always points in the same direction, to the north. It does not matter where the sun is; the compass needle always looks the same way. So then I know which way the wind blows and when to set or raise sail and where we are going at all times, night or day. And Captain Youssef uses other instruments, equally as shiny and bright as this one and maps to plot our route. Surely you have seen the Captain pondering over the maps in his quarters?'

'Oh yes,' said Mila enthusiastically. 'I remember Trader showing me and telling me about maps.'

'A trader?' said Brahim. 'Your people do trade with the merchants of the Mediterranean?'

'Yes,' said Mila. 'And you speak Trader's language. I am glad. There are so many words of your tongue I don't understand.'

'Yes, I learnt it long ago,' said Brahim. 'There are a few who can speak the *common tongue* of Isaac. It comes in useful in our *business*. Youssef insists we must communicate with other *merchants* as well as we can.'

'One day I would like to see Trader again,' said Mila.

'Perhaps, Mila. Perhaps one day. And look also!' Brahim cried, pointing out across the starboard bow.

Mila stared out to sea but saw nothing at first, until the huge dark fins and shapes appeared arching over the surface of the sea and submerging again followed closely by many others, surfacing and submerging in giant elegant rolls.

'What is it?' said an astonished Mila as one leapt out from the water.

'Whales,' said Brahim. 'Brothers of the sea. They follow us from time to time, or so it appears. And they are another way of navigating. Depending upon the time of year, we know which direction they travel and so we can set a course by them.'

'Where are they going?' said Mila.

'Who knows, other than the whale?' said Brahim. 'But they are on a journey as the rest of us in this life are. And do any of us really know where we are going in the journey of life?'

And Mila also was curious of Captain Youssef's maps, and Youssef eventually took heed of his inquisitiveness and was surprised at how well the boy understood the geography of coastal outlines, land relief and the concept of compass points in relation to the instrument itself.

'I would like one of these to take to my people one day,' Mila would say. 'Then I would never be lost in the ocean again.' At which Youssef would smile and Julieta would shrug her shoulders dismissively.

'You still be stupid child and go fishy fishy in big storm,' she remarked.

Over time Mila learned all about the Seyaad. Julieta instructed him in the art of rigging, which sails needed to be up and others when to drop according to the winds and how to grease and operate the windlasses and inspect the ropes, repairing and binding the worn and frayed ones. At other times he would mend dropped sails, repair barrels and fetch water for Brahim or grease and polish the cannon rifling instructed by Anas, the ship's gunner.

'Every day,' Anas would insist. 'The guns gather rust if they are left, so you grease the barrels like so, every one, never forget. The guns are useless if they are not cared for.' And Anas would dip a long pole bound with rag at one end into a barrel of oil and plunge it back and forth down the cannon barrels. And then the gun's powder chambers would need carefully polishing. It was hard work, running down the length of the deck attending to each gun and Mila felt his arms grow strong over the passing days. And each day in turn, to Mila's delight, Anas would test one of the guns with a small powder charge.

'It is magic!' Mila would shout as the cannon boomed. 'You are making lightning and thunder like the gods, Anas.'

And all the time Mila would watch in fascination at Julieta's agility, scampering up the riggings to untangle ropes or kicking out sails that had become stuck, swinging from one rig to another and walking unaided along the crossbeams. She caught Mila staring at her one day and quickly clambered up past the crow's nest to the very top of the mainmast as it swayed long and wide in the rolling breakers. She pulled the bandana from her head and let it flutter in one hand like a red rippling flame that droned in the breeze as she held on swaying and singing into the wind.

Youssef appeared shaking his head at the girl's antics and waved her down. 'If you want to do something useful you can show the boy Mila the crow's nest. The two of you can take a shift at watch.'

Julieta quickly scampered back up the rigging followed by Mila who shinnied up the rope nervously looking down as the mast swung back and forth ever further out over the sea as he climbed. Julieta laughed as he finally made the crow's nest, hauling him over crouching into the wood basket fixed around the mast.

'Here boy,' said Julieta producing a small brass telescope from her sash. 'Look through like this and see for ships coming.' She extended the telescope and demonstrated, looking through the eyepiece. Then she passed it to Mila. Mila examined the instrument closely, not quite understanding what Julieta had just shown him. He raised the telescope close to his eye and looked through the large end at which Julieta laughed and reached over, turning the telescope around in his hand. 'Oh, you real dumb boy!'

At first Mila wondered what the instrument was all about as he looked out to sea, until the ship's foremast and sail came into his sight. He jerked his head back, banging it on the side of the nest and dropped the telescope. Again Julieta laughed. Mila picked the telescope up again and looked through, grinning as he swung the instrument one way and another, looking out, across and up at the gulls that hovered over the ship then down at Brahim who smiled and waved at the two as he steered. Mila reached out to Brahim as though he could touch him as he watched him through the lens and leaned over the edge of the nest. Julieta quickly grabbed him and pulled him back down.

'Remember, Mila,' she said. 'It look very close, but if you fall when looking through spyglass it just as far to fall…dumb boy.'

That evening they ate silently at Youssef's table and Youssef eyed the two children closely.

'So, Mila,' said Youssef as he finished his meal. 'Where are we going? Do you know of our destination?'

Mila's hand stopped halfway from taking a mouthful of bread. 'No, Captain Youssef.' It was a question that Mila had pondered over the days but was too nervous to ask the Captain of. And Julieta was dismissive of him whenever he'd asked her, as if she herself wasn't even certain.

'Well,' continued Youssef, 'let me show you.' He stood up and walked around the table to a heavy wooden-fronted cabinet, stroking Julieta across the shoulder as he passed. Unlocking the cabinet with a key, he produced a scrolled map and a carving of a sea-turtle, which he placed upon the table by leaning over Julieta who now stopped eating and sat very still staring down at her plate.

Youssef resumed his seat at the opposite side, placing a lamp at one edge of the map, unfurling it and placing the carving at the other edge.

Mila had not seen the highly polished statue before that

shone so brightly in the dim light of the cabin and stared in fascination at it.

'Impressive, isn't it?' said Youssef. 'Extremely valuable, carved from the purest purple jade from Bursa Hamancik, Turkey.'

'It must be a very fine carver that made this,' said Mila gently touching the statue.

'Indeed it was...*whoever* he was. We have many fine objects aboard this ship by many fine craftsmen,' said Youssef, leaning forward and laughing. 'We just don't know where they are! Oh, but we do promise to look after them on their behalf!'

'We have many fine carvers in our tribe,' said Mila. 'They would be most pleased to make a carving such as this. Injua the old one who was once a fisher makes fine wood carvings.'

'I'm certain he does,' said Youssef dismissively, rapping his knuckles on the map. 'But what have you learned from my maps? If I show you where we are on here would you be able to tell me where we are going?'

Mila stared at the browned paper that covered most of the table. The representation of its distinct black outlines of coasts, islands and water had become familiar to him with Youssef's instruction. He pointed to the compass symbol at the top. 'That way is north, as Brahim says. But without compass I don't know which way the ship is sailing.'

'Good lad,' said Youssef. He produced a small brass compass from his tunic, placed it down on the map followed by a slim dagger which he punched into the map. 'There! There is where we are, boy!' he stated forcefully, pointing to the dagger. 'Now you tell me where we are going.'

Julieta stared at the dagger, her wide eyes betraying her apprehension at Youssef's mood as Mila slid the compass over. Mila stood up and turned the map around so the compass symbol was at the top then placed the compass next to Youssef's dagger turning it slowly as Brahim had once shown him until the compass and map symbol were aligned. The needle was opposite in position. He pointed behind to the fore of the ship. 'We are going north,' he said.

'Indeed we are,' said Youssef. He stretched his arms out wide arching his back and clasped his hands behind his head, leaning onto the bench-back and placed his feet upon the table.

Cautiously, Julieta resumed her meal, careful that Youssef might take offence at her for leaving the food that he had provided.

'But yesterday Brahim said we are going South?' said Mila.

'Correct again,' said Youssef. 'You see, we had word of a British merchant clipper on its way back from the East Indies, stopping for rest and even more cargo in the Azores. An Indiaman clipper so laden with gold, fine cloth, preserved delicacies, oils and spirits, so heavy and slow that it can barely sail the seas. But somewhere on the course we missed it, so now begins the race. We take the ship before it comes into their territory. We are fast and can catch them, but we are no match for the British Man o' War gunnery should it come to that. But then after that, we don't head for your little island, Mila. That is just one of many of our hidings, the more the better, should one be discovered, or we are spied upon unbeknown to us. We head back South, to the Azores once again! How's that for impudence! A little hidden cove on the isle of Sao Miguel. Shoved away once again in their own back garden, until such a time as I grow weary of such trade and go and collect my share of booty and live as rich men live, surrounded by beauty, finery and elegance! What do you say to that, my little woman, eh?'

'Yes, Captain Youssef,' Julieta muttered as she ate without looking up.

'You see, Mila, one day you will understand; there comes a time in a man's life where he desires more than riches. There is love. And a man cannot indeed be a man without the presence of woman.' Youssef sat upright and leaned across the table, staring at Julieta. 'And a man without a woman is nothing! Is that not right, Julieta? Look at me girl! Am I so vile you cannot bear to meet my eye?'

Julieta stopped eating again and looked at Youssef, her voice trembling, 'No, Captain Youssef.'

'And you, my little boy Mila,' continued Youssef, turning. 'Perhaps we can take you to the *great civilisation* that Brahim tells me you wish to see? How would you like that?'

'I would like that very much Captain Youssef,' replied Mila, now unsure of the Captain's mood.

'Yes,' said Youssef, pulling the dagger from the map, then stabbing it down hard again in another position. 'Here is where it all begins,' he said pointing. 'The Pillars of Hercules. The gateway to the *great civilisation* itself. From there we dock a while in Tunis, wait and see. Others may be on the lookout for us after this little boarding party!' He laughed aloud.

Then, slowly and purposefully Youssef placed one hand on the dagger. His mood suddenly darkened. 'But first, Mila, I can't make any such promise until you are *honest* with me.'

'I don't understand,' said Mila suddenly nervous of the Captain.

'Come, come, boy. You tell lies. You say you were not a slave, but we have seen the remains of many slaves on your little island. You jumped ship along with the rest of them, correct? Although how you managed to slip chains I can't imagine, but you jumped, am I not right, boy Mila? You were the lucky one, correct? The only survivor, yes? Come, boy, there is no point in denying it.'

Mila nodded guiltily.

'And you hide something from me,' hissed Youssef, leaning further forward, the reflection of the lamplight's dancing flame gleaming in his eyes.

'No, Captain Youssef.'

'Liar!' Youssef bellowed, slamming his fist down hard upon the table making Mila jerk in fright and Julieta let out a little cry of dismay. 'I've seen the way you walk, the way you hold yourself at work and in the rigging. You conceal it from me. This thing must be very important to you to conceal it among your privates! What value is it to you? Show it to me now, boy!'

Mila looked awkwardly at Julieta who shook her head, not understanding what Youssef was saying.

Youssef withdrew the dagger from the table, pointing it at Mila and Mila slowly, reluctantly withdrew the leather pouch and took out the Yoonir pearl, holding it out in the palm of his hand.

Youssef gasped at the sight of it glowing in its opacity, reflecting all the colours of the surrounding cabin in the lamplight. 'Where did you get such a thing of beauty as this? Surely it must be stolen!'

'It was given to me,' said Mila.

Youssef burst out laughing. 'Who would give a thing of such value to a mere slave-boy! You lie to me again!'

'It was given to me by Kobina,' said Mila. 'He was a great warrior with his people. He told me it would bring great fortune for those that depart with it wisely.'

'And so he departed with it to you? And for what reason? What was so wise that this *Kobina warrior* would hand it over to a slave?'

'He gave it to me for helping his people to escape from the slavers.'

'You?' said Youssef incredulously. 'You managed to slip the chains of many slaves? And for what? So that they might all drown and feed the vultures of a forsaken island?' And Youssef burst out in hysterical laughter, slapping his thighs. 'What good fortune it brought to them!'

Suddenly Youssef stopped laughing and pointed the dagger

again at Mila. 'You take me for a fool, boy. You would have me believe that you could outwit the entire crew of a slave ship? You jumped over along with the rest of them yes, of that I have no doubt, but you were not the liberator. You were the thief! You are far too clever, boy. An English speaking slave boy is a rare thing in this world. You've been about this world before and lived off your wits thieving. I think you were likely some rich merchant's houseboy at one time. That's before they tired of you and sold you on again, but not before you thieved this gem from them unnoticed. No doubt they'd like to get their hands on you now, once they discovered the theft! Given to you by a *great warrior*, indeed! What nonsense! Only a complete fool would depart with it willingly. And now it is time to depart with it once again…wisely of course. Give it to me, boy!'

Mila still held the pearl tightly.

'Let me explain to you what I mean by *wisely*,' said Youssef menacingly. 'I told you we would be porting in Tunis? Oh, well let me try to remember what this famous port is actually famous for? Ah, yes, I recall a very nice slave market there. A fine stout boy built up strong with good work and my food should fetch a pretty price. Particularly an unmarked, English speaking one.'

Julieta gasped in dread. 'No!' she pleaded.

'So, my little Julieta,' Youssef responded. 'Suddenly you feel sorry for this *foolish child savage-boy*? Perhaps then you should go also? He turned his attention back to Mila. 'A *very* pretty price for two, I should think; an English speaking black boy and a multi-tongued Spanish girl. Not that you would be together. You, boy Mila, would be shipped to the colonies and whipped mercilessly in the fields by day and sobbing by night, regretting the day you ever set eyes upon this pearl. And you Julieta, at best a house servant, sweeping and scrubbing, no more riding the waves and singing into the wind as you so much enjoy.

And at worse? Life as a concubine somewhere in the Far East, never to see the free world again, at mercy of your master to do as he will, whatever his desire, and believe me, you will have no right or power to desist…as you do here.'

Slowly Mila reached out his hand and Youssef snatched the Yoonir pearl from it. 'A wise bargain, young Mila. This beautiful stone shall be locked up safely. And should our good clipper we pursue prove to be of bounteous *trade*, once we have safely stowed our bounty on Sao Miguel, you might have your freedom. We shall see.'

Youssef stood and rolled the map up and placed it along with the pearl in the cabinet, locking it in with the key. 'Oh, and one more thing…mention the pearl or this little transaction to anyone, including your trusted new friend Brahim, and I feed you both to the sharks. And now my little ones, off to bed. Plenty of sleep; there may be some fun and games for you to see tomorrow.'

But Mila could hardly sleep. He felt strange without the Yoonir pearl after carrying it for so long and he wondered if he had really parted with it wisely and what Kobina himself might have done in his situation. He had no choice. To be a slave or not. And could he really trust Youssef? And the events of the night had prompted him to overcome his fear of asking Julieta questions. And one question above all still mystified him.

'Why do you steal?' he whispered from his hammock.

'You steal, also,' Julieta answered. 'You take pearl from master or slaves, I don't know.'

'But I told captain Youssef the truth.'

'Maybe,' answered Julieta. 'But steal is the way of Barbaries. That's all they do. I don't know why except to eat.'

'But I still don't understand. Who are they? Where do they come from?'

Julieta sat up. She also was beyond sleep. The mood of Captain Youssef had deeply disturbed her that night.

'Barbaries are Moors,' Julieta whispered. 'Islam people. They used to steal for big Sultan man in Tripoli many years ago, but Sultan man say if merchant ship countries pay gold to him then people like Captain Youssef stop attacking. Then there was big war and Barbaries supposed to stop, but Youssef not stupid. He still take from gold ships for himself and men and Sultans not know about this or maybe they no care. Youssef say this is his *payment* for when he old. So, Barbaries don't do like before, they no take slaves for ransom. They just take enough gold and things. Many merchants no want to say anything, they smuggle and no pay tax to Sultans, so they no complain. Brahim tell me this. So Youssef only take some, not everything from merchants. Youssef no want to be seen or known. And so men listen to Yousssef and work for him, even though it still dangerous. There are ships with guns that still look for Barbaries. But there much riches for men and they like, they no want to go back to sheep and goat herds in dusty mountains.'

'Oh,' said Mila. 'Islam is about spirits, I know this. Brahim has told me about the wonders of Allah. But there are others on the Seyaad that are not like Brahim. Isaac is different,'

'Isaac is English man who used to be slaver,' said Julieta. 'But he steal gold from slave ship master and run away living as merchant. One day Youssef's men capture him and take his gold. They beat Isaac until he say he Islamic man. He *turn Turk*, as my people say. But he not true Islam man, he only stay for gold. Other men here for same reason, Barbaries take anyone who *turn Turk*. Isaac has no soul, no heart, he evil. English people hang Isaac if they find him.'

'You are also Islam?' asked Mila.

Julieta snorted scornfully. 'No! My people good Christian people. I good Christian girl. My father very wealthy, send me to good schools and learn many language, even Barbary speech and English. Father insist and say this is how we trade with many countries with many languages and I must learn, so many merchants to speak to. Too many for young girl, so not perfect. But Captain Youssef try to make me Islam, but I say no. Many years ago my father tell me they drive Moors from our land of Spain. Push them back to desert beyond beautiful field and mountain of Andalucia, back to Isalm lands. That why I never be Islam. They try to take Julieta's people and land.'

'Yes, I know about Christian people,' said Mila. 'Trader has told me about this.'

'Stupid trader man again,' Julieta mocked.

'Is this why you are angry?' asked Mila. 'Because they once were your enemies?'

'Yes,' replied Julieta. 'I am angry sometimes, when I think about my people.'

'Why don't you go home? You must have a family.'

'Oh, you being stupid child again,' said Julieta, lying back down in her hammock. 'I lose my family. No more family, nowhere to go. I am Barbary now. Forever.'

Mila lay quietly for a long while watching the stars through the little glass panes of the fretwork as they appeared in the night sky. Although he could sense the sadness in her voice as she spoke of her family, Mila's curiosity overcame his apprehension of Julieta's mood. 'Julieta…are you still awake?' he whispered.

'Yes, Mila, but we sleep now. Captain Youssef have big plan in morning.'

'But I want to know,' Mila insisted. 'What happened to your family?'

Julieta turned over in her hammock to face Mila, his swaying hammock barely the faintest silhouette in the darkness as she spoke. 'My people were merchants, father was man with own ship doing trade from port of Coruna with my brothers. He sell much good Spanish wine, cloth and oils everywhere, even Americas. One day I ask father to take me with them on voyages. He no want to take me at first. But I have no mother, she die before I remember and father agree when I beg him. I no want him to leave me in big house with servants and teachers.

'But one day Captain Youssef's men catch us in ocean. My father brave man and he fight before men board, shooting guns, but no one hurt, but Youssef's men win and they take what they want, not all but plenty of fine things and gold. They going to go then and leave Julieta and family alone. But two men, very bad one English like Isaac and other Moor like rest. They angry that father fight them. They shoot father, and stab older brothers before Youssef can see. Youssef already on Seyaad ready to sail and he get very angry at this when he find out. He shout at men and say we are Barbaries not murderers. He want to show Julieta his *justice*, he say, so he make big example of men, bind them in ropes and stand them together on deck. He come out from cabin wearing *thobe* and turban, carry scimitar sword, and make big ritual. First he bring sword back and slice head off English man with one swing. Head rolls on deck at feet of other man, still blinking eyes and mouth opening like head trying to speak and other man cry like little child. Then Captain Youssef bow down and give sword to Brahim and Brahim cut head off Moors man with one swing. Then Youssef make big speech to men who afraid now.

'Captain Youssef take pity on Julieta and say I must come with him now, he have no one, no family to give Julieta to. So I have nowhere to go. I live like Barbary now.'

'I'm sorry for your family,' Mila whispered after a long silence.

'Time to sleep now, Mila.'

8.

The following morning the wind had whipped up hard and the Seyaad skipped across the white-crested rollers at a flying pace. Men were racing about the deck, pulling at riggings and cranking the windlasses eagerly. Julieta clambered among the riggings looking out for tangles while Mila oiled the squealing winches and smoking brass eyelets as the ropes sung through them as the sails arose into the turbulent sky.

Captain Youssef stood on the foredeck observing the waves through a spyglass. 'We can't be that far behind now,' he said to Mehdi.

'Are you certain that you have plotted the course correctly, Captain Youssef?' said Mehdi.

'As certain as I am stood here on this ship!' Youssef handed the spyglass to Mehdi. 'I know the routes of this particular vessel; I've studied its movements for months just waiting for this particular cargo to be loaded. Fat she is! We should run this one down within the day. Keep watching, Mehdi. Rough as it is, get Anas to send the young ones up to the lookout. The rest of you!' he bellowed. 'I want every man at his station! We keep the Seyaad flying! A feast for all once we finish the job!'

The crew cheered and yelled their enthusiasm at Youssef's command.

The crow's nest creaked and howled in the mainmast and sails rippled deafeningly as the nest dipped in the waves leaving Mila feeling weightless. Each sway sent them down so far that Mila thought each time they would be dunked into the sea before it swayed suddenly the other way forcing him down to the side of the wooden basket. Julieta danced around the mast as it swung, singing into the wind and laughing at Mila who hugged the mast tightly with both legs and hands.

All that day the Seyaad glided briskly with a strong breeze behind, but as the evening drew in there was still no sign of the clipper. The breeze began to drop. The sky cleared leaving the heavens bright with stars and by the time a thin sliver of moon appeared over the horizon the sea was calm.

Youssef was worried. The ship's stores were getting low and he had allocated much time and research, querying traders and merchant companies on land, disguised as a buyer or trader himself to learn the routes, times and cargoes of the clipper. A few of the men had objected, although admitting that the rewards would be vast and untold, some suggested that the pursuance of such a large ship of the English line was risky. 'We should stay as our usual *trade*, cut the smaller merchants free of some of their wares, many of whom have stolen themselves, then run,' some would say. 'They will simply be grateful that we haven't sunk them and they will count their losses and blessings,' others would agree. But a clipper of the British Empire? That would draw attention. It was dangerous, some tried to warn 'The English have built a naval fleet like no other,' Mehdi had said. 'A fleet that won a mighty war on the French some years ago, but still rules the seas to this day.'

But Youssef was adamant. He spoke only of the riches and his plan to hide out and lay low in the hills of Dalwah, Syria until notice of their actions was long out of sight and mind. Then their rewards would be shared, they would be wealthy men and could return to their families and live the life of Sultans.

But the men were now visibly unhappy. A stationary ship

breeds familiarity. And familiarity breeds contempt. Sullenness and resentment pervaded the atmosphere as they went about their duties. And always there was the presence of Isaac, who would leer at the children from the riggings with looks of menace and hatred. Youssef was wary of the men's mood and that of Isaac in particular, sending the two children up to the crow's nest as the ship drifted by day.

Mila was happier this time, climbing the riggings eagerly with Julieta, as the sails fluttered in the weak winds and the mainmast held but a gentle rock. He played with the spyglass, which still amazed him, spinning around in the nest, looking at everything and anything.

'Don't fool with glass!' Julieta scolded. 'Look for ships, Mila, always look. You have spyglass first until sun high, then Julieta watch.'

And so they took it in turns, Mila watched the horizon, occasionally waving at Brahim as Julieta lay back, with her feet overhanging the basket, grumbling at Mila's fooling, then, Julieta would watch a while. The day wore on and the wind picked up modestly enough to raise three masts of sail, but still nothing was seen.

'It is not good,' Mehdi complained. 'The ship may be far ahead by now, perhaps in English waters even. Perhaps we should go, look for other quarry.'

'But this wind I feel coming from the South,' answered Youssef. 'It is building and it is behind. It will not have reached the English clipper yet. It still flounders as we have and now the gap must close. It is reasonable logic, Mehdi. By the time the breeze reaches them we will be bearing down its neck and by the end of this day we will be rich men all! See that the men are at their stations, Mehdi!'

'Yes Captain Youssef.' Mehdi grumbled, bowed and reluctantly conveyed the Captain's orders.

By the time twilight descended and the sun skipped its rays

horizontally across the gentle swell, nothing had been seen. Youssef was resigned to another night of bitter disappointment and a darkening mood of his men. Reluctantly, he admitted to himself that Mehdi's advice was probably right. He was about to call the children down from the nest when Julieta, leaning over the basket edge, cried out as loud as she could. 'Ship, Captain!'

A frenzy of activity rippled through the crew below as Julieta stood shouting and pointing in the direction of a tiny black dot where the pink sky touched the sea. 'Mehdi!' cried Youssef. 'Bring the scope from my quarters immediately!'

Mehdi dutifully obeyed, rushing and carrying the large brass instrument followed closely by Anas with the tripod, which was quickly set up on the foredeck. After a long sweep of the horizon, focusing and shouting accusations at Julieta that she was mistaken, Youssef finally located the dot. But now with the telescope's wider and superior objective, the dot was no longer a dot, but the distinct outline and silhouette of a large ship at full sail.

Mehdi leaned over Youssef's shoulder. 'Is it her?' he whispered hopefully.

The men gathered around Youssef as he observed and after a tense silence he stepped back from the scope rubbing his eyes. 'I cannot commit with a yes or no. She is too far in this light. But this looks promising. She has picked up the wind as we have. If it is her we should soon catch it. We shall follow her into the night, full sail, Mehdi. Get Anas to take over from Brahim, let him rest for the morning. By the down of the moon I shall take relief of the helm. In the meantime, Mehdi, stay on its course. Whatever mere flicker of candlelight it throws never lose it. Watch it always! By first light we shall know what manner of vessel it is. And Mehdi? Break out the rations, feed the men up! We shall all need our strength for the task ahead. And also, Mehdi,' said Youssef, grabbing Mehdi by the arm and whispering, 'See that Anas has the guns clean and ready for priming by first light...should they be foolish enough to try and resist.'

Mila awoke with a start in the early light to the sound of much shouting and banging. Julieta was out of her hammock and peering through the cabin window. 'Quick, Mila,' she said rushing over and dragging at his arm. 'Get up quick! We help men now.'

Dashing out onto the deck which now rolled and dipped upon the swell under a cool stiff breeze, the children could see the Seyaad had all but caught up the ship Julieta had spotted earlier. Men were working frantically at the winches and ropes as others gathered at the portside pointing and calling out orders. Captain Youssef stood stern and proud in his robes and turban at the helm alongside Brahim. His arms crossed and sword drawn, Youssef stared ahead steadfastly as the Seyaad pursued. Brahim swung hard at the wheel, veering the ship in then out on course with its prey as it chased, but now they gained no more as though the clipper had found new life in its sails.

Youssef jumped down from the foredeck waving his sword, shouting frantically. 'Mehdi! The wind has caught them up! They're getting away! Send them a reminder of who we are! A two gun salute! Brahim! Full starboard! And, Anas, waste no iron, but double the powder charge! We don't want to sink them, but let them hear us loud and clear from here to Tripoli!'

Brahim had no sooner swung the wheel full right with the Seyaad broadside to the clipper's rear deck, when there followed a *boom* so thunderous that it flung Mila to the deck with shock.

The Indiaman clipper *Escalate* suddenly seemed to flounder, as Brahim drew the Seyaad around still in full pursuit. Three of the Escalate's sails rippled and fluttered as the men on board abandoned their posts in terror at Anas' second booming salute and the Seyaad soon drew level. Mila and Julieta dashed to the side rail to get a better view. Now many of the crew of the Escalate seemed to have disappeared.

Youssef joined the men at the rail as the ships ran alongside each other. 'Ah, these merchant men!' he cried. 'They are not warriors but mere mortals never having heard the sound nor smelt the odour of saltpetre! But be cautious still, Mehdi, their shutters may be up, but another small reminder of our *peaceful* intentions might not go amiss.' He raised his sword high into the air and the other men followed, drawing swords and flintlocks as they shouted and cheered and waved at the remaining crew of the Escalate.

The Seyaad drew nearer carefully guided by Brahim until close enough for ropes to be launched. Youssef strode purposefully along the line of men at the side shouting orders, words of encouragement and warnings of respectfulness of their quarry. 'We shall be quick and efficient above all. Remember, we are no longer under guidance from Tripoli or other, but are united unto ourselves, so we do only what is necessary. We lessen the chance of drawing attention to our existence and pray that these merchants are just grateful to have escaped with their lives. No man shall use force except in self defence, but we shall be vigilant! Some may be armed and be foolish enough to resist. Otherwise do not abuse or take advantage of the persons on board the vessel other than to relieve them of certain cargos of which I shall be the judge of what constitutes necessary taking. And no man shall steal for himself alone.'

Youssef stopped by Isaac, who smirked derisively back at him. 'That smile can be removed with a sword, Isaac, if necessary,' Youssef muttered. 'What you take belongs to all of us.' He turned to address the rest of the crew sternly. 'Concealment will be dealt with harshly! Is that understood by all?'

'Yes Captain Youssef,' they cheered, waved and clattered swords together.

Youssef suddenly spotted Mila and Julieta at the end of the row of men. Hurrying forward he cried, 'What are you two doing here? This is no time for children! Hide yourselves away immediately!'

The children scurried off to the aft deck, ducking behind barrels secured to the side of Captain Youssef's cabin. As they peered over the barrel edge, Julieta placed her arm over Mila's shoulder. 'Watch and learn now, Mila,' she whispered. 'This is big catch, bigger than Julieta ever see.'

The two ships were drawn together, hastily secured by Youssef's men, some of whom had already jumped aboard the Escalate. Youssef and a small gathering of the Escalate's crew were talking as Youssef's men dashed about the deck disappearing below and into cabins, some shouting for others to come and look or cheering at their finds. Chests were removed, passed carefully from one man to another and slid across to the Seyaad's deck. Sacks were removed, which the children could only imagine the contents of, and were thrown roughly over to their ship. Long reels of brightly coloured cloth were taken along with many baskets.

Most of the talking the children could not hear, except for a man in uniform waving his arms at Youssef and Isaac and shouting. The man jabbed a finger at Isaac. 'This is a bloody disgrace!' he roared. 'And a fellow Englishman at that! I'll see you hang as God is my witness, I will. Bloody Turk of a turncoat! You have no right, there are treaties in place!'

'Stuff your bloody treaties!' Isaac cried, drawing his flintlock, but Youssef quickly grabbed his gun hand, lifting it above Isacc's head. 'Bloody fancy rich bastards in your fancy silk knickers,' Isaac continued. 'Stuff the lot of you!'

'Hung from the highest gallows of Newgate, I tell you!' the

man defied. 'I'll see you all in hell, for that matter. An Englishman at that! Bloody traitor to the crown!'

The rest of the Escalate's crew were gathered up onto deck and guarded as Youssef himself inspected the ship from top to bottom, saying what could and should not be taken. It was a long time before they were finally finished and ready to depart the clipper. The uniformed man still threw curses at them, at Isaac in particular as the rest of the Seyaad's crew re-boarded. Youssef bid them a final farewell with a deep bow and *'ma'a as-salahmah, rihlah sa idah,* good-bye and happy journey, it's been a pleasure doing business,' at which Isaac burst into fits of laughter.

As the Seyaad sailed away into the afternoon on board all was quiet until the Escalate was once again a mere dot on the horizon.

'I think we can relax,' said Youssef, placing his hand upon Mehdi's shoulder. 'Cause for a little celebration, I think.' Youssef raised his sword high into the air, twirling around at the rest of the crew, before sheathing it with a broad smile. 'Rejoice and be happy,' he called. 'The job is done! Brahim, set a course for Sao Miguel!' At which the crew cheered and bowed.

The celebration and feasting lasted long into the evening with Youssef joining his men in the main galley. Mila and Julieta dined alone at Youssef's table on smoked fish, preserved fruits, beef, and bread with honey, smiling at each other as they listened to the background noise of much laughter and pounding of benches along with the crash of metal coins on tables. 'That's the sound of gold, Mila,' said Julieta. 'Gold make men happy, happier than food or anything.'

'I am worried, Julieta,' said Mila.

'What? What you worry about?'

'This is very nice food, better than anything I have had since leaving my people. But the food is stolen.'

Julieta tore a small lump of bread off and threw it into Mila's face laughing. 'I know it stolen. It is way of Barbaries. If you don't want then you starve. Julieta have no choice, I can't leave and get food myself, so I have to eat Barbary food. Come, Mila, eat now and don't worry, men not take everything from clipper and clipper won't come back, they too frightened of Barbaries.'

'But it is because of stealing that I am here,' said Mila, who'd stopped eating altogether. 'I took something from Trader who trusted my people and now I am lost.'

'Never mind stupid trader man, Mila. He never find you now.'

'But I *want* to find him,' said Mila. 'So that I can tell him it is safe to return to my people and that the thing I stole is safe with Nnamdi of the Baja people.'

'So what you steal from trader man that so valuable you go floaty in big storm and nearly drown?'

'A net,' said Mila quietly. 'A fishing net.'

Julieta burst out laughing. 'Oh, now I know you real stupid child! You nearly be slave-boy, nearly drown, then nearly starve for fishing net?'

'It was for my people that I went looking for Trader. They need Trader to come back and see that we are honest and can do trade again.'

Julieta shook her head and sighed, 'Oh well, you Barbary now. Maybe you never go back to people. Eat now, Mila, is good food, yes?'

'Yes,' replied Mila despondently, and resumed eating.

It was long dark and the children were still up and talking before the noise began to subside and Youssef appeared in the cabin. 'You should sleep now,' he said. 'There will be much work for you in the morning, Julieta. Mila can take his place in the nest alone, I think. I will be taking a shift from Brahim tonight. When I come to sleep in the morning I want you two to be up and lively.'

But again Mila couldn't sleep and the thought of his destiny as a Barbary pirate troubled him. 'Julieta?' he whispered from his hammock.

'What now, Mila,' said Julieta rolling over. 'You heard Captain. We plenty to do in morning.'

'But I have to know. Do you think Captain Youssef will keep his word and free me when we reach the *civilisation*?'

'Who knows? Why you worry about that? You rather be slave-boy?'

'No, but I don't understand *freedom*,' said Mila. 'It is a word Kobina used and is for slaves. Kobina asked me to free him and now he is dead. If I am free, where will I go? I don't know the way to my home and I don't know the way to the *civilisation*. Youssef says he may show me the *civilisation*, but now I am lost.'

Julieta sat up reluctantly. 'Captain Youssef may free you, Mila like he say, but I don't think so. He send you up to crow's nest in morning. That good sign, it mean he trust you to keep good spying on ocean.'

'But might he sell me to slavers, like he once said?'

'No, he just scare you. He want you to be Barbary now…and maybe he want you for something else.'

'What do you mean?' said Mila.

Julieta spoke very quietly now and Mila could barely make out the words. 'Maybe he want you for boy boy.'

'I don't understand. What is boy boy?'

'Maybe he like you like body. Like men like woman, only they like men.'

Mila was shocked. 'I have never heard of such a thing. Are you certain that he would want this? This is very strange. How can someone…'

'Oh, you very dumb child, Mila,' Julieta hissed. 'I know you from forest and never hear about big world. But some men like that. I see it on ship but men don't see me and don't know I seen them, but some do it.'

'But I am not a man yet.'

'So? It don't stop captain Youssef try to touchy touchy Julieta. I only girl but Youssef want me as woman. He try many times.'

'Youssef wants to *join* you? Like my mother and father together?'

'Yes, yes! You understand now, child Mila? Youssef want to *join* me you say, I say he try to poke, but I scream once and say I scream again if he touchy touchy anymore. He stop then and leave alone. Men on Seyaad don't want Julieta on board anyway. They say is bad luck for woman to be on ship, so Youssef not want to upset them. If Julieta scream men will come and mutiny. So now I think Youssef wait until I woman…or he wait until we on land and away from men then try again, I don't know. It don't matter anyway, I say to Youssef I tell Brahim about touchy touchy if he try again. Brahim is maybe only good man on ship of all men. Brahim look after Julieta always, he say. Youssef get really angry about this and just say: 'One day my little Julieta, one day and you will be mine.' He leave me alone then.'

'But what if Captain Youssef *wants* me?' said Mila gloomily.

'Who knows? Go sleep now Mila.'

9.

Captain Youssef roused the two children at first light, tired after a night of high sea at the helm. True to his word, Mila was sent to the crow's nest with the spyglass and Julieta was set to work helping to sort out the booty from the clipper. There were foodstuffs to store, some deep in the galley in the coldest part of the ship. There was cloth reels to stack, gold coins to count and store, perfumes, precious exotic oils and spices to stack in boxes and bottles and intricate trinkets of precious metal to itemize and decide upon their future in the markets of Tunis or Tripoli. But most of all there had to be decided how much and what was to be hidden away on the island of Sao Miguel. This brought about heated arguments, many of the men wanting to take some of the spoils to their homes and share with their families, some of whom were very poor. The fighting caused Brahim to rouse Captain Youssef who was angry at being disturbed and settled the matter with a slam of sword upon bench and a stern lecture about the dangers of flaunting their wealth so soon after a very high profile hijacking. 'There will be eyes everywhere,' he emphasized. 'Of that you can be certain. We make for Sao Miguel with haste. Your time will come soon enough!'

In the meantime Julieta gathered some food items together in a basket which she tied to her waist and clambered up the riggings to Mila. 'Here, Mila, look what Julieta bring you. Good things to eat.'

Mila looked into the basket and uncovered the cloth, staring at the array of unfamiliar food. 'What is it?' he asked pointing.

'Things from clipper, very nice things like we don't have for long time. Here try cheese,' she said, and broke off a piece handing it to Mila.

Mila bit cautiously and smiled. 'This is very good!'

'Is made from milk. Now try this,' Julieta handed him a strange looking piece of shriveled fruit and Mila smiled again as he devoured it greedily. 'Date,' said Julieta. 'Very special dry fruit, so last for long time on voyage. Now this one,' she said passing him a small black fruit.

Mila bit into the fruit and spat it out immediately with a scowl.

Julieta burst out laughing and poked him in the ribs playfully. 'Olive,' she said. 'You no like olive? Very special fruit from my country. It very good for you, keep you strong and live long life my people say.'

'It's horrible!' said Mila, picking bits of the remaining fruit from his mouth. 'It's not fruit, there is no sweetness in it.'

'Ah, well you want sweet? Julieta bring you very, very special treat from *civilisation*. Here, try this one.' She handed him a piece of a soft, spongy square, the like of which Mila had never felt nor seen before. He squeezed it in his fingers and white dust floated away from it in the wind. He smelled it cautiously and instantly thought of the wild flowers on the forest edge of his home. He took a small bite and smiled as broad a smile as he'd ever done since leaving home. The sweetness sent a surge of elation through his entire body as he gulped down another piece.

'Turkish delight,' said Julieta. 'Kings and queens send merchants many miles and pay much for this special food from markets in Istanbul. You enjoy Mila. Let Julieta watch ocean for a while.'

Julieta helped Mila finish the food. They lunched on the fruits (except for Mila and the olives) and cheese along with fresh cornbread, saving the remaining candy for last at which Mila, replete, sighed his contentment. After a long while of taking turns with the spyglass, the sea calmed and a warm breeze lulled the nest into a gentle rock. Julieta lay back letting her legs dangle over the edge of the nest as Mila watched the ocean. As the sun beat down he tired and sat down next to Julieta and talked about what may lay ahead for them after the voyage to Sao Miguel. Julieta drifted as Mila spoke and before long both had fallen asleep.

They were awoken late in the afternoon by the rippling of sail and a heavy sway of the nest as the wind picked up again, and the sound of angry voices bellowing their names out and cursing. Mila shot up and looked down at the men who'd gathered at the aft and others who stood at the foot of the mainmast waving fists and cursing at him.

Captain Youssef had run quickly from his quarters and was now calling and waving them to come down from the nest. 'Damn you foolish children! Are you both blind?' He bellowed and pointed out to sea.

Julieta grasped tightly onto Mila's arm as he strained his eyes struggling to focus them after his sleep. There was another ship, closer this time than the dot of the clipper Julieta had spotted previously. Mila grabbed the spyglass and gasped. There were two more ships further behind. They were coming towards them.

Youssef was livid as the two scrambled down the riggings. He grabbed Mila roughly by the arm shaking him. 'Curse you slave-boy!' he shouted. 'I might have known. I thought I could trust you! What were you two doing up there? Playing foolish little boy girl games, I suspect. And now we have visitors upon us.' He shoved Mila to the deck and drew his sword, pointing it to his throat. 'I should feed you to the sharks.'

'Do it, Captain!' declared Isaac. 'Told you first time, he's nothing but a stinking nigger. Should have left him to rot with the other slaves on that stinking island.'

'I shall deal with you later, boy,' said Youssef. 'The both of you!' he snapped at Julieta. 'By the first rise of moon, if we are not out of sight of these voyagers whatever their business is, I shall throw the both of you over!'

Brahim suddenly called out and Youssef ran to the starboard. Brahim surveyed the ships through the large telescope. Youssef bent down very close to Brahim and whispered. 'What manner of vessel is it?'

Brahim shuddered. 'Frigate, Captain Youssef.'

'I don't understand, Brahim. Who are they? What flag do they fly?'

'Americans, Captain. Gunships all three. Very fast.' He looked at Youssef uneasily.

'We have no business with them,' said Youssef. 'What are they doing with gunships in these waters? I don't understand? The war ended many years ago. And our ships have paid the American merchants no attention since. It's too risky to stir up hostilities with them again.'

'Perhaps the English clipper has passed them by?' said Brahim.

'But that's just by the way. They wouldn't wage a fight for the sake of an English merchant. They have nothing to do with them.'

'All the same, Captain, what are we to do? I have doubt that we can outrun them.'

'Perhaps they're just curious, Brahim. We just watch and see for now. Show no sign of aggression and sail away.'

'Sao Miguel, Captain?' said Brahim doubtfully.

'Too risky,' said Youssef, looking through the telescope. 'We cannot port up there for now. They will only watch our every move and learn our business. Curse those children! This is a bad turn of fortune indeed.' He stood and faced the men who'd gathered around. 'Brahim, set a course for Tripoli. I doubt they'll want to follow us once we're through the Pillars. The rest of you,' he called, 'man your stations! We fly like the wind and outrun these leeches!'

The rest of that day and long into the night the Seyaad skimmed the waves at full sail and the gunships followed just keeping pace with them. In the first light land could be seen ahead and Youssef breathed a sigh. But as they approached and the Seyaad flew, the gunships appeared to suddenly make haste and the gap began to close. They were still some miles from the Straits and what Youssef deemed to be the safety of the Mediterranean waters when the American vessels had caught them up.

'What now, Captain?' Brahim asked uneasily as he steered. The front runner of the three had drawn broadside barely fifty yards away from the Seyaad.

'Steady, Brahim,' Youssef said calmly. 'They have done nothing yet and their shutters are up. So I suggest we try to confuse them, send them on a chase they won't forget. We are by far the more agile vessel, wouldn't you agree, Brahim?'

'By far, Captain,' said Brahim proudly. 'Nothing turns and tacks as quickly or easily as a Xebec.'

'Then if we can't outrun them, we outmanoeuvre them. Brahim, show this side leech our backsides, sail close to the outrider and make them think we're going to collide at the last minute! Frighten the cursed crew to death, I say!'

'Yes, Captain Youssef!' Brahim cried excitedly as he spun hard on the wheel sending the Seyaad tilting alarmingly as it turned away from the broadside gunship. Mila and Julieta clung hard onto the starboard rail as the sea rushed up to meet them on the ship's turn. Julieta cried out gleefully as the ship dipped and swayed back up but Mila hung on fearfully until the ship had righted once again.

Then the Seyaad poised and bore down quickly upon the

rear gunship straight ahead, the crew of which worked frantically to spin away from its path. At the last second Brahim spun again at the helm and the Seyaad dipped to the sea on its port side, the rising hull just nudging and skimming the gunboat's side as it flew past. The crew of the Seyaad cheered and jeered at the gunboat as their ship righted and sailed quickly away leaving the gunboat floundering, its crew in total confusion. Then the Seyaad went for the main ship that had caught them up originally. A sudden huge sea swell lifted the Seyaad as Brahim steered, sending the vessel bearing down upon the gunship like a giant whale as it cut straight across its front bow, narrowly missing as the Seyaad flew past. Again, Youssef's men cheered and Julieta danced about the deck as Brahim headed for the third vessel which turned away frantically in the opposite direction. All three gunships now floundered and faced in different directions as Brahim reset his course for the Strait.

'Brilliant work, Brahim!' Youssef declared, slapping him across the shoulder. 'It will take them a while to untangle themselves now! Keep us flying, Brahim!'

The gunships drifted into the distance as they sailed on. The cliffs of the Strait and the Pillars of Hercules now appeared like two blue giants ahead. But before long the gunships had rallied and were in pursuit again. They were still another mile or so from the Strait when once again the first gunship was broadside of them, this time further away, wary that the Seyaad might make a sudden turn again.

'Damn them,' said Youssef. 'Cut between them, Brahim; force the two followers to flounder again. It's our only chance. They may try to blockade us otherwise, should the others catch up.'

Once again Brahim took his ship into a deep turn, rushing past the aft of the front gunship. The two following ships slowed as intended, but the front ship spun herself and gave chase as Youssef cursed and gave orders for the cannons to be manned as the gunship closed in once again behind them.

Youssef ran to the aft of the ship, waving his sword and cursing the nearest pursuing vessel. The vessel drew very near then tacked to the Seyaad's starboard as though once again attempting to draw broadside. Youssef stood watching, his arms crossed defiantly as the gunship suddenly banked away.

Mehdi had come up beside Youssef, observing the unexpected change in direction of the chasing ship. 'It looks as though they've finally given up, Captain,' he said, joyfully. 'Look, she turns and runs like a whipped dog!'

Youssef was about to agree with Mehdi when, in the blink of an eye, the gunship's shutters dropped and a full side of cannons appeared.

'Allah, have mercy!' cried Youssef, running up the ship. 'Brahim! Full portside, now!'

The first shots were launched with a resounding *boom* from the American naval gunship *Walter Scott*, two twenty-four pound cast iron balls that screamed across the water with a sound that reminded Mila of the screeching birds in the forest near his home. The first shot sailed through the rear riggings and far into the sea beyond. The second one swiped the midmast, sending chunks and splinters of wood flying high into the wind. The mast momentarily stood, defying gravity, and trembling with a ringing quiver that ran down to the deck before toppling in half, dragging sail and rigging crashing below and sending Youssef's men scattering in all directions. The Seyaad dragged, its mainsail crippled as the gunship rallied and soon drew broadside.

Anas and his men were in disarray. In a blind panic, several charges were launched which sailed high over the bow of the gunship. Three more were fired, more hopefully than accurate, as the Seyaad dipped port side in the ocean swell, falling short of their target and into the sea.

A third shot, carefully recalibrated by the *Scott's* master gunner, smashed through the Seyaad's hull, shattering a strut in the galley below Mila's feet. The deck gave way and Mila slipped into the gap grasping frantically at the edge.

Julieta, who was frozen in shock, quickly snapped out of her trance, rushing forward grasping and pulling at Mila's arm, the ship now listing as it took in water. 'Quick now Mila, we must leave ship!' she shouted as Mila struggled from the gap and splayed out upon the deck.

But Mila scrambled to his feet, dashing into Youssef's quarters as Julieta screamed hysterically at him. He looked round quickly before picking up the jade sea-turtle, pounding and smashing a hole with it into Youssef's cabinet. He threw the carving to the floor and grabbed the Yoonir pearl, still in its skin bag and dashed out onto deck straight into the arms of Isaac.

'Now my little thief!' Isaac cried as he held Mila in a bear-hug. 'What are we stealing here, eh?' Mila kicked and squirmed and bit but still Isaac would not release him.

'Give it to me now and I let you go!' Isaac screamed. He spun Mila round grasping him in a headlock, desperately trying to reach for his knife and struggling to keep his balance at the rapidly tilting deck. Mila cried out in pain as Isaac's arm crushed harder. Suddenly the knife was out as Isaac rocked and staggered about the deck with Mila.

Julieta rushed up behind as they struggled and swiftly and as hard as she could, swung her right foot up between Isaac's splayed legs and Isaac collapsed to his knees doubled over and howling like a dog.

'Run quick now, Mila,' Julieta cried as the crippled ship now creaked and groaned its dying message. 'Seyaad is dead, we must leave now!'

They scrambled as quickly as they could, sliding and

clambering up the tilting deck and straddled the side rail. Mila sat for a moment watching the black water bubbling and seething below as the ship rapidly sucked in the ocean.

'Foolish child!' Julieta screamed. 'Jump, Mila, jump! You want to die?' She drew her arm back and swung, striking Mila hard across the side of his face with her hand sending him tumbling and bouncing head over foot down the hull and into the sea.

Mila surfaced with a cry of stinging pain and a sea of stars bursting before his eyes at Julieta's strike. He swam blindly before banging his head into a piece of mast which he grasped onto desperately. Another volley of shots struck the ship's powder store and the Seyaad erupted in a ball of fire sending pieces of flaming debris raining down, hissing into the sea all around him. As Mila looked around, a plume surged upwards into a huge ball of black smoke, blotting out the sun in the sky, from the last of the Seyaad's foredeck, which now slipped slowly and silently into the deep.

Julieta was nowhere to be seen.

10.

Mila cried and cried as he floated and drifted away from the bubbling site of the ship as the last cries of the drowning crew faded. The coast was near, and he could have swum the distance clinging to his piece of mast but he no longer cared. Heartbroken and lost once again, he cursed the Yoonir pearl. Convinced that if he had left it in Youssef's cabin and not been delayed by the struggle with Isaac, he and Julieta would have had time to jump ship and clear before the explosion. Now she was certainly dead and his life once again seemed to have no purpose and he had failed. The image of Nnamdi's face, shaking his head and bowing in disappointment and the death mask of Kobina haunted him as the day turned to night, and as the tide and currents carried him away, he lost consciousness. In the morning the coast was still there but further away and had become unfamiliar, the blue giants of the Strait and the entrance to the *great civilisation* had gone and he wondered how he had managed to stay afloat still clinging to the mast piece.

Several times that day he fell into sleep. And each time he dreamed that the Yoonir pearl was playing tricks upon him. As he drifted into the strange place between sleep and consciousness he imagined that the pearl, tied to the string of his pantaloons, was bumping and nudging him in the groin from beneath, or even nudging him to the surface as he slipped into the water. And each time he grasped back onto the mast. As night fell he once again lost consciousness and the pearl bumped him again but he no longer cared nor had the spur to try and survive. As he slipped into the cold deep and the last image of Julieta faded from his mind, a huge surge from beneath lifted him from the water, throwing him across the mast with a crash that woke him fully.

He cried out in pain. 'Oh shark or whatever you are, please eat me or leave me to my death!' He lunged forward across the mast to try once again to sink into the deep and end it all and flopped onto solid wood. The mast was bumping a section of deck or hull of a ship, of which he could not tell. But he lay there not caring, staring up at the stars and drifting at last into deep dreamless sleep.

He awoke blinking into the sunlight, his 'raft' grinding and churning the sand and pebble. Foam washed into his face and eyes and throat, awakening him in fits of coughing and choking. As the sea receded, leaving him on a sloping beach, he imagined he could hear laughter or the cackle of bird or the chirp of monkey coming from the sea. A spout of water and a dark shadow disappeared into the depths as he rubbed his eyes wondering, only to see a whirlpool of bubbles slowly fading into the gentle surf.

On the breeze the smell of smoke drifted and Mila thought immediately of people and wondered if he might be on the same coast as his home. He set off wandering in what he felt was the direction of the smoke. It was a long walk and afternoon before he could see a thin blue column drifting up and away into the wind. Further on was a cove with a ship anchored and a large cabin inland from which the smoke rose. He hastened forward around the cove until he realised that the ship looked familiar. He remembered the flag, the red stripes and blue as Brahim had skimmed against its hull. He stopped and considered. If they knew he had been aboard the Seyaad they might capture him as a slave or even kill him. He knew nothing of the attackers other than that they had sunk Youssef and all his men. But perhaps they knew about Julieta, or even picked her up in the sea? Maybe he could pretend he was nothing to do with Youssef. But then he had to find out about Julieta and if she was there she would surely acknowledge him and they might both be slaves. Or dead.

He had to try, he decided. And he had to eat sometime soon. He hastened again as close as he dare, then hid himself in the woods until evening, thinking it was best to watch and observe first before approaching the cabin from behind. It seemed deserted, but the column of smoke suggested otherwise. For the rest of the daylight, whether anyone came or went he couldn't tell. There was no door to be seen from his vantage point behind the building nor did there appear to be any windows. As darkness fell, he emerged from the woods and sneaked stealthily around to the front corner of the building, dropping onto all fours as he peered around the corner. A man in blue and white uniform with a rifle by his side stood very still and erect on the decking in front of the entrance. Mila was transfixed and couldn't decide if the man was a slaver or not, his dress was similar to that of the slave ship captain.

Suddenly another man emerged from the door behind and the first man stepped sharply forward with a high knee lift, stamping his foot to the decking and spun precisely to his right looking straight at Mila. But before Mila could duck back around the corner, he was spotted.

'You, boy!' the officer cried. 'Halt now!'

But as Mila ran back towards the woods a crack of gunfire shocked him sending him flat on his face. The two men were quickly upon him lifting him to his feet and frog-marching him through the entrance.

A long line of men stood wearing chains at their feet and hands with their heads bowed. At the front of the line a man sat at a large desk and another stood at attention by his side with a musket held across his front. Mila was dragged to the front of the queue and left standing shivering before the officer at the desk. One of his captors spoke: 'We found this one skulking about outside, Lieutenant.'

'Well, speak up boy,' said the Lieutenant. 'Are you one of this scurvy bunch?'

'Bloody right he is!' shouted one of the men in chains and Mila spun round at the familiar voice. 'Slap the little thief in irons along with the rest of us!' declared Isaac.

There were others from the Seyaad among the men who joined in calling and shouting at Mila. 'Curse the son of Satan!' one cried. 'Should never have been on board, brought us bad luck, the boy is evil!' said another. 'See you in hell!' screeched another.

The officer with the musket marched swiftly forward first striking Isaac hard with the butt of his rifle before kicking and striking others. 'Silence!' he bellowed.

'Is this true, boy?' asked the Lieutenant.

'I was with them,' said Mila. 'It was not my choice; they captured me from my island.'

'So a slave boy then? You have done well to survive, but unfortunate to have ended up here. What am I to do with you? You are no use to me here; you may as well go...unless you want to hang like the rest of this vermin.'

'I have nowhere to go,' said Mila sorrowfully.

'Well, you should at least consider yourself lucky and not one of *them*,' said the Lieutenant gesturing to the far side of the cabin.

In his state of fear, Mila hadn't noticed the line of shrouds lain out in a row by the wall and at first still didn't understand, thinking they were provisions taken from the ship. But from one shroud in particular, there protruded the familiar black boots of Captain Youssef.

'Go take a good look, boy,' said the Lieutenant. 'This is the fate of pirates, to die either by sea or by gallows.'

Mila went over to the line of corpses, tugging cautiously at some of the shrouds. Even though he recognised the boots, he still found it hard to believe until he saw the death mask of Youssef. Then there was Mehdi further down. But Brahim was not here. And he knew without looking any further that Julieta couldn't be among them. 'There was a girl?' he said, looking around at the Lieutenant.

'I know nothing of any girl,' said the Lieutenant.

'Fried like a little Spanish omelette!' Isaac cried delightedly at the look of despair on Mila's face. 'Went up like a firework, she did! Oh yes, I saw it all! Another piece of Spanish garbage we never wanted on board in the first place. Got exactly what she deserved! Curse the wretched bitch!'

Isaac collapsed to his knees at another blow from the armed officer followed by several kicks. The others stood silent but smirking at Mila's misery.

'Get the boy out of here,' said the Lieutenant. 'Send him on his way before I change my mind.'

'But I have nowhere to go,' said Mila. 'I have no one. I am lost and hungry.'

The Lieutenant beckoned forward one of Mila's captors. 'Give him some food and a bunk for the night. If he's still here by reveille he can hang on the gallows along with the rest of them.'

At first light Mila was shaken from his bunk, having spent most of the night crying and tormented by the last images of Julieta. He was given a breakfast of watery porridge and bread and a pouch of water for his journey and led outside.

'Follow that path,' said the officer pointing through the woods. 'Beyond the trees it leads through hills and down to a market town by a port. You should reach it by noon. It's easier than following the coast, there are places along that way where the cliffs are impassable. Perhaps some trader will take pity and employ you or you may get taken in by a wealthy merchant as a houseboy if you are lucky. But be warned; the market is full of scoundrels and possibly slavers. You have no slave markings; that makes you fair game for kidnapping. Try not to be seen away from the market by day and by night hide yourself away carefully.'

Mila looked questioningly at the officer and asked, 'What will happen to the men?'

'They will be put to death for piracy,' said the officer. 'Hung on ropes by the neck from a high gibbet until they are all dead. You see, these Barbary pirates were supposed to have ended their attacks in these waters years ago, after the war. But some of them are just plain stubborn, like the captain of that bunch you were caught up with. That's why we have to keep our ships looking out for them.'

'If my friend Julieta was here would you hang her also? She told me she was a Barbary...just like the men.'

'The girl you asked about? Well, I don't know about that. I guess she was about your age then?'

Mila nodded despondently.

'That would be up to the Lieutenant,' said the officer. 'I never heard of hanging a young girl before. And the Lieutenant is letting you go free yourself, although I guess that's because he believed you when you said you weren't one of them. But she's not here anyway, that guy I rifle-butted said she was blown up. Well, I guess I'm sorry about that; it's one of those things that can't be helped. But those guys in there...well they're pirates. They don't care nothing about stealing or killing and it's just as well you got away. Looks like the Good Lord is looking after you alright. Sure is a shame about your friend though.'

Another officer stepped out briskly from the cabin standing to attention and the sound of a bugle ripping the early morning air with reveille sent the forest birds crying out from the trees into the sky.

'Go on now boy,' said the officer, 'before the Lieutenant sees you and changes his mind. And good luck to you.'

'Thank you,' said Mila, as he set off walking, and although his heart was heavy with the memory of Julieta he turned and managed a smile at the officer. 'Thank you for not hanging me.'

11.

All that morning Mila followed the path through woods and grassy valleys and up and down barren and dusty hillsides. He'd barely slept in the officer's bunkhouse, but the food he had been given the evening before and in the morning had rejuvenated him. And as true as the officer had said, Mila made his way up the last hill as the sun reached its zenith.

There were strange and enticing smells drifting over the summit as he climbed and the hum-drum of voices as though far away and yet near. He scrambled the last few feet to a rocky summit high above where the path now weaved in and out in its descent coping with the steep gradient.

The market town and port of Ancen Medina sprawled out before him like one of Captain Youssef maps, only a very brightly coloured map. A map that moved. Flags and banners fluttered in the breeze and bright sun below. Flags were everywhere. Flags of all colours. Colours Mila had never seen before. Banners of all shapes. Long thin banners of orange, purple and green. Triangle banners of yellow, blue and red. Narrow banners as long as their poles fluttered and waved like snakes crawling in fields and red and orange banners that split into two or even three sections that looked like dancing flames in the wind. There were stalls and people everywhere. People in white or black robes. People in many coloured robes and vests and jackets that looked to be adorned with gems or gold, Mila could not tell from his vantage point. And there was food; the scent of spice and roasting meat and bread from smoking ovens and spits filled his nostrils as he scrambled and stumbled his way down the hillside. He had found it at last.

The *great civilisation*.

Mila wandered through the narrow spaces of the market turning and looking at everything at once. Merchants shouted their wares of leather, metal bowls and beaten copper. Women in brightly coloured shawls interwoven with golden braid or dotted with beads held up fruits and vegetables calling and beckoning traders and passers-by to sample their produce. Crabs crawled among other shellfish in metal pots. More fish hung from strings over smoking braziers. Hens in cages squawked along with the cacophony. More hens hung by their feet from stall rails fluttering in their attempt to escape, while others turned on roasting spits above hot wood embers. Buyers walked through the melee carrying baskets and fluttering chickens, stopping and bartering with stallholders in a language that Mila recognised from his time on the Seyaad, but still understood only a little of. Some shouted at each other in their deals or smiled and laughed as coins and wares changed hands. And others cursed Mila as he bumped into them as he tried to look at everything at once. He stopped by a fruit stall staring at the familiar red and green of apples stacked high along with other fruits he had never seen before as colourful as the banners waving and rippling above his head. The elderly woman looked him up and down, deciding his worth before shooing him away like a fly with a wave of her arms. Further on a man turned a roasting goat on a spit over hot coals as traders haggled for the best cuts of meat in dishes before them. Mila stopped and stared longingly at the array of cooked meats, reaching out. The man stopped turning the spit and leaned over to Mila. 'Dirham, dirham!' he shouted opening his palm then shoved Mila back away from the stall.

Towards the far side of the market a crowd of men had gathered, some shouting and others shaking their fists at a frightened looking man in ragged robes. The crowd surrounded the man, pushing and shoving him to the ground. As he struggled to his feet he spotted Mila in the crowd and broke free from the others, running towards him shouting and Mila began backing away nervously.

Suddenly a hand slapped itself firmly on his shoulder and Mila spun around. At first Mila thought he was staring at a spirit-god, the bright white of the man's suit shone and dazzled his eyes in the bright sunlight. A burly man with a reddish and tanned face stood looking at him. His bushy white moustache, all white suit and open white shirt gleamed in the sun against his colourful complexion, shaded by a wide brimmed straw hat. He stepped forward in front of Mila, grabbing hold of the ragged man by the sleeve and his pursuers stopped abruptly, angrily gathering around him and Mila. The man removed his hat, waving it about, pushing some of the crowd back away from Mila as he appealed to them in their own language to be calm.

'*Walikann alrrajul hu alllas!* But the man is a thief!' one of the crowd protested.

'*W lrrajul hu alkadhdhab!* And the man is a liar!' said another.

But the strange man that had stopped Mila managed to quieten the crowd with his words. He reached into his pocket and gave coins to the man who had accused the thief.

Slowly the crowd moved on muttering between themselves as they dispersed and the ragged one bowed gracefully before the stranger. '*Shukraan lakum w bark allah fikum,* thank you and god bless,' he said before running swiftly away into the throng of people.

'You boy, come with me,' the stranger said. 'Never mind them. I need a good stout lad like yourself to help me with a few things.'

Mila followed the man to a place at the back of some stalls where tethered donkeys tied to a large flat wagon covered in canvas fed and drank water from buckets.

'Here boy,' the man said, untying the front ropes holding the canvas cover. He gestured Mila to the other side of the wagon and together they rolled the heavy canvas back. 'Now I'll need a lift,' he said. 'Don't worry; I'll make it worth your while.' Then the man removed his jacket and Mila helped him with a long table and some strong steel legs which the man assembled before they carried it together between stalls, all the while the man arguing with other merchants to *give him room,* or *this is in your people's interest,* he would say. Large pieces of metal objects and instruments, some of which reminded Mila of Captain Youssef's quarters were arrayed on display on the table along with maps and posters. A canvas canopy was erected overhead. And lastly, there were the strangest of objects that were the heaviest of all. There were several pieces of bright metal, the shape of which Mila had never seen anything like in his so far strange life. The pieces were heavy and they struggled with them, all the time the man protesting *not to drop anything under any circumstances.* When at last everything was off the carriage and either on the table or underneath it, the man sat upon a stool and fanned himself with his hat in the shade of the erected stall.

'Well, that took a bit of doing,' the man said as he stood holding out his hand and shaking Mila's. 'And well done to you kind sir. Well then, I suppose a half dirham or so is in order for that worthy effort, but first introductions I think. Billington's the name. Barclay Billington, chief rail engineer to his Majesty William IV. You see, young man, all this land will...oh but wait, I haven't asked you your name, have I? Although I don't suppose you understand what I'm saying.'

'I am called Mila.'

'Excellent!' said Billington. 'And a fine name at that for a fine young man. West African, I think, by the sounds of it. And you speak the lingo quite well. I wasn't expecting that.'

'Trader taught me,' said Mila.

'A trader, eh what?' said Billington. 'Oh, I expect you get a few of them down your way. I've seen some of your folks craft in the markets all over these great islands and ports. Well, it seems you've come to the right place at the right time. There's a few here who speak the language, largely thanks to pioneers such as myself, but also because there are so many different folk with different tongues no trade whatsoever would get done if there wasn't a common one, or *lingua franca* as they once called it. But never mind that for now. Why don't you run and fetch us both something to eat and drink?' He handed Mila a couple of coins. 'Some bread and a little cheese and a cut of that fine meat I noticed you eyeing up earlier. And there's a merchant over there with some wine,' he pointed. 'And something you might like yourself? Oh, whatever you desire, young Mila.'

'What do I do?' asked Mila, looking at the coins doubtfully.

'Oh, I see!' Billington said. 'You aren't familiar with money? It's quite simple. You just point to what you wish on the stall and hand the coin to the merchant when he gives you the bread or whatever. Then he should give you some smaller coins in return. Then you go to the next merchant and do the same. And if they're honest – and believe me, they mostly are around here – they will give you the correct change. You see, young Mila, there is a powerful man ruling these lands and he doesn't take kindly to swindlers. Perhaps I shall tell you more about him later. Off you run now.'

Mila soon returned and the two feasted on the best meal he'd had in days, all the while Billington talking about his business and the clutter of metal spread upon his stall.

'You see, Mila,' Billington explained between mouthfuls, 'all across this savage land there will one day be a railroad, from the mighty Atlantic to the Red Sea and beyond. All the ports of India and the Far East and their markets will become available to his Majesty without the need to navigate these savage waters and their pirates. I don't expect you understand all that, but I will explain as we go along...that's if you don't mind helping me a bit longer, young Mila?'

'I don't mind,' replied Mila, chewing the succulent meat. When he had finished eating, he asked Billington why the crowd of men had been so angry at the one that had ran towards him.

'Ah, well,' said Billington. 'The man was not only a beggar but a thief also. He saw you and tried to claim that you were his poor, starving son and that he was stealing food for you only and not for himself. As I explained, the people here are most trusting and a thief is not welcome. There are harsh punishments in these lands for thieves and I could see that you were not one yourself, but was about to be caught up in the fracas. I decided to pay the merchant the small sum he was owed before things got out of hand.'

Billington then set about assembling the various pieces of metal knelt on a cloth on his hands and knees, all the time talking as Mila watched in fascination at the variety of Billington's strange tools and how the shiny pieces could be put together without rope or binding. 'You see, Mila, a train is much like my wagon, only much larger and there are many wagons joined to it that the people can ride in. Now the first wagon isn't drawn by donkey such as mine is. It has a life of its own. It has a heart that drives it like your very own legs drive you forward.'

Eventually, Billington stood up panting, wiped his hands and forehead with a towel and placed the tools on the stall. 'And this is it!' he said at last.

Mila stared at the strange machine in wonder. 'What is it?' he said.

'This, my boy, is a steam engine!' said Billington proudly. 'This is a machine that will pull many wagons across many miles of desert in a fraction of the time of sailing the

Mediterranean.' He pointed to one of the posters of trains on display. 'Just like that, Mila. Tracks will be laid and the great iron horse will cut across these lands like a great steaming chariot! But this is only a miniature, a very small engine in comparison. You see, it is my duty – endorsed by his Majesty King William IV himself – to convince these people of the benefits of the railroad. Can you imagine it Mila? Look at this market! This will be a tiny thing by comparison once the trades of the Far East have easy access to the port here. Ancen Medina will be a huge and wealthy metropolis one day. And it is my job to prove just that to these people. First Ancen Medina, then further afield, I must travel these lands convincing all across it that access for the rail is paramount to their wealth and prosperity.'

Mila stared in curiosity at the poster of the great train billowing smoke from its huge stack. 'How does it move?' he asked.

'Ah well, now there comes a little demonstration. Look under here,' said Billington, kneeling again and pointing to the largest section of the engine. 'This is a boiler and under here is the firebox. That is the heart of the engine, where the energy comes from. And once the steam is created by the boiler, it pushes this rod.' He propped the rear of the engine upon a wood block and grabbed the engine's piston rod pulling it out from the cylinder. 'This makes this flywheel rotate. Come, come, Mila. Have a look at how it works.'

Mila knelt down and Billington took his hand, placing it on the cold steel part. 'But you see the interesting thing about the flywheel,' said Billington, 'is that if you spin it once,' he gripped Mila's hand making him spin the wheel, 'it keeps on spinning several times. That's the cam, you see? It's the weight at one side that does it. You spin it once and it carries on because the excess weight at one side pulls it round by *centrifugal force*. It's the offset weight. The faster it spins the heavier it becomes creating even more energy. It's the very force that keeps us on this Earth, Mila.'

'I don't understand,' said Mila, watching the wheel turn and slowly come to a stop.

'Watch Mila,' said Billington standing up. He picked up a wine gourd Mila had brought him earlier. Slowly he tipped it until a little wine spilt from the spout. 'You see how the wine spills out when it's tipped?' Then holding the gourd by its leather thong, Billington swung it around his head. 'Look Mila! The wine stays in! Even though it's tipped! That's centrifugal force! And that saves energy. The steam gives the energy to the wheel and the centrifugal force of nature helps it along. Do you understand?'

Mila shook and scratched his head and frowned.

'Mila, have you ever wondered why you can only fall down but never up? But if I tied you to a rope and swung you like the gourd, of course if I was strong enough, that is, then surely you would rise up?'

'Oh yes!' Mila exclaimed. 'Now I see!'

'So on with the demonstration!'

By now a small crowd had gathered, somewhat bemused at the array of curiosities and Billington's strange actions with the gourd. Billington charged the engine's firebox with coal and a little lamp oil to get a small flame going. Within a few minutes the engine began to hiss and steam before the boiler started rumbling under its pressure. Just for effect and amusement, Billington pulled the little lever releasing the pressure valve and the engine hooted sharply, making the crowd jump back in fits of both alarm and laughter.

'And now my dear folks,' called Billington, 'bear witness to the greatest invention of the modern age. An age of great wealth is soon to be upon you!' Another two hoots of the whistle and Billington slowly released the piston valve and the engine crawled forward. The crowd gasped and clapped at the magic, following Billington and Mila as the engine gathered pace.

'Clear away! Clear away!' Billington shouted as the crowd grew larger, some crowding in front of him and jumping back as Billington pushed them aside. Others ran in front of the engine as it quickened. An Arab man in robes, fascinated at the machine, stepped just in front of Billington causing him to stumble. The engine sped off pursued by the crowd of cheering Arabs and merchants.

Billington jumped to his feet chasing after them. 'Don't touch! Don't touch it!' he cried.

The engine struck the legs of a stall, sending metal pots and vases scattering across the ground. The stallholder cursed and kicked at the engine before trying to pull it out from under his stall before jumping back in pain at his burnt hand, much to the amusement of the crowd who now cheered and laughed as Billington carefully dragged the machine out by the rear wheels and doused the firebox.

'Well,' said Billington, 'that's one dissatisfied merchant I'm going to have trouble convincing, eh what, young Mila?'

The rest of the day Billington spent wandering the market, and although many of the travelling merchants understood the *common tongue*, he respectfully addressed as many as he could in their own language as he handed out copies of the rail posters. Mila followed and watched in fascination as Billington slowly weaved through the crowd gesticulating with his hands and arms explaining to the many merchants about the benefit of the *great railroad*. At one point he asked Mila to mind the stall while he went down to the port to talk to the merchant sailors and fishermen with the message.

'Nothing is for sale,' explained Billington. 'You must understand that, Mila. It is for display only. They should understand you if you just wave them off with one of my flyers, and even the thief we encountered earlier is unlikely to be interested in something he can't eat.' And true to his word, proud that Billington had trusted him with such an important task, Mila spent the late afternoon stood in front of the stall trying his best to explain with hand gestures to the many curious passers-by not to touch anything. '*Bikham? Bikham? Shoo hada? Shoo hada?* How much? What is this?' many would ask poking and prodding the many instruments and displaying handfuls of coins 'Sorry, no, sorry no,' Mila would reply and kept repeating for a long while in Billington's absence, waving his arms at those that did touch or handle the instruments and drawings, giving them free posters as Billington had instructed.

In the evening Billington thanked Mila for his services. 'Well, I expect you'll be wanting to return to your family or people now, eh what? Perhaps you might want to assist me again tomorrow, mind my stall for an hour or two while I try to convince some more of these people that I'm here in their own interests?'

Mila thought for a while as Billington stood smiling with his hand extended to shake. He thought about what the officer at the camp had told him about being wary of strangers. But Billington was no slaver, he could tell that. For the first time since he left his home he felt a warmth and trust for this strange man all in white with a face the colour of red leather and his magic machine.

'I have nowhere to go,' Mila said.

'Oh dear, oh dear,' said Billington. 'That will never do. But I'm afraid you can't just stay with me, I'm a guest at the Oasis Faraj and I'm certain they won't accommodate a lone young lad at such a hotel, fine young man that you are. You see, I'm only here for another day or so, until I've struck a deal with the *great one*, as they refer to him around here, then I must move on by ship to the next part of this vast land with my machine and what-not convincing others and securing contracts to allow his Majesty access for the railroad. Oh, I don't suppose you quite understand what I mean but I shall explain it as best as I can as we go. In the meantime we should have a little walk and see if someone will take you in for a night or two.'

Mila followed behind as Billington wandered the market speaking to the various stallholders packing their wares away for the night, until they approached the fruit stall tended by the elderly woman that had shooed him away earlier. Mila stopped a few paces back, worried that the woman might shout and wave him away again as Billington spoke to her in her own language. The woman glanced at Mila and shrugged her shoulders then nodded her head and bowed as Billington spoke and handed her some coins.

'Well, that seems to be settled,' said Billington, beckoning Mila to come forward.

As Mila cautiously approached, the woman eyed him up and down, then smiled and reached into a basket, tossing him a shiny red and green apple.

Billington laughed. 'This is Amira, Mila. And the apple is a gift, a mark of respect for not pinching one from her stall earlier! She speaks only a little of our language, but is quite willing to give you a place to bed down for the night, for a small fee. She's a widow, and lives in a dwelling within an orchard not far from here. And not only that, but it seems we've been invited to supper!'

Amira finished packing the rest of the fruit and Billington explained as they walked from the market, insisting on wheeling the stall himself. 'You see, Mila, it seems though I've only been here a short while, that I've already caught the people's attention with my engine display. People are talking and realise that I'm an important person, even though some don't quite understand just yet. So, when the local people invite you into their home, you don't refuse, you accept. That also, is a sign of respect in these parts.'

They arrived shortly at a stone and clay dwelling, Billington huffing and puffing from the exertion of pushing the stall. 'And of course, young Mila, in return, I must insist upon demonstrating the Englishman's form of respect, and that is to always help a lady with a heavy burden! That, Mila, is how we gain the friendship of people we have never met before!'

Engineer Barclay Billington drank the remaining wine he'd purchased that day sat in the comfort of a cushioned chair in a corner of the humble dwelling. A single oil lamp cast a flickering shadow of his burly frame on the wall as widow Amira went about sweeping sand and dust from the doorway, sorting a warm blanket for Mila and preparing a meal for her two guests, all the while chattering in her own language to herself and Billington as she went. Mila sat upon floor cushions dining on smoked fish, figs and still warm stone-baked flatbread that Amira had made fresh that evening in her little oven, listening in fascination at the white-haired man enthusing about many things Mila didn't quite understand or had never seen but tried hard to imagine.

'Oh, Mila, the countryside of England is such a beautiful land of green hills and mountains with sparkling waterfalls and cool glens. And in the winter months the hills are beautiful and white with snow.'

'What is snow?' asked Mila.

'Ah, well,' said Billington. 'Of course, I should have realised that you would never have seen such a thing in your world. A wonder of creation it is. When it becomes very cold the rainfall, you see, it freezes. I don't suppose you understand what that means either, but I shall try to explain. The raindrops become solid and form themselves into beautiful patterns like, like...some of the patterned woven cloth you see in the market. Beautiful little patterns falling across the hills of England. Such a wondrous thing it is to behold!'

Mila tried hard to imagine tiny patterns of white cloth falling from the sky and wanted to ask more, but Billington just carried on capturing Mila's imagination with tales of a land that seemed like a magical spirit world to him.

'And such a land of wealth was created by the science of industry,' said Billington. 'Yes, the railways in England span the country bringing trade and goods to all the remote corners of the greatest country in the entire world. And at its head is his Majesty King William IV. Oh, to see His Majesty the King, Mila. To be in the presence of royalty! I have only met him once and that was on the business of the railroad; after all, it is to be *his* railroad. Although they say he's a bit new to the job, having not been King long, I don't believe for a minute that he'll be anything other than a most magnificent head of state for England. And to see him in all his regalia, flowing with grace and dignity, Mila, one cannot help but bow down in absolute awe at his presence!'

'I would like to see snow one day,' said Mila. 'And I would like to see the King, such a fine man who is the Head of such a great tribe called England.'

Billington slapped his thighs and burst into deep laughter. 'The head of the tribe indeed, of that he certainly is! I suppose I *could* bring you back to England with me, but a boy of your colour would find it difficult to fit in, very difficult indeed. But one day all that will change. You see, Mila, once these vast lands of Earth are traversed with rail, people will be able to travel all over to places they have only dreamt about. It's not just the trade that's at stake, but all the different cultures of the world will know about each other. They will be given the opportunity to meet and learn all about the diversity of mankind. And when that happens there will be a new world order. There will be understanding and tolerance and there will be peace, harmony and much more happiness upon Earth.

How can we possibly understand the true value of all men if we do not travel? The railroad will provide that understanding, and all because of the science of rail engineering. Won't that be a wonderful thing, young Mila?'

'Yes, Billington,' said Mila. 'Then will there be no more slaves?'

Billington sighed and leant forward pouring another cup of wine. 'Slavery is a vile, vile thing, Mila. Those that perpetrate it will one day pay for their acts. The trade itself has already stopped back home, but there are still many doing it illegally, especially to the Americas. But again this movement will surely develop as our understanding of each other progresses. But first things first. It's going to be a long process which starts with the securing of land contracts. And the most important of those begins tomorrow hopefully. You see, the so-called *powerful one* I was telling you about should arrive here by then. The agents for the Rail Company have filled me in on this chap. He's a very important person who owns much of the land around here including this market town. Not quite a Sultan but very wealthy just the same. He's, how shall I put it? Something of a rogue he is, as we shall see. Apparently he travels much with this *entourage* of oddities, strange people and such like, rather like a circus. But I don't suppose you know what that is, but you shall see. Something of a hobby of his and a way of generating favour amongst the people as well as a little extra wealth...for those that like that sort of thing. Anyway, Mila my boy, I'm forgetting my manners! I've told you my business and a fine and patient audience you have been. And a well trusted aide also you have proven to be. I like to think of myself as a good judge of character and so I've proved it. I knew instinctively what a fine fellow you might be. But now you must tell me your own story. Surely a stout lad as your fine self, so far away from home must have a tale or two?'

So Mila began his story, starting at his life in the village helping Injua fishing and his duties as a watcher running the shores looking for the tall sails of the slave ships. And then, doubtfully at first, he told him of the theft of Trader's net, wondering how Billington might react to having befriended a thief. But Billington just nodded and hummed or tutted at Mila's admission. He told Billington of the slave ship, but not about the slaves drowning, lest Billington think him to be a fool, but his eyes gave him away here as he became tearful at the memory of the event. Nor did he recount the part about how he killed slave driver Briggs. He worried that Billington might consider him to be dangerous and a murderer without conscience. And he left out the part of the Yoonir pearl, still unsure of its destiny. Billington hummed and growled his despise of slavery again, and was astounded that anyone could escape from slavers unaided and eyed Mila sceptically, but said nothing. Mila told him of his time on the island and Billington's eyebrow raised as he commented on Mila's strength against the odds.

'A common man wouldn't last the week!' Billington exclaimed. 'An absolutely astounding tale! Do carry on, young Mila!'

And then Mila told Billington of his time on the Barbary ship and Billington was so amazed and enthralled at the adventure that he said very little throughout the story other than to utter the odd phrase such as: 'truly incredible,' or 'remarkable.' When Mila came to tell Billington of the death of the Seyaad his words became broken and he began to cry as he recounted how he had lost Julieta in the fireball, and Billington almost had to dab his own eyes at the tale of tragedy.

And then, after much consideration, Mila told him of the miracle of his survival being lost and floating in the sea for yet a third time and how, even though he had lost hope and wanted to slip into the deep forever, that somehow he was pushed to the surface each time he let go.

'I could see nothing at all,' explained Mila. 'I could only feel it beneath me, until on the second evening it pushed me onto a piece of wood big enough to float on without sinking.'

'And what was it?' Billington asked in wonder.

'I don't know,' said Mila. 'At first I thought it was sharks playing with me before devouring me. But then, I think it was the power of...Yoonir.'

'Yoonir?' said Billington. 'Ah, I have heard of this myth. The Yoonir star that guides. Some of your people's tribes believe in its power over life and death. Well, I'm afraid I can't subscribe to that sort of thing. The Yoonir is merely another star, a sun in the heavens, much like our own sun and one of myriad suns in the universe. Science tells us that, young Mila. No doubt your folk use its brightness to guide your way by night, but that's all its power is.'

Mila was puzzled. 'If the Yoonir is like the sun, why is it not warm?'

'Ah well,' explained Billington. 'It's like a fire, you see. The nearer you are, the warmer it feels and the brighter it is. But if you walk a long way from it, it looks small and you feel no warmth. The Yoonir is simply a sun like the very one above us in the day, but it is much further away. And that's science again. The Yoonir is so far away that the warmth cannot reach us. Do you understand now?'

'Oh yes!' said Mila. 'But what is *science?*'

'Science? Why, science is everything, Mila. Everything in the world that we see, all living creatures, the sky, the ocean, the deserts. Everything can be explained by science. And those that can't be explained now will be explained one day. And I, as an engineer am privileged to be part of that progress of understanding. That is why I am here, to bring this part of the world up to date with the modern technology of science and all its benefits.'

'Is *science* a god?' asked Mila.

'Well, I suppose it is something of a god to me,' said Billington, 'although it doesn't quite fit that definition. As far as you're concerned, Mila, then I suppose it is. It all must seem like magic to a lad such as you who's never seen the industrial world.'

'Then *science* must have saved me. Science is a very good spirit to be like the Yoonir star.'

'Well, I think science *did* save you, Mila. But I think it was science of a different nature that was looking after you that night. I've heard of this thing before, stories of men drowning and suddenly being helped ashore. I didn't believe it then but your story has a familiarity about it and has certainly made me reconsider. You see, Mila, I think you were being kept buoyant by a dolphin, or perhaps even a group of dolphins. That's the tale I've heard, that they can look after those in difficulty at sea. And if that's the case then you truly are blessed with good fortune! And hopefully that means some of that will rub off on me when it comes to finalise the contract! Well, thank you Mila for that remarkable tale, certainly one for my memoirs when I return eventually to England. But before all that there is tomorrow and that is where the first step of the great Trans North Africa Railway begins!'

Billington stood, somewhat unsteadily from the effects of the wine and thanked Amira once again for taking Mila in for the night. '*Taetani bih balnsbt li,* look after him for me,' he said, handing Amira another coin before departing for his hotel.

12.

In the morning Mila stirred from his bed of cushions and blanket to the sound of commotion in the market. From the window of Amira's dwelling he could see men running between the stalls and shouting.

Billington grumbled and snorted to life from his luxurious bed on the first floor of the Oasis Faraj hotel, and quickly gathering his clothes and dressing, hastened towards the commotion. A large group had gathered at the edge of the market shouting abuse and Billington pushed and struggled to get a view. Men were throwing stones and swearing at the thief that had been there the day before. Billington spotted Mila in the crowd and pushing between the ever increasing throng of people, grabbed him by the arm, and marched swiftly from the melee.

'What is going on?' asked Mila.

'Come on away now young Mila,' said Billington. 'It's not something we have jurisdiction over in these lands. Bloody fool ought to have known better than to have come back. You see, the people here, the Arabs and Berbers and all the other hard working folk that have come from far and wide to sell their wares, well, they don't take kindly to thieves. He had his chance and I tried to save his hide once, mainly for your sake, but to get involved again, well that would make me look like I condoned what he was doing. We must mind our business, unfortunately.'

'What will they do?'

'Well, with a bit of luck they will just drive the poor beggar from the area with a few cuts and bruises. Hopefully, for his own sake he'll run fast and far.'

Suddenly, there was another commotion at the other end of the market. Trumpets sounded and men were calling. The gathering of stone throwers stopped and ran in the direction of the sounding horns.

Firstly, two camels appeared carrying the trumpeters. Bare-chested in turbans and wearing white pantaloons, they blasted their notes, waving the people aside and shouting as they made their way between the stalls: '*Intabih! Intabih!* Look out! Look out! *Salaam! Lau samaht! Naql janba min fadlik!* Hello! Excuse me! Move aside please!'

There followed a long wagon, drawn by donkeys, the fore carriage of which carried a dark, smiling, portly man with neatly trimmed black beard and moustache, attired in flowing white robes with red vest and matching red fez upon his head. He waved to the crowd as he passed, occasionally throwing a coin or two as they cheered. Then there followed several more tented wagons, that passed like floating marquees above the mobbing merchants and customers as they squeezed their way through.

'And there you have him, Mila,' said Billington as the entourage passed. 'The man I must do business with. Abram Faizan himself. Well, we'll give the chap chance to settle in a bit; then I must arrange a meeting. In the meantime, I think breakfast calls.'

Later in the morning Billington set up his stall again and left Mila in charge to hand out posters to all and curious that passed as he went to visit the camp being set up at the far end of the market. He returned after midday with a meal of cheese, flatbread, honey and figs and they dined at the stall while Billington talked to the people that stopped and pondered the array of instruments and his steam engine. And he talked about the contract he was on the verge of completing.

'It's all in hand now, Mila,' Billington explained. 'Just a few little areas to iron out and then my work here is complete. Perhaps after lunch you might like to have an amble over to the odd fellow himself and have a look at the bit of a sideshow he's got on. Somewhat entertaining I suppose, for these people here. However, I personally have no time for such frivolity. Seems like nothing but a freak show.'

After his meal, Mila made his way to the end of the market. A huge white marquee had been set up in front of the covered wagons. Red, green and blue triangular banners fluttered in the wind on poles that protruded from the top of the marquee. Posters stuck to boards on stands depicted Abram Faizan himself as a huge figure surrounded by a collection of 'wonders' as the poster described. A crowd was gathering chattering in anticipation at what might be to come.

Eventually Faizan emerged from the marquee onto a platform erected at the front to cheers from the crowd. *'Salaam! Salaam,'* he cried. Mila watched a while in fascination as the man gesticulated enthusiastically with his hands and spoke in the language he recognised from the Seyaad. He was about to turn away when Faizan broke into the language of Trader. 'Many greetings to the good people of the beautiful town of Ancen Medina! I speak to you, my many, many Arabs, Berbers, Nomads, Europe people and all my other travelling merchants and guests from afar in the *common tongue,* that all may understand and enjoy what is to come!'

The crowd cheered even louder as Faizan continued.

'Far and wide I, your faithful servant Abram Faizan, has wandered in search of the wondrous and extraordinary curiosities for your entertainment! And today of course is no exception! For starters, there is as usual my beautiful harem!'

Faizan gestured to his aides dressed in all white robes and turbans with daggers tucked into their sashes. The two bowed deeply and drew back the curtain of the marquee.

The women, dressed in flowing robes of many colours, and adorned with many fine jewels peeped out shyly from the marquee, giggling under their veiled faces. There were gasps of admiration from the men of the crowd before the women disappeared quickly back into the marquee.

'Ah, but later, later my good men folk,' Faizan enthused. 'You will have your chance to admire my beautiful ladies at your leisure! But first today, my good friends of Ancen Medina, I bring to you one of the truly wondrous creatures of this world!'

Again Faizan gestured to his aides who brought out a stand with a poster attached and the crowd pushed and jostled to look, gasping in awe at the picture of Faizan dwarfed by a truly huge man that stood towering above him. 'Today, my people,' called Faizan, 'I bring you the Greek giant of Pelopennesus, the great and mighty Andreas!'

The crowd cheered and jumped. 'Bring him out! Bring him out!' they cried.

Faizan held up his hands calming the crowd. 'Ah, but Faizan has gone to hard work for your entertainment. Such things do not come cheap! But I say to you my good people, that I still have a bargain for you. You all understand a bargain?' Faizan implored, opening his arms. 'You are merchants and tradesmen! You recognize a good deal! And today, my good people of Ancen Medina, I offer you not only the opportunity to meet the giant Andreas, and all the wondrous creatures of my travels, but also my beautiful maidens will dance for you! And all for the meagre sum of one dirham! Is that not a bargain?'

The crowd nodded and enthused, many holding up their coins and pushing forward.

'Orderly, orderly, my friends!' called Faizan. 'There is plenty of time, one at a time.' And Faizan's aides collected the coins in a pot as the people filed by into the marquee, until Mila came to the front of the queue.

Faizan stopped him dead, pressing the palm of his hand on Mila's chest. 'What, no dirham?' he said. 'You expect Faizan to allow you for free because you are but a young man? Be off with you insolent boy!' And Faizan pushed him aside roughly.

But Mila was curious and eager to see the giant and stared in wonder at the poster, unable to believe that such a huge man could possibly exist. He thought about asking Billington, if he might give him a coin to enter the marquee, but he also realised that Billington was dismissive of Faizan's 'sideshow' and that Billington had been more than kind so far having fed and found him somewhere safe to sleep.

As the crowd was preoccupied with Faizan as he addressed them, Mila slipped quietly between some stalls and around to the back of Faizan's wagons. He crawled underneath until he reached the narrow gap between wagon and marquee and carefully pulled up the canvas, poking his head inside. To one side of the marquee Faizan's maidens danced and swayed upon a stage to the music of flute-pipers, occasionally uncovering their beautiful faces and dark glinting eyes as the men enthused and admired as they passed. Another stand displayed snakes in many glass cases and strange reptiles some of which looked familiar to Mila but were much larger and deadlier looking. In a cage next to these were birds of blue and gold, the like of which Mila had seen before in the forests near his home. But as the crowd filed past some of the birds would flap their wings and then speak in Arabic to the surprise and entertainment of many. Then suddenly, 'Faizan the great, Faizan the all powerful,' one squawked in English. Mila was so amazed his head sprang up against the marquee apron straining his neck, nearly causing him to cry out.

But there in the middle of the marquee sat the giant. And each time a few of the crowd passed he would stand up and tower over them. Some of the people looked fearful at the giant in his strange outfit of animal skins; he was almost twice the height of some and his head reached high up near the apex of the marquee. Then he would sit again. He was eating but for a few seconds only, before Faizan's aide would tap him with a stick and order him to stand. And each time he stood, he would pick from a bowl full of very large copper rings and place one upon his forefinger as Faizan's aide would ask the crowd to marvel at the size of the giant's fingers, and if they would like to purchase a ring for a very modest sum as proof of their seeing this marvel of the world? And then the giant would sit again and eat a little before the aide's command to repeat the performance.

And he was chained. Despite his fixation with the man's massive frame and height Mila couldn't help but notice that the giant had nowhere to go and was to his mind, a slave.

Later that evening Mila told Billington about the giant and Billington was both bemused and annoyed. 'You must be careful, Mila. Faizan is most revered and powerful in these parts. You do well not to cross him. And getting a sneak view of his show was quite dangerous. He does not like being done out of a single half dirham.'

But that night Mila couldn't sleep. Every time he shut his eyes he saw the giant Andreas, his huge frame seemed to fill the marquee and Mila tried to imagine him inside Amira's humble dwelling, his massive torso crushing the chair and his head bursting through the ceiling as he stood. And he thought about the chains and about what Billington had said about slavery. It was no good. Mila had to get to know the giant and his tale.

He slipped out of the dwelling in the dead of night as Amira slept and mumbled in her sleep. The bright stars and moon lit his way to the back of the marquee, the only sound being the dogs on a hillside howling at the brightest of the heavenly bodies. Slipping under the canvas he wondered if the giant might even be there at all, or in one of the tented wagons, or even if the wagons were long enough for him to sleep in at all. But he was in luck. The giant snored and grunted on a straw bed scattered with goatskins, his silhouette rising and falling like a midnight ocean swell with each breath.

'Giant?' Mila whispered. 'Giant, are you awake?'

Andreas suddenly snorted and spluttered. '*Pooios einai ekei?* Who goes there?' he called out in a language Mila had not heard before.

'Be quiet, giant. I am Mila, a friend.'

'It speaks the *common tongue*, I hear,' Andreas grunted in English. 'Whoever you are, I should be the judge of you being friend or foe. So what is the meaning of this intrusion? Speak up or I call for Faizan, and in that case we shall both be in trouble.'

'I wanted to meet you,' whispered Mila.

'Then come back tomorrow and pay your dirham like the rest,' Andreas growled.

'But you are a slave, giant,' said Mila. 'No one should be a slave. I was once a slave, I think. But now I'm free. How is it that a man of your size can be a slave? It must have been very hard to catch you.'

Andreas sat up and lit a lamp, holding it up to survey Mila in the low light. 'Impudent boy! I am no slave. Come closer where I can see you.'

Mila approached cautiously and sat upon the bare ground nearby. He could see the giant's fair-skinned face now, framed in flowing black curly hair and beard. It was broad and strange, his jaw seemed wider than his brow. But he was kindly looking, not fierce as Mila had imagined from the poster which made him to look like a terrifying monster. 'But you have shackles,' Mila said. 'That means you are a slave.'

'Hmm,' said Andreas. 'You might think so, little one, but

that is all part of the show. If the people see me chained they think it is because I am fierce and dangerous and that makes it more entertaining. But also Faizan says they are for my own protection during the show. If one of the visitors to the show should taunt me, and that has happened before, and I lose my patience then I don't know my own strength. I might accidentally hurt someone, he says. So he keeps the people well back out of touching distance.'

'But no man should be in chains,' said Mila. 'It is the same as being a slave.'

'But look, little one,' said Andreas, stretching out his massive legs into the lamplight. 'I am wearing no chains now.'

'Good,' said Mila. 'I am glad. Slavery is a vile, vile thing. You can go now and no longer be a slave.'

'Go? Go where? What do you mean?'

'You can go home to your people,' said Mila. 'If you are no longer in chains it means you have freedom and are no longer a slave.'

'You don't understand, little Mila. I can go nowhere. This is my home now. I can never return to my past home.'

'But why not?' said Mila. 'You must have a family. I have a family somewhere, but I am lost now in the *great civilisation* and don't know how to get back, but one day I hope to find them again.'

'I once had a home.' said Andreas. 'I lived in a home in the foothills of my country, a beautiful land of green and gold with forests and blue mountains and the bluest of seas imaginable that you could see from above the olive trees on the slopes below.'

'Perhaps we might look for your home again?' said Mila. 'I could help you, or maybe one of the boats in the port might take you back?'

'No, little one, that can never be. My family could not keep me. You see, I belong to Faizan now.'

'Then that means you really are a slave?'

'I suppose in a way it does,' said Andreas sadly. 'Faizan bought me from my family. When my mother and father saw how big I was growing and how much it took to feed me they despaired. My family are but poor farmers barely making a living from a little smallholding. I was eating everything they could produce; such was my size and appetite. They sold me to Faizan's show that passed by long ago. My poor mother was broken-hearted, but they had no choice. Faizan promised that I would be looked after well. And I suppose he does that. At least I'm not hungry and Faizan makes much dirham from my appearances. He even teaches us the *common tongue* as we so speak. He says this is the tongue of the *modern world* and we must be part of it. I suppose this thing called a *railroad* he speaks much about on our travels here is part of it.'

'Yes, I know about the railroad,' said Mila. 'I have been helping Barclay Billington. He is very proud of the Head of his tribe called the King and the railroad machine.'

Andreas smiled. 'Billington? Yes, that's the name Faizan speaks much of. You must be honoured to be his aide?'

'Yes,' said Mila. 'Billington has been very kind to me.'

'Well, whatever this railroad is about, it is nothing to do with us here in Faizan's show. We are here simply for the entertainment of the people. So this is my life for good. I can never go back; my family would starve should I return.'

'But Faizan makes you work and stand and sit and put rings on even while you are eating from morning until night,' said Mila. 'You do not have time to rest and sleep in the sun after a meal? That is what my people do. Then they can work harder when the magic of the food and rest gives them strength. Eating in chains is what slaves do.'

'Indeed it is, little Mila. You are quite right in saying this.'

'Perhaps one day?' said Mila.

'It can never be,' Andreas said gruffly. 'Be off with you now, boy. I have much to do in the morning and I don't need anyone to remind me of my miserable life or my lost home.'

Mila slipped quietly back to the dwelling and tucked himself into his blanket without disturbing Amira who still slept soundly. He found it difficult to sleep at first, still thinking about Andreas as he slipped in and out of dreams about the poor giant and his sad family at having to part with their son. He dreamt of Trader and sailing upon a warm blue ocean taking Andreas back to his own tribe and introducing the giant to his mother and father who shook their heads in disbelief. And he dreamt of Julieta floating upon the sea, calling out to him in despair. And as Trader's boat sailed by he leant over the edge reaching out his hands, but could not touch her, and each time the boat circled he would try to catch Julieta but each time he was just out of reach and Julieta eventually slipped into the deep never to be seen again.

And in the early light he woke up crying.

Later that morning Mila helped Billington roll the steam engine out by the stall. Billington cleared the way for another demonstration, this time for Abram Faizan himself who now made his way with his aides through the crowd. As Faizan walked, he extended his hand to the many people who kissed it and bowed in respect as his aides waved horsetails before him shooing flies away.

'So, this is your mighty machine, Billington?' said Faizan.

'Indeed it is, your Excellency,' said Billington. 'This is but a very small version and I can assure you that the great locomotive itself, every inch as large as shown on the drawings we have perused is now being built in the great British city of Newcastle. Indeed, it has been designed at the works of none other than Robert Stephenson himself, son of the great George Stephenson, and undoubtedly the greatest pioneer of mechanical engineering technology of all.'

'Enough of your waffling, Billington,' said Faizan. 'Show me this quickly, I have a show to provide and time is money.'

And once again, Billington fired the engine's box and hooted the whistle before releasing the engine on its way. This time the crowd stood well back as the engine crawled along steaming and whooshing as the piston gathered momentum. The man selling pots and vases stepped out in front of his stall wary and making sure that the engine passed safely by. As the engine picked up more speed Billington ran in front of it and blocked its progress with his legs, locking the piston and releasing the boiler valve as the machine billowed and whooshed at the escaping pressure.

'So, as you can see,' said Billington, 'the machine keeps gathering pace. There truly is no limit to how fast it can go. And a very large machine as we are building will be powerful enough to transport hundreds of people, all your entourage and luggage and your harem at once in a fraction of the time you take to cover these vast and barren lands between towns. The markets of the world will be at your disposal within days rather than the weeks it must take you to access them. And no donkeys or camels to feed on the way, no diversions in search of water holes and pasture or carrying bulks of animal feed. This is indeed the age of the machine, Faizan. Be part of it before others should pass you by.'

'I am impressed, Billington,' said Faizan. 'Perhaps we have a deal. We should discuss it tonight in my villa. After the show, of course.'

Billington was very pleased and the following day a deal was struck. He began to dismantle the stall and Mila helped him to load up his wagon and ready for his onward journey seeking out more land access contracts. In the afternoon Billington gave Mila a few coins for his help.

'Perhaps you would like to see Faizan's show before he leaves town?' said Billington. 'At least you won't have to sneak in. I'm here for another night or two and then well, I'm afraid I must be on my way. But you go off and enjoy yourself for now while I finish tidying up, eh what?'

Mila made his way to Faizan's marquee and again Faizan was up on his platform, doffing his fez, bowing, opening his arms and addressing the crowd as though *he* was *their* servant. But today was different. Faizan had a new attraction that the people hadn't seen the previous day. The strange man stood tall and menacing looking; his dark face seemed even blacker than Mila's own skin as he frowned at the crowd. He was dressed in a single leopard skin loincloth and a headdress of many finely coloured feathers. He had a spear with more feathers tied to the hilt near the long, sharpened bone end, which he held at his side, occasionally lifting it above his head and gesturing to throw it into the crowd as Faizan spoke and the people enthused with gasps of admiration.

'And so my good people!' Faizan declared. 'Once again I bring you not just entertainment but a challenge! Remember Faizan's last challenge? Last time I brought to you the *wrestler*. The great 'Stone of Rome.' Ah, but he was not a giant, barely the size of me, Faizan himself. But could anyone rise to the challenge? Merely to put this man onto his back was all that I asked to win the challenge. Many of you tried but not one could manage this simple feat! But now I admit this was most unfair. The Stone was a very cagey grappler with much experience and many clever moves. Indeed I had seen him in the arenas and knew what he could do. But I thought at least one among the magnificent people of Ancen Medina might accomplish the task and at least I would have felt a little fairer about taking money? But no, it was not to be.' Faizan removed his fez and shook his head and bowed as if in apology.

'But now my good people of Ancen Medina, I bring to you

a much simpler challenge! I introduce to you the great Ethiopian warrior and runner, Gabra Adunga!'

Adunga stepped forward, holding the spear across his chest and bowing before the crowd as they clapped and cheered.

'The challenge is quite simple this time,' Faizan continued. 'And one that will not involve any such bruises or cuts as there were last time! A thousand apologies!' He laughed, removed his fez and bowed again to the crowd. 'My challenge is simply to race against Gabra Adunga. And the winner, should it be one of you, my beautiful people, will have their choice of my treasures.'

'Anything?' someone from the crowd asked.

'But of course!' said Faizan. 'Whatever your heart desires! A beautiful maiden, perhaps?'

'What manner of race will it be?' asked another.

'The contestants will simply follow the road out of Ancen Medina and around the far hill,' said Faizan pointing. 'It is about seven miles. And the first one back to the market is the winner. A very straight forward challenge, no broken bones, nothing to lose but a wager and perhaps a little tiredness. What do you say my good people.'

'A wager?' another man asked. 'What wager are you asking for?'

'Whatever you can afford, my good people!' said Faizan. 'A dirham, perhaps? No? Maybe a half dirham? But wait! You haven't heard what I am offering! For every dirham you place on any challenger whatsoever among you, Faizan will give you ten in return should the challenger win. Ten dirham! Think about it my people! What you can buy with ten dirham! Or even five dirham should you be cautious and only wish to place half a dirham! Still a tidy sum, yes? And of course, the challenger himself gets anything he wants, that is Faizan's promise!'

The crowd mumbled among themselves, some shaking

their heads or sighing in disapproval. 'It is not right, Faizan. You know the teachings,' one shouted.

'Ah, but of course I understand the laws of Allah,' replied Faizan. 'When we play anything for money it cheats one of the people, this I understand. It is a loss that is harmful for those that lose. So Allah, the good and only God told his prophet that it is restricted. Of course I know this! But look at me. I am a wealthy man. It is surely no loss for me and I simply provide entertainment for you. But, of course, it must be paid for at a very small cost, the same as looking at my show, it doesn't come for free. And such a small cost! One quarter of a dirham, perhaps?'

The crowd stood silent other than a few whispers. Faizan was getting worried that his investment in Adunga may have been wasted.

'This is a sporting competition!' Faizan blurted in exasperation. 'Not a gamble! And of course, all the money will go to good causes...of that you can be assured. It is not for *me*, my good people.' Faizan spread his arms wide then removed his fez, placing it across his chest and bowing gracefully. 'I have no need of money. Your wagers will be collected for the poor and beggars of your fine town. Surely Allah provides for charity, does he not?'

At that very moment a flock of birds flew up from a nearby stall and Faizan pointed at the flock shouting: 'Look my people, surely it is a sign? A sign of Faizan's word!' And the crowd began to rouse and talk again, some nodding their heads in agreement at Faizan's sudden turn of face and began to come forward to offer small 'donations' to the competition.

Soon a small pot held a few lesser coins and Faizan was disappointed but addressed the crowd once again. 'But we have no challenger as yet. And the challenger must make a wager himself. There must be a challenger who can wager enough against my offer of any of my possessions to make the race worthy of Adunga's effort. A simple collection between only a few of you, even, and there should easily be enough for your challenger at so little expense. And of course, should your challenger win, your money is returned! Think of it my good people, not only your money back, but anything your challenger asks for and I, Faizan the honourable, will grant it. Surely one of you is stout and fast?'

Faizan pointed to a man in the crowd. 'You my good friend! A sheepherder, I believe? Surely a man who spends his days marching the mountains and chasing off wolves could rise to this simple task?'

The shepherd simply shook his head.

'Anyone?' beseeched Faizan. 'Gabra Adunga is a mere mortal like any of you. Surely someone? Then I'm afraid that your meagre donations must be returned until we find a challenger. Ah, such a great pity that the poor will lose out. I am an honest man and will not hold your monies.'

The crowd began to file a queue and Faizan's aides started returning their coins when Mila stepped forward to the front of Faizan's platform. 'I will race the warrior,' he said.

The crowd suddenly hushed and Faizan looked down from his platform at the boy with disdain. 'You?' he said. 'What manner of joke is this? The boy without a single dirham who wanted to see my show for free? Be off with you insolent child!' And the crowd laughed.

'But I wish to challenge the warrior,' persisted Mila. 'I am a runner. I have done many runnings for my tribe.'

'Perhaps,' said Faizan dismissively. 'But you have no money. The challenger must lay a wager himself otherwise the race is not worth it for a few small coins. You must present at least ten dirham for your place in the challenge.'

Mila held out his hand with the few coins Billington had given him.

Faizan looked at the coins derisively. 'You call this

miserable sum a wager? I said ten dirham! What is wrong with you boy? Can you not count?'

'It is true,' said Mila. 'I don't understand money.' He reached into his pantaloons and untied the skin bag from its cord. 'But I have this,' he said, holding out the Yoonir pearl. 'This is my wager.'

The crowd gasped and Faizan stood frozen in amazement. The pearl took on a new brightness in the afternoon sun, it dazzled and shone with burning colours that seemed to flow about its surface like many coloured seas upon a globe. Even Mila was surprised at how much brighter it seemed, as though the pearl was speaking to him in colours and glows.

'Where did you get such a gem?' Faizan gasped and reached out his hand to touch the pearl.

Suddenly a hand from behind grabbed Mila's outstretched arm firmly by the wrist. 'I'll look after this, Faizan,' said Billington, snatching the pearl from Mila's hand.

'But the boy has made his wager,' protested Faizan. 'You cannot go back on a wager; that is the dealing of thieves and vagabonds!'

'I realise that,' said Billington. 'Unfortunately I was just a second too late to stop the boy from this foolish act. But just the same, I shall be the holder of the wager...unless you think I can't be trusted.'

'But of course, Billington,' Faizan laughed uneasily. 'We have a deal, of which I am most pleased. You are a kind and honourable man.' Faizan removed his fez and bowed gracefully. 'And the race shall begin forthwith.'

'This wager is huge,' said Billington. 'You of course realise that this gem must be worth many thousands of dirham. You will at least grant me time with the boy before we start.'

'As long as the race is done this day,' said Faizan. 'That is the challenge. Then you shall have your time. But the day is getting on and we should start soon.'

Billington pulled Mila aside sharply dragging him away from the crowd. 'Whatever were you thinking of, Mila? And where did you get this gem? Why didn't you tell me of this before? Do you realise that this pearl may be worth the entire wealth of Ancen Medina itself? And now you are willing to hand it over to one of the biggest scoundrels in the Eastern world? For what? Whatever are you doing?'

Mila began to cry. 'I'm sorry, Billington. I want to go home. You are going tomorrow and I am lost, and Faizan said the challenger would be granted anything they wished for.'

'How on earth do you think you can win your way home with this scoundrel?' Billington scolded. 'The man is a travelling show; he doesn't go about providing boats for young homeless lads. Even so, where would he take you? You don't even know where you are from exactly, do you, Mila?'

Mila shook his head.

'Oh Mila, whatever will you do next, bet my steam engine? The Rail Company warned me to be wary, to curry the man's favour, yes, but with caution. And I warned you as well, Mila. But where did you get this gem? Oh, never mind that now, you have a competition on your hands.'

'I will miss you, Billington,' Mila sobbed.

'Oh dear boy!' said Billington, hugging Mila. 'It's such a shame that you have gone through so much to have it end like this. I'm so sorry I can't take you with me, but I must travel alone. I may stop a day or two longer at most, if only to see you cared for. Perhaps I can convince Amira to take you in for good? You are after all a fine hard working lad.'

'Thank you, Billington,' said Mila wiping his tears.

'Now then, Mila. We have a race to win. Tell me something, and you must be completely honest with me this time. You told me about you being something of a runner yourself, is that right?'

'Yes, I am the tribe's *slave sighter*. The tribe counts the days that Trader says the slave ships will come our way and I run the shore looking for them so that I can warn the tribe before they reach us.'

'Yes yes, you did tell me that,' said Billington. 'I seem to remember even though I'd had a spot too much wine. Very good, so far. And tell me, Mila, how old are you?'

'Trader says I am *fifteen*...or maybe *fourteen*. I forget. Maybe I am both.'

'Excellent, excellent,' said Billington. 'And how far can you run?'

'I run to Baja village. Trader says this is *fifty miles.*'

'Good heavens! I didn't think any man could run that far. And how long did this take, Mila? How many hours?'

'I don't know *hours*. Trader has not taught me about *hours*. I run from morning to the sun being at highest in the sky.'

'Even more remarkable,' Billington whispered. 'That might equate to anything between four and seven hours, depending on the season. If I know anything about athletic feats then I know this is something of an exemplary performance.'

'And we were carrying a net,' Mila added.

'We?' asked Billington.

'Yes, the net was very heavy and my friend Obi helped me carry it.'

'So the two of you, carrying a heavy net ran about fifty miles?'

'But Obi fell down and couldn't carry any more so I carried it alone for...I don't know...*miles* I think.'

Faizan called out: 'It is time, Billington. The race cannot delay any longer!'

'You must at least give me time to *prompt* the boy,' Billington shouted. 'It is obvious your man is a seasoned runner. To make this competition at least somewhat fair you must give me a few minutes.'

'Very well, Billington,' said Faizan, rubbing his hands

together and smiling wryly at his aides.

Billington ordered Mila to strip down to his loincloth then knelt down, and taking a cloth tape measure from his lapel pocket, took hold of Mila's leg. 'Now hold still, Mila,' he said, as he made various measurements.

Billington then stood and measured Mila's full height, then knelt again, producing a pencil and scraps of paper from his pocket that had some detail of the steam railway on it. Finding a blank sheet, he began scribbling furiously, stopping only to take more measurements around the diameters of Mila's thighs, calves, feet and buttocks.

'Very good,' Billington mumbled enthusiastically. 'Excellent in fact. Now stand on your tip toes, Mila.'

Mila obeyed, wondering exactly what Billington was doing. A crowd had gathered around the two, equally as flummoxed as Billington continued his measurements of Mila's body and flexed various parts of his legs. He then spent several more minutes scribbling, rubbing out and rewriting calculations, sweating and mumbling numbers to himself. Eventually he sighed pleasingly, stood up and grabbing Mila by the arm again, dragged him back to Faizan's platform.

'And now, Faizan,' said Billington, 'in the name of true sporting etiquette, you will let me inspect your man.'

'What is the meaning of this, Billington?' Faizan demanded. 'You do not trust me? He is a mere mortal after all.'

'It is common procedure where bets are laid,' answered Billington. 'At least in a *civilised* country, that is. The competitors and their agents must be allowed to assess the competition, it is only fair. Obviously you *do* consider yourself to be civilised? You have every right to assess the boy in return.'

Faizan stared at Mila and scowled derisively. 'I don't think that will be necessary, Billington. He is a mere nothing who will be swept away like a leaf in Adunga's wind.'

Adunga grinned, and bared his teeth at Mila as he growled and pounded the spear hilt against his chest.

'Then you will have no qualm in me examining your man,' Billington stated, stepping up onto the platform.

'But of course, Billington,' Faizan said doubtfully as he removed his fez and bowed.

Billington repeated his routine on Adunga, who often repelled or drew back his leg, or flinched in protest at being handled as he frowned at Faizan questioningly. Faizan looked over Billigton's shoulder worryingly as Billington scribbled his calculations. It was taking longer this time and Faizan began to fret and protest at the delay, but Billington just grumbled for silence and muttered about *civilised* sportsmanship. At last Billington had finished and stood up. 'Faizan!' he declared. 'Let the race begin!'

'Excellent, Billington,' replied Faizan with a broad smile, tipping his fez in honour.

'And just to make it interesting, Faizan,' added Billington. 'I'll have a hundred dirham...on the boy!'

13.

A ripple and gasps of astonishment ran through the crowd followed by heavy chatter.

Faizan was rendered speechless for several seconds. 'Are you serious, Billington? A hundred dirham? That is a small fortune.'

'And if you're an honourable man, you'll take my wager, unless of course, you doubt your man.'

'But of course, Billington,' said Faizan nervously. 'A hundred dirham it is. You are good for it then, I presume?'

'The Rail Company pays me well and the honour of both myself and his Majesty King William are at stake. I swear by both.'

'Then it shall be done!' Faizan declared.

The crowd stood silent for several seconds, then there was a hum of chatter and discussion among them, the words *Billington* and *wise man* or *magic machine* could be heard drifting between them and many a head nodded in agreement. Suddenly many rushed forward to Faizan clutching coins and shouting: 'The boy, the boy! The boy Mila!' Coins were thrust in Faizan's direction. Coins of all denomination. Dirhams and half dirhams and quarter dirhams along with much shouting and pushing, all in a last desperate attempt to back *the boy Mila*. Faizan desperately tried to calm the crowd, worried at the sudden turn in interest at the boy, at first declaring that the boy's wager would be the only one accepted for that day. But the crowd were having none of it, betting of individuals had already been accepted and many shouted angrily at Faizan, reminding him that to turn down the opportunity to 'help the poor' was offending them, and that he had already promised odds of ten dirham to each one dirham bet.

In the meantime, Billington had dragged Mila away from the melee and knelt down on one knee, massaging each of Mila's legs in turn. 'Now listen to me carefully, Mila. You are quite capable of winning this race. Oh yes, believe me, you have a distinct leverage advantage over this Adunga chap. He also carries some weight around the buttocks. He may be a fast runner, but I believe Faizan has only pitched him against peasants and merchants so far. And do not be put off by his ferocious look, that's all part of Faizan's show. And if what you tell me about running the shores of your homeland is true, then I'm certain you can do it. Remember, Mila, what you have been through already. This is a mere nothing by comparison. You, my boy, are a true survivor!'

Billington stood up and placed his hands on Mila's cheeks and kissed him on the forehead. 'And when the race starts you will run like the wind!'

Faizan had relented and the last of the bets were being laid. He turned to Adunga and whispered: 'I do not trust this man Billington. He is very wise and knows something we don't. I want that pearl at all costs. See that the boy does not return. Whatever it takes, kill him if you must but do not let him finish the race.'

Another whisper was given to one of the aides who ran through the restless crowd waving an orange rag tied to a pole to a place on the edge of the market. He stopped by the last stall, stabbed the pole to the ground and called out: 'The race will proceed at my command from this point! From here the competitors will follow the path out past the port of Ancen Medina along the coast and around the mountain and back to the market. Whosoever lifts the flag first shall be declared the winner! Competitors shall come forward!'

Gabra Adunga sprang forth out of nowhere and without further word Faizan's aide had picked up the pole, waved it above his head and dropped it again and Adunga had sprinted off along the path before anyone realised the race had begun.

'Bloody cheats!' Billington grumbled. 'Go Mila!' he shouted and Mila set off in pursuit to the cheers of the crowd.

Adunga had left a substantial distance between the two and Mila was well past the port and out onto the hillside path before he could see him. Mila felt comfortable in his run, the heat of the market was replaced by a cool breeze that drifted down from the mountain and seemed to be lifting him from behind like the sails of the Seyaad. He carried on, trying to assess if he was gaining on Adunga but for a long while the gap remained the same. Then came a steep incline and Mila noticed that the distance had lessened once they were on the descent and he put in a spurt downhill. Another mile on flat grassy plains and Mila was nearly level.

He came close upon Adunga's shoulder. 'You are a very fine runner,' Mila said, and Adunga looked around in amazement.

Mila drew level. 'In my tribe we have running competitions but we do not race. Whoever is the finest and most beautiful at running and pleases the rest of the tribe is the winner. I have never won such a competition. Usually the prize goes to Jaji who is most graceful when he moves.'

Adunga snarled at Mila and put in a short spurt leaving him behind, but Mila soon caught up. 'You are a great runner, Faizan says. And you are a very fine runner also. You would win the competition in my tribe. I am very pleased to meet someone who is both great and fine. One day when I return home I will tell my people of the time I met the great Gabra Adunga and was honoured to run with him.'

Again Adunga sprinted off, this time leaving Mila far

behind, but little by little Mila caught him up.

'I have an idea,' said Mila. 'We are both very good runners. If we decide to finish the race together then there is no winner. Then Faizan might grant me my wish, if I give him the pearl, and I can go home. And you will still be a great and fine runner.'

Adunga was getting extremely agitated by Mila's endurance and could not understand how he kept catching him up. The extra bursts of speed had sapped his legs and Mila's persistent talking had infuriated him. He swung his arm out catching Mila across the face, sending him sprawling onto his back sliding on the ground and sped off.

Mila sat up, his lower lip bleeding and gravel burns stung his back. For a minute he felt dazed and hurt in body and heart, but gathered his wits and set off again in pursuit of Adunga. Now his thoughts were of Billington's words and his *magic* and *science* and the steam engine and Billington's belief in him as the winner. He thought of Julieta and his sense of loss, and he also saw a vision of Billington's saddened face at him losing the race. He thought of his time on the island and the slave ship. He thought of Brigg's *scourge* thrashing his back and how it now stung once again from Adunga's attack. And now he was angry.

Now the path curved and Adunga had been out of sight for a long time. Mila wasn't certain but from his days learning about *miles* from Trader he thought that the race was not far from finished. He put in short bursts on the bends until Adunga came into view and soon he was nearly level once again. He said nothing, unaware if Adunga knew of his presence or not. He recalled the old man Injua's words of warning many years before: *Beware the tail of the ray from behind, the ray will know you are there and will flay and sting when you least expect.*

The path had narrowed and Mila could not safely pass

Adunga should he try to strike out again. He held onto his position just behind matching Adunga's pace hoping the path would widen soon.

Something in Adunga's psyche alerted him, suddenly realising that Mila was shadowing him. He glanced around as the path began to widen where it drew away from the mountainside. Adunga ground to a halt spinning round and barring Mila's way. He drew a small dagger from his skin loincloth. 'Ignorant child!' he seethed. 'You dare to challenge the great Adunga? Be put out of your foolish life now!'

Adunga lunged with the dagger towards Mila, but Mila sprang out of the way. Spinning around, Adunga leapt and missed Mila again. As Adunga staggered off balance, Mila kicked him hard in the buttocks sending him face down in the dust. He jumped onto Adunga's back and sprang off down the path.

Soon the path widened into road onto the flat away from the hills where the clay-brick dwellings appeared and peasants attending flock and field looked up in bewilderment at the *runner*. Mila imagined a time when he ran hard in desperation after sighting the tall sails of the slavers so very near his village. He glanced around as though the slavers were there, sailing quickly along the path behind him. Adunga was running again, but some way behind. Ahead, a goat herder began to lead his drove across the road, unaware of Mila's rapid approach. Mila weaved and wound between and leapt over the bleating animals that scattered and ran in dismay. Over a small rise the market came into view. Arabs, Berbers, citizens and merchants and peasants had begun to line the road cheering Mila. Soon the cheering rose to a deafening crescendo as Mila approached the first stall. The orange flag, obscured by people, was nowhere to be seen. A last glance around and Adunga had gained considerable ground on him and was sprinting furiously. Mila cried out as he burst forward with one last surge, his eyes bulging with the strain, his legs felt to be burning like the lightning tree on his island. People screamed at him but he no longer heard words, it was like the shrill cry of Billington's steam engine.

The orange flag suddenly appeared before him as the people parted and he almost missed it as the last man obscuring it from view jumped out of the way and Mila snatched it up and collapsed into the grasp of many hands lifting and cheering him. Seconds later, almost unnoticed by the crowd, a furious Gabra Adunga sank to his knees at the finish, pounding his fist into the dust in anger.

The people were rapturous as they mobbed Mila and Billington fought his way through. 'Give him air! Make way; let the boy breathe, for pity's sake!'

Billington laughed and hugged Mila as the crowd released him. 'You did it, my boy!' he cried as he laid Mila gently on the ground. 'I told you you could do it! Now stand back everyone!'

'I win,' Mila panted before passing out.

14.

A jubilant merchant sang the praises of Mila's victory and his own small fortune of winnings as he ran through the market to fetch water. Mila soon revived with Billington's attendance. Billington bathed his head with cool water and a cloth, and sitting up, Mila took small sips smiling between each one.

Some of the crowd had gathered around Faizan's platform declaring their winnings but Faizan himself was out of sight, having assisted his aides with dragging Adunga into the marquee. Others of the crowd were getting restless, urging Mila to now go and claim his prize from Faizan, curious as to what it may be. 'A pretty maiden!' some suggested, at which some of the nearby women giggled. 'Gold!' said others. They could wait no longer despite Billington's protests and lifted Mila carrying him to the marquee and platform. Setting him down on his feet they began to chant: 'Mila, winner! Mila winner!' until Faizan appeared from the marquee.

'My very good people of Ancen Medina!' Faizan called. 'How very good of you to turn out for this excellent competition today!' Faizan removed his fez, twiddling with it nervously before bowing deeply. 'It seems at first suggestion that we may have a winner.'

Now the crowd hushed followed by low mumbles and chatter and discernment at the mention of the word 'may.'

'As excellent as the competition was,' continued Faizan, 'I'm afraid there has been some *deception.*' Adunga appeared from the marquee his face still betraying his anger. 'It seems that the boy Mila has attacked my runner causing him to fall, whereupon he assaulted him, leaving him lying in the dust long enough to gain a distinct advantage to attain a win that could not possibly be achieved otherwise. Speak now, Adunga!'

'It is true,' growled Adunga. 'The boy is a cheat.'

'So, my good people,' said Faizan. 'I'm afraid the race has been declared void. In truth, my man is the winner by default, but I am an honest man and will declare that there has been no winner, and therefore all wagers are also void.'

A wave of audible disappointment and frustration ran through the crowd as Billington pushed his way to the front.

'Abram Faizan!' Billington declared, pointing and wagging his finger. 'You're nothing but a scoundrel! You may deem these people to be savage but they're not stupid. Are you really trying to convince them that this mere wisp of a boy could overcome your strapping great athlete? Don't be absurd! If he had indeed done that then he could only have done so if he caught your man up. And if he could catch him up, after that ridiculously unfair start, then surely he could pass him and win the race. I'm afraid your man has proven himself to be a liar by his own words. So, I suggest you pay these people out like the *honourable* man you claim to be!'

Now the crowd's tone changed to a combination of protest and triumph, many of them patting Billington on the back and declaring Mila as the true winner and demanding payout of their wagers. Faizan stood silently fiddling with his fingers, glancing between his man Adunga, the crowd and Billington, who stood firmly with his arms crossed awaiting Faizan's reply.

'I may remind you, Faizan,' said Billington. 'That this deal with the railroad has yet to be finalised. It can just as easily be torn up.'

Faizan gasped. 'You would not do that!'

'Try me, Faizan. I may be a contractor and achiever of deals with the mighty, but there are things in this life that mean more than money, and that is honour! And you, my *honourable* friend, stand to lose much more than I. All I have to do is go back to England and say that *the great Faizan* has refused the contract. And you will be the greatest loser. There will be no rail access for you to the east. No easy marketing, having to traipse across desert by camel and donkey, whilst all around you others become rich beyond your dreams, perhaps even rich enough to buy you! I can just as easily start the links from Oran or Algiers, and Ancen Medina will be left a barren place in the midst of wealth, if you so wish.'

There was a long silence and then the crowd erupted, shouting demands. Faizan nervously considered Billington's words as he shooed Adunga away into the marquee waving his fez angrily at the runner. He held up his hands to silence the crowd. 'Very well, Billington. I see that you are a hard man to deal with, and I respect that. I will honour all wagers.'

Again the crowd began to cheer and praise Billington with many a pat on the back before he calmed them with a wave of his hat. 'And of course, Faizan,' he said, 'you will honour the boy's wish.'

The crowd cheered even louder and chanted Mila's name, some lifting the exhausted boy above them and throwing him into the air in jubilation.

'But of course,' said Faizan reluctantly. 'We must ask the boy.'

The crowd hushed and pushed Mila forward, whispering suggestions to him or chuckling in anticipation at Mila's wish to come.

'Well, child,' said Faizan. 'What so be it? What item of Faizan's would you like to claim as your prize? Perhaps I might make a suggestion or two?'

Mila looked around at the crowd smiling and giggling and egging him on, then he looked at Billington, also smiling in anticipation.

Then Mila looked up at Faizan grinning from ear to ear at him. 'I want the giant,' he said.

There was a silence followed by a murmur of confusion from the crowd. Some were not certain of what Mila had said, others had heard but were in disbelief. And others laughed as though the boy had made a joke.

Faizan was certain it was a joke and laughed out loud. 'Very good, young Mila! Now please, tell Faizan what you *really* want?'

'I want the giant,' Mila said louder.

Billington grabbed Mila by the shoulder. 'Mila, what on earth are you doing?' he whispered. 'Now is your chance. Faizan is honouring his debt, largely thanks to me. He will see your passage home, or somewhere whereabouts. Now tell him this.'

'But I want the giant,' said Mila. 'He is a slave and Faizan makes him work all day, even while eating. No man should be a slave. You told me that, Billington. It's a vile, vile thing. I want the giant to be free to go home with some money for his poor family, and I want to go home also.'

Faizan was getting impatient. What little he had heard of the whispered conversation between Mila and Billington convinced him that the boy was either delusional from the stress of the race or making fun of him. 'Billington! Make the boy decide, and no more ridiculous suggestions!'

Billington straightened up and removed his hat and looked around at the puzzled faces surrounding him. 'I'm afraid it's true. My boy Mila wants the giant. He wishes him to be a free man. And he requests passage back to his own land.'

Faizan's face turned from one of bemusement to one of rage. 'The giant is not for sale!' he bellowed. 'Or bargaining! Besides, that is two requests. I only promised one prize to the winner. Not that I truly consider your boy to be the winner anyway, Billington. I think that the boy's request is outlandish and stupid. What could you possibly do with a giant?' he said, glaring menacingly at Mila.

'Set him free,' Mila muttered.

'Free?' Faizan exclaimed, standing upright and proud, spreading his arms wide. 'He is already free! He is not a slave at all as you suggest!' Faizan gestured to his aides and shortly after Andreas appeared to the gasps of the crowd who had not already paid to see him inside the marquee. 'Well, boy, ask the giant himself.' But Faizan asked on Mila's behalf. 'Are you not a free man, Andreas?'

Andreas looked out across the crowd, then at Mila, frowning in his confusion.

'The boy wishes to purchase you,' said Faizan amusingly.

Andreas turned to Faizan. 'Why?' he asked.

'The boy thinks you are my slave,' said Faizan. 'An insult indeed. Only the lowest of the low are considered as slaves, is that not right, Andreas?'

Andreas glanced again around the crowd and grunted, 'I am no slave, a slave to no man.' He beat his chest with his hand. 'Who could look at me and say I am a slave? I am Andreas the giant. No man makes me a slave.'

Faizan's aides emerged from the marquee to escort Andreas back inside. 'So, you see my good friends of Ancen Medina, Faizan the honourable does not keep slaves. Therefore, the giant does not truly belong to me and I cannot include him in this bargaining. I suggest, Billington, that you take this boy away for the night and have a good talk to him about what he really wants. In the meantime, Faizan the honourable will honour all bets. Even though the race was most unfair you can see that Faizan is truly the greatest friend of the beautiful town of Ancen Medina!'

The crowd surged forward at Faizan's words mobbing the platform cheering and waving, declaring their small and large bets as Faizan's aides tried to calm the people into an orderly queue.

Billington pulled Mila aside and away from the crowd. 'Well, young man,' he said. 'I think we need a little talk.'

Billington was in a most jovial mood that evening as he, widow Amira and Mila dined on *ferakh maamer*, a dish of chicken stuffed with couscous, raisins, orange flower, almonds, slow cooked in honey, garlic and spices lovingly prepared by the wife of a merchant who had done particularly well from Faizan's challenge. Others had gratefully brought soups and spicy sausage and sweet flatbreads such as *halwa chebakia*, deep fried dough soaked in honey and sesame seed, and still others brought wine to the dwelling, all praising Mila's victory and Billington's stand-off with Abram Faizan. Many had offered coins also but Billington had assured them that this was not necessary as he had done quite well out of the bet himself, but he did accept a gift of new clothes for the boy.

'The great runner must look his greatness!' the merchant woman enthused and bowed before Mila.

At first Mila was reluctant to depart with the old sea damaged clothes that Julieta had given him many weeks before, But Billington explained that to not be seen in the woman's gifts would be taken as an insult to the merchants. So, he changed into soft new pale blue cotton pantaloons and shirt and ate the most delightful foods he had ever had in his life, regaining his strength after the exhaustion of the race while Billington celebrated with copious amounts of free wine and food.

Once the last of the callers had been and both Billington and Mila were replete, it was only then that Billington broached the question of the pearl. 'Faizan will certainly not forget about this, Mila,' he said. He poured another cup of wine and reached into the lapel of his jacket and produced the pearl which he held up to the lamplight admiring the opalescent glow of its many subtle colours. 'Yes, mark my words, Mila. Faizan will still want this desperately. Something of a tricky if not dangerous situation, eh what? A young boy in the possession of such a thing of inestimable value, and him wielding so much power in these parts he'll naturally think that this should belong to someone of his own stature. So, now it's a case of what we should do with it? Well, we'll just have to stash it away for tonight and sleep on it. In the meantime, young Mila, perhaps you ought to tell me exactly how it came into your possession?'

Mila told his story once again, but this time without leaving anything out. He recounted the true events in the hold of the slave ship, admitting that he, himself, was not chained. He then told Billington about Kobina, the great white tattooed warrior reduced to his pitiful destiny in a stinking place of disease and then the Yoonir pearl. Mila explained the pearl's meaning to Billington as told to him by Kobina, and how Kobina had promised him that the pearl would protect him and bring good luck to those that parted with it wisely. Then, with apprehension and some misgivings, Mila told Billington about Briggs. He sat trembling as he remembered the shock of what he had done and related the details of how he took the life of the slave driver, worried about Billington's reaction, but Billington just nodded sympathetically and prompted the boy to continue. Finally, after struggling to describe the details of how he managed to unchain the slaves, he then became tearful as the memory of the drowning flooded back, the guilt he had felt on his island and the horror of the bodies washing upon the shore.

In the end, Billington was gobsmacked, not with shock, or horror at Mila's tale, but at the boy's fortitude. 'Well, that is one immense tale, I must say! And I told you, Mila, you are a true survivor. This will be one jolly good tale to tell at the

Gentlemen's Club once I return to England. I should imagine that they will find it very difficult to believe, but I shall swear upon my life of its truth, I can tell you that, Mila. And the story is far from over. You are still young and the adventuring spirit remains within for a very long time, I can assure you. I mean, look at me Mila? I'm very nearly an old man, but still I wish to travel the seas and see the mountains and deserts of this great Earth and marvel at the wonders of science. Oh no, your story is far from over,'

'Yes,' said Mila. 'That is what Nnamdi told me. He said the tale never ends.'

'Nnamdi, eh?' said Billington. 'I imagine this is the spiritual leader of your tribe, Mila?'

'He is the wise man of the Baja people. He guided me after I had failed to reach Trader in time with the net.'

'Oh yes, but of course, the trader. Oh well, you never know, you might see him again one day, although I doubt it very much. This is a great big world, Mila, and the markets across the Mediterranean are vast and wide. But, stranger things have happened.

'And speaking of strange things, why on earth did you ask for the giant? And it's hardly a 'wise' way to part with it, giving it over for a travelling show attraction. Such an absurd request, I can understand your sympathies, but it seems Faizan is not willing to bargain on this one. You've rather upset him, I can tell, indeed he thinks you've tried to make a fool of him in front of his own people and that's a rather dangerous thing to do. And besides, the giant is free to go when he wants; you heard it from the giant himself, indeed. I should forget about the giant and tomorrow we'll go back and arrange some sort of passage for you. Perhaps there is a navigator in the port who knows the shores of your land and can escort you somewhere near to home. That would be the best bet. I'm sure Faizan will be agreeable to such a request as your prize. In the meantime I would forget what you said about the giant. Faizan will never part with him. So don't you think that would be the best solution, Mila?'

'Yes, Billington,' answered Mila reluctantly.

'Which leaves the question of the vast richness of this pearl,' added Billington. 'It's no good in our hands as such. We must secure it somewhere until we can decide what to do with it. And it's no good to me, I could never keep it. Oh, I used to dream of such wealth in my childhood, but I realise now, even though I am somewhat well off, that there are things in this life that are so much more important. I suppose you have learned that lesson already Mila, having been through so much, and one day you'll realise the full importance of that lesson. So we best sleep on it and see what the morning brings. Oh well, time for me to go, but first, in order to secure the pearl, we must be one step ahead of Faizan.'

Billington drained his glass and standing unsteadily, whispered to Amira in her own language. 'You will keep this safe for me. Faizan will never suspect that I have let it out of my sight. I doubt he will try to steal it, but if his men come in the night, they will naturally come to me first. You are an honourable woman and I trust you.'

Billington slipped the pearl, still in its skin pouch, silently to Amira, almost unnoticed by Mila. '*Aeaddak, Allah sawf harasatuh,* I promise, Allah will guard it,' Amira replied, quietly stashing the pearl behind a stone in a tiny hollow in the wall behind her oven.

'Yes, Faizan will be after the pearl,' Billington whispered as he bid goodnight. 'Perhaps safer in a bank vault in port, we should do that first thing in the morning. But then Faizan may still be able to get his hands on it, he's very powerful, you know. And I should forget about the giant, young Mila. You are very young, so much to learn, such a vast world. Oh yes, Faizan will plot something, he'll want that pearl, but I think we've outwitted him, if only for the time being.' And Billington departed for his hotel, leaving Mila wide awake on his bed of cushions.

No matter how hard he tried, Mila couldn't sleep. Billington's final mumbling words before sleep filled his mind and the thought of Faizan *the most powerful,* plotting and taking the Yoonir pearl deeply disturbed him. He imagined Faizan's grinning fat face and nobly trimmed beard removing his fez and bowing apologetically as he snatched the pearl from Billington before glaring in hatred at Mila and saying: *this can only be for a noble person, things of great beauty and wealth are only meant for me and not mere slaves!* And Billington's words, saying to forget about the giant and Faizan being not willing to *bargain on this one* haunted him. And Billington saying: *things in this life that are so much more important.*

And the image of Andreas loomed so large in his mind that each time he closed his eyes he could only see the poor giant being made to act out a display of his huge size before the many Arabs, Berbers, Nomads and curious merchants that filed past. And the story of Andreas' family having to sell him made Mila so sad that each time he began to slip into sleep, an image of a father and mother parting with their only son seemed to emerge out of the blackness of the night, and Mila would awaken and think of his own family and how much he missed them also, and a great sorrow for the giant would come over him. And this in turn brought images and memories of Kobina and the slaves and the promise he had made to Kobina, *to depart with it wisely,* until he was overwhelmed with such sadness and grief that Mila felt as though his heart would burst if he did nothing to help Andreas.

He considered for a long while as Amira slept, then very quietly he crept up to the oven by the wall and slipped his hand behind, removing the stone from the hollow. He knew what he had to do. He grabbed the pearl, and not for the first time he pondered the question of whether he was doing the right thing by taking something that he knew he wasn't supposed to. He never really understood why he was doing this thing tonight, other than the fact that he didn't want Billington to know – at least until he had done it. The pearl was of no use to Billington himself, he had said as much. But something else drove him that night, he couldn't tell what it was, just an instinct, as he slipped out of the dwelling. It was as though the Yoonir pearl itself was willing him and that one way or another – either by Faizan or himself – he would soon no longer be in possession of it, and if it was by Faizan, his promise to Kobina would never be fulfilled.

There were no dogs howling that night and the market was unearthly silent as the moon crept over the horizon and the star of Yoonir itself hung high above drifting between the clouds.

Once again he scurried under Faizan's wagons, but this time he stopped short at the skirt of the marquee. There was the pale glow of lamplight filtering through the canvas and voices could be heard. Faizan's voice was raised and angry. There was the sound of *swishing* wooden sticks upon flesh and Andreas crying out in pain.

'He is useless, Faizan,' said one of Faizan's aides. 'Why don't we get rid of him? The people are bored of this *giant*, and are no longer willing to pay the same money to see him.'

'I agree,' said the other aide. 'Useless.'

'Not until he answers me!' cried Faizan, and the stick could be heard lashing Andreas again. 'Why did he ask for you? Answer me now!' and either Faizan or Faizan's aide struck again.

'I do not know!' Andreas squealed with pain.

'He lies, Faizan,' said an aide. 'I noticed the boy peeking in here during the show. He has been again sometime, I am certain, I know not when, but he must have. Why would the boy ask for something he has not seen before? The giant has asked the boy to help him escape, it is obvious.'

'And where do you think you will go?' Faizan cried. 'You think this Billington will take you and the boy to England, is that it?' Again the stick found its mark and Andreas begged for mercy. 'You will answer me!' Faizan cried again. 'A simple slave boy with a pearl the value of Ancen Medina itself and he wishes to risk it for a useless piece of scum as you? What manner of joke is this?'

'I swear, I know nothing of this,' sobbed Andreas.

'I will have that pearl one way or another,' Faizan seethed. 'With that pearl I can say to hell with Billington's railway. I shall be the richest man in all of Morocco, the entire East even. I shall buy my own railway!'

'Yes Faizan,' said the aides.

Again the stick came down and Andreas cried out as Faizan screamed at him. 'And you, you worthless dog, will be thrown into the desert like the useless piece of garbage you are. Just like that feeble Adunga who has cost me the pearl, I will dispose of him also! The people have lost interest in you. You eat as much as a herd of cattle! How can I afford you! So what am I to do now? I cannot just take the pearl from Billington.'

'Perhaps you could just trade the giant for the pearl?' said one of the aides. 'The boy was willing to risk it in the race. He obviously does not understand its wealth.'

'No, that would never work,' said Faizan. 'The people understand its value and now Billington himself holds the pearl. He would never agree to such bargaining and I would look like a thief before my own people.'

'Perhaps you could set another challenge?' said the other aide.

'What do you mean *another challenge?*' said Faizan.

'If the boy really wants the giant, then you could ask him to put up the pearl again as a bet. He seems determined enough to have the giant – and even Billington agreed that if that is what the boy wants, then he must have him.'

'Excellent idea,' said Faizan. 'But how would I get him to agree to one more challenge?'

'You appeal to the people, Faizan,' said the aide. 'They like to see your challenges, and to get them on your side shouldn't be difficult. You are a great appeaser, Faizan, and the boy was a cheat in the race. You simply have to convince the people of that.'

'And what about Billington?' said Faizan. 'I've just told you it is *he* who now holds the pearl. He is not stupid enough to let the boy risk it again.'

'But the pearl is rightfully the boy's,' the aide explained. 'The people know this. If Billington refuses the boy's will, he will be the one seen to be a thief before your people. They will believe he covets it for himself.'

'You are a genius!' exclaimed Faizan. 'But we need to think of a challenge, one that the boy can't possibly win. Come, we will depart to my villa to discuss this excellent idea and leave this useless piece of dung to weep like the big woman he really is!'

Mila waited a long while after Faizan and his aides left, listening with great sorrow to the giant's sobbing alone in the dark. He never imagined that a man so huge and strong could actually be able to cry at all, and he began to weep a little himself before steeling his nerve and slipping under the marquee skirt.

'Giant,' whispered Mila. 'Do not be sad. I am sorry that you are so sad.'

Andreas rolled over on his bed in surprise and anger. 'You again!' he hissed. 'Why have you come back? To torment me with your idle talk about my past? You are the source of all my misery! Be gone before I crush you like a leaf!'

'But I come to help you,' said Mila.

'Yes, and Faizan beats me for it! Because you ask for me as a prize! What kind of fool are you? And what can you possibly do? Where would I go? Can you navigate a boat? And why would you? You have nothing to gain and much to lose by crossing Faizan.'

'I cannot navigate a boat,' said Mila. 'But I can help. I do this because you are a slave even though you say you are not. Faizan beats you like a slave. He owns you like a slave. You have nowhere to go but wherever Faizan goes. But I can help you go back to your family.'

'I can never go back,' Andreas grumbled. 'Did you not listen to me the first time? I belong to Faizan now and I'm tired of your childish obsession with me. I have a show tomorrow and Faizan will be angry again if I am tired and cannot perform. You should go now before he finds you here or we will both be beaten.'

'I know you do not believe me, but this is how I will help you,' and Mila revealed the pearl. Although the marquee had plunged into darkness since Faizan and his aides had departed with the lamp, the pearl seemed to glow with a faint iridescence of its own. Mila held it up to his face, smiling, so that the giant might see the sincerity in his eyes. Then he held it to Andreas' face which beamed with astonishment.

'This is the Yoonir,' said Mila. 'It is the pearl of which Faizan speaks. He plans to take it from me tomorrow, but I can't allow that or my promise to Kobina will not be fulfilled. With this I shall buy your passage back to your family and to my home.'

'It is so beautiful,' Andreas whispered, reaching out his hand to touch the pearl. 'So many colours...it is like the mountainside of my home, with the trees and orchard fruits and the blue sea...as though it looks into my soul. It is no wonder Faizan wants it. Its value must be beyond everything

Faizan owns. Where did you get this?'

'It was given to me by a great warrior for freeing him as a slave. The Yoonir is the star of his people. I promised that I would depart with it wisely and that I would know when that time was.'

'This slave was called Kobina, you say?' said Andreas. 'And this is the promise you gave him that must be fulfilled? And you bring it to me, right under Faizan's own nose, inside his marquee? And you think that you know that the time to fulfil that promise is now? For me?'

'Yes,' said Mila. 'I am certain that the time has come. And Faizan will have the pearl if it is not done tonight.'

'Then, I think you are a fool, boy,' Andreas growled. 'And a dangerous fool at that. Where do you think I can go? Look at me! I can be seen for miles, everyone that would bypass me would stop and stare and say: 'Look at that giant! He must belong somewhere!' And everyone would talk and talk spreads like fire in dry brush and no matter where I was I would be known and Faizan would find me.'

'But I can buy your way home, far away from Faizan,' said Mila. 'You will have wealth from the pearl and Faizan will not need to buy you again. A merchant will sail you to your land and your family will be able to feed you and look after you again and you will be happy.'

'And when will you do this?' said Andreas sarcastically. 'Take me down to the port in the morning? Just lead the great giant out by the hand with Faizan's blessings, carrying the pearl that he would slaughter half of Ancen Medina to get his hands on, down to a merchant sailor and hand the pearl over for a sail over the Mediterranean? You are indeed a fool for even bringing this thing here.'

'But I must do this thing tonight, before Faizan even knows, or he will take it from me. You will not be seen in the dark and by morning light you will be far away at sea.'

'Then be off with you, foolish child!' Andreas grunted. 'And good luck to you and your pearl! The first merchant boat you arouse under the moonlight and they will deem you to be a thief in the night and slit your throat and take your pearl, and then your promise will be worthless and no doubt any slaughter in the night will catch the attention of Faizan and the pearl will be his in the end anyway. Something like this will always belong to someone like Faizan and not mere paupers or slaves!'

The moon hung low above the hillside, silhouetting the ramshackle buildings and homesteads and shimmering upon the water by a gentle breeze that rippled the seaport of Ancen Medina as Mila made his way to the moored boats. Everything seemed silent and dead to the world as the boats gently bumped the wharf, straining against their lashings as he silently padded the wooden walk. There was nothing. As far as Mila could tell, the merchants and sailors were fast asleep and Andreas' warning about his throat being slit seemed a possibility, should he try to awaken anyone. With a heavy heart and Andreas' words ringing in his ears he was about to return to the market and Amira's dwelling when a faint light at the furthest end of the wharf caught his attention. In curiosity and hopefulness he jogged along the jetty as silent as a night creature to the boat. The faint glow of a lamp lit the inside and Mila stepped very gently onto the deck careful not to rock the boat. Through the smallest of slits in the cabin curtain Mila peered inside. A figure in a simple hessian robe with a hood concealing his face was seated on a bench, quietly mumbling to himself as he counted gold coins on a table into a chest.

Mila was uncertain and afraid, but determined. Gently, he tapped at the cabin door. He heard the scuffle of the man and the clink of coins falling onto floor, followed by more scuffling and then silence. Mila heard nothing but the gentle lap of wave and breeze and bumping of boats for what seemed ages. Even the noise of his own breathing and race of his heartbeat seemed glaringly loud in the dead silence surrounding him. When the boat man eventually spoke he jumped back in alarm.

'Who is there?' the man hissed.

'I am a friend,' Mila answered as loud as he dare.

'It is late,' said the man. 'Only thieves and vagabonds skulk in the dead of night. State your business or be off before I slice off your arms, thief!'

'I am no thief,' said Mila. 'I want a voyage for a friend. I have wealth and can pay you well.'

The man opened the cabin door a crack and peered out. 'You are not even a man. How can you have wealth and how can you pay me?'

'You must trust me,' said Mila. 'I can pay you. I do this for me and for a friend who wants to go home to his family. He is a good man.'

Cautiously the man opened the cabin door further, looked swiftly around outside and dragged Mila into the cabin. His drawn sword pointed straight at Mila's face as he motioned Mila to the cabin's table. 'Be seated,' he said.

Mila sat and the man sheathed his sword and sat on the bench opposite, his head bowed, the hood still concealing his face. 'And where does this 'friend' wish to go?' he asked.

'It is called Pelopen..,Pelopennesus, I think. And I wish to go home to my own people of the Mjumbi.'

'Pelopennesus? I have heard of this place. But I was not planning to go to there or to Greece, even, and I know nothing of any Mjumbi people. Do you even know where this is?'

Mila shook his head.

'So, what *wealth* might a mere boy pay me?' said the man sarcastically. 'With kind blessings, or the goodness of his heart? The *wealth* of his soul, perhaps?'

Cautiously, Mila reached for the pearl tied by the string bag concealed in his pantaloons. The man quickly placed his hand upon the hilt of his sword, ready to draw.

'Do not worry,' said Mila. 'I have no knife, I am not a thief,' as he laid the skin bag on the table.

'That is a small purse of coins for two voyages,' said the man.

Mila picked up the bag and tipped the pearl out into the palm of his hand and the man sat up sharply, his hood falling back from his head as the pearl refracted the light of the oil lamp into a myriad of colours onto his astonished face.

Mila gasped as the man's face was clearly revealed. 'Brahim!' he squealed with delight.

The man leapt across the table, grabbing hold of Mila and clasping his hand tightly over his mouth. 'Silence, boy!' he hissed. 'Awaken anyone at your peril!' He carefully removed his hand from Mila's mouth. 'What did you call me?'

'You are Brahim,' Mila whispered.

'And you are mistaken, boy! I have never heard this name before, and you do well not to speak that name again anywhere. Now tell me, where did you get this pearl?'

'It was given to me by a great warrior for releasing him from slavery,' Mila whispered cautiously. 'Then it was taken from me for a while by Captain Youssef on the ship Seyaad. And you were the navigator...and there was a girl...Julieta.'

The man tightened his grip on Mila. 'And you talk in riddles, boy. I have never heard of such things. My name is Elijah, a simple travelling merchant. And there is nothing to stop me slitting your throat here and now and taking this pearl for myself. And you are a very naive boy for coming here.'

'But you will not do this,' said Mila. 'I know you are a good man and you would already have done this silently if you wanted the pearl. I ask only a voyage for my friend and myself for the pearl.'

'You are far too trusting,' said Elijah, releasing his grip on Mila. 'But I am indeed, as you say an honourable man. I have no need for great wealth or power. The freedom of the waves and the beauty of the sea are my riches. Go, and I leave you to take your pearl to your friend, I will not steal it from you. But hasten your return; I have only come to Ancen Medina to purchase this boat. I sail tonight.'

'The pearl is worth much,' said Mila. 'I have heard it is worth the value of Ancen Medina. You must promise to share the wealth of the pearl with my friend. He travels back home to his people who are poor. He must never be poor again, so his family do not have to sell him again.'

'I cannot do as such,' said Elijah. 'I cannot split the pearl in half. That would render it valueless. But I have gold, much gold in dirhams and others. For this pearl I will give passage for your friend and yourself. And I will give your friend gold, enough gold to feed not just his family, but his children and their children and their children again. Enough gold for a thousand years. I have enough gold to do this. They will never be poor again.'

'You are a simple travelling merchant,' said Mila. 'Where did you get so much gold?'

Elijah glared at Mila. 'Do not ask that question! I have gold and am willing to part with it for the pearl. I am handing over the worth of Sultans in gold for your pearl which I could take easily from you now! You need not know any more than that!'

'And when the time comes, you must part with the pearl wisely, that is what Kobina said to me.'

'And you believe that *you* are parting with it wisely?' Elijah said sceptically. 'I can see that you are indeed a charitable one, with a heart as big as my chest of gold. Allah indeed shines upon you, boy. But I cannot promise to part with it wisely. I will part with it for riches and wealth, but I will use those riches wisely. I too, have a heart, and there are many good people that live by the heart alone and have nothing more. These are the people that deserve wealth, and shall have it by my hand. You must go now, and be quick!'

As silently as a fox, Mila ran the wharf to the portside and up the slope to the market of Ancen Medina and the marquee. He slipped quietly under the skirt and found Andreas asleep and gently snoring. Excitedly, he shook the giant into a grumbling awareness. 'Giant,' he whispered. 'It is done. You can go home.'

'What are you talking about?' Andreas groaned.

'There is a merchant boat that will sail to Greece if I trade for the pearl. But we must go now. The man sails tonight.'

Andreas sat up. 'You cannot be serious? Who would sail in the dead of night?'

'But it is true. He wants to depart very quickly.'

'And how do I know this isn't some trick? This could be one of Faizan's men. He has spies and collaborators everywhere. This is how he controls the people.'

'But I know this man,' said Mila. 'Even though he pretends to be someone else for a reason I don't know. He is an honourable and trustworthy man and a great navigator. I have been on his ship and seen how he sails.'

'I don't know about this,' Andreas grumbled doubtfully. 'Are you certain of this? It must be a trick. And how will I live? How can I go back to my poor family and expect them to feed me? I have no money, Faizan only feeds me; he doesn't pay me.'

'Believe me,' said Mila. 'The man is honest. He had the chance to steal the pearl from me if he wanted to do so. I was alone with him on his boat and showed him the pearl. But he didn't take it from me. And he has gold, much gold which he says he will share for the pearl. But we must go soon. If we don't go quickly the man will sail and Faizan will have the pearl and you will continue to be beaten like a slave or Faizan may even dispose of you.'

'Beaten?' Andreas muttered, considering Mila's words. 'My beating was nothing compared to that of Adunga's, the poor wretch. He lost Faizan the pearl and now he cowers in pain and blood in a wagon and probably will be dumped in the desert somewhere for his effort. And now you bring the pearl to me? You are indeed a very brave and good-hearted, if not foolish boy.'

'Please, giant,' Mila pleaded.

After a long contemplation, Andreas stood up, grumbling, and walked to the front of the marquee, pulling the skirt high enough for Mila to nearly walk through. 'Then show me the way to this man,' he grunted. 'And if he proves to be a spy I shall crush him like a leaf.'

Mila padded stealthily as a nocturnal creature in search of prey along the wharf, but Andreas creaked the wooden boardwalk underneath alarmingly with every step. Elijah was already aware of their presence before they reached the boat and sat out on the deck waiting as Andreas' huge frame obliterated the glow of moonlight on the wharf as they approached.

'You did not tell me about this!' Elijah hissed, backing away nervously. 'He is the size of three men!'

'This is my friend Andreas,' said Mila. 'He is a slave of Abram Faizan, who beats him like a dog.'

'Faizan!' Elijah gasped. 'I have heard that name. He is a powerful figure in these parts. They say he owns the people, even. You ask me to steal something from him? That is very risky indeed!'

'But you will have the pearl,' said Mila. 'That will mean you will be richer and more powerful than Faizan.'

'Then I agree. I shall take the pearl and your friend to his home. And I shall take you to your own people. But come, we must go now!'

'I cannot,' said Mila. 'I must let Billington know what has happened to the pearl. Faizan will accuse him of hiding it and taking it for himself. The people will not trust him, and the railroad might not be built and they might think Billington has disposed of me to keep the pearl. Billington has been good to me and does not care for wealth, only for his railroad and King William, the head of his tribe in England.'

'Again, you talk in riddles, boy,' said Elijah. 'I know nothing of this 'Billington' or *railroads*. But very well, I shall return in some days time and look out for you. I will be as a simple beggar merchant selling trinkets from a bag. You must follow me then to the port, keeping your distance. And you must not acknowledge me as a friend until we are far away at sea.'

'And you must give all the gold to Andreas in trade for the pearl,' said Mila.

'You are far too trusting, boy. I am still a stranger to you. What if I decided not to hand over the gold?'

Mila took hold of Andreas' enormous hand and quietly slipped the pearl into his fingers, which easily closed over the skin bag and pearl together. 'This is yours now, giant Andreas. I think I am parting with it wisely. When you reach your home and your mother and father see you with bags of gold and hug you once again, then you may give the pearl to Elijah. If he does not give you the gold then you may crush him like a leaf.'

Andreas growled at Elijah, who glanced at the giant fearfully. 'It shall be done,' Elijah hissed. 'But we must go now quickly, the night has ears!'

'As you insist on staying behind,' said Andreas, 'you must run and tell Billington what you have done as soon as we are away. Faizan will be furious when he finds out and Billington must hide you away until Elijah's return.'

Andreas bent down and picked Mila up under the arms like

a child. And like a doting father or mother would embrace a child in their arms, he hugged him gently to his chest. 'I will never forget you for this, little one. There will always be a home for you in my land, should you ever decide to come.'

'And I must go to my home,' said Mila. 'Elijah has promised this to me. You must remind him of this before you give him the pearl.'

'I am a man of honour,' said Elijah. 'As Allah is my witness, I shall return for you. But if you are no longer in the town, I shall not linger. It is too risky for me. We must go now, quickly!'

Mila watched for a long while as Elijah's boat and the huge silhouette of Andreas waving upon the moon-sparkled water disappeared beyond the far rock jetties of the port of Ancen Medina. But Mila was not heavy-hearted as he realised that he would never see the pearl or the giant ever again. He skipped along the wharf and up the slope to the market, still dead and still with an unearthly silence without baying dogs on the hillside or the faintest of fluttering of canvas or banners in a breeze. He wanted to tell Billington straight away but realised that the residents of the Oasis Faraj would be angry at being disturbed. As soon as the faintest light came he would go round to the hotel and explain things. And with that thought, he slipped quietly back into Amira's dwelling, nestled himself onto his bed of soft cushions, wrapped the blanket around himself and fell fast asleep.

In his sleep, Mila saw a vision of Andreas stepping off a boat from an ocean of unimaginable blue onto the shores of his home, a golden beach that swept up into green hills of fruit and olive trees under a cloudless sky. But instead of a sun the star of Yoonir burned as bright as day upon the land. And Andreas carried a chest of gold so heavy that even he had trouble carrying it up the hill to the little farmhouse. As he lay the chest before the feet of his mother and father, they cried in joy at seeing him once again and hugged him as Andreas too cried like a child who had once been lost.

And Mila also saw Elijah ruling over a land even larger than Faizan's. But Elijah was not Faizan. Elijah was humble and kindly and ruled with benevolence, the people prospering as he showered them with his wealth. He visited pauper and peasant, tended the sick and poor with the blessings of a god that Mila never grew to understand even during his time on the Seyaad, and Elijah built schools and places of worship, that the people might worship his god and not him for their prosperity.

15.

Billington dressed for the day and took his early morning coffee in the hotel lounge before making his way round to Amira's dwelling, where Mila still slept soundly after his nocturnal escapades. Amira had barely welcomed him in and closed the door behind, when there was loud banging upon it and the sound of raised voices.

'What in blazes is going on!' Billington growled, throwing open the door.

Faizan, his two aides and another man stood outside. Faizan's face betrayed the anger boiling up inside him. 'Where is my giant?' he seethed.

'Your giant?' replied Billington. 'I have no idea what you're talking about.'

'Andreas is missing!'

'Well, you can see he's not here,' said Billington, stepping aside and gesturing inside with his hand.

'I can see that, Billington! Do you take me for a fool?'

'Well, if you're not a fool, explain yourself.'

'The boy knows something about this. He asked for the giant and now he is gone. Bring the boy to me now!'

'Oh, this is ridiculous!' Billington declared. 'Mila has been here all night, correct, Mila?'

Mila was wide awake now, and very frightened, having realised that he hadn't woken in time to explain things to Billington. He stood up from his bed, trembling and silent.

Faizan turned and gestured the fourth man to step forward. He was stern-faced and unemotional, dressed entirely in black robe and black turban, with a long, thin grey beard that ran down below his waist. He carried a large black book that he hugged to his chest with folded arms as he bowed respectfully before Billington.

'This is the magistrate of Ancen Medina,' said Faizan. 'He has the authority to question the boy, and when I say 'question,' I mean in any way that he and his sheriffs feel is necessary to reach the truth. So, to avoid the unnecessary inconvenience, I shall simply ask him myself. Where is my giant?'

Billington turned to Mila questioningly, whose face was now etched with guilt and fear. 'Andreas has gone home,' Mila mumbled.

'Oh, so you admit it?' said Faizan. 'You have encouraged my giant to run away. And did you tell him which way to go, and how? And did you pack him with a wagon load of food? Is he going to walk across all the deserts of the Middle East? Or shall he simply swim the entire length of the Mediterranean?'

'A merchant sailor has agreed to give him passage,' said Mila.

'I see,' said Faizan, sarcastically. 'A simple merchant sailor with nothing better to do and no particular port to go to and sell his wares, has agreed to take the most conspicuous of cargoes, big enough to sink a small vessel, across the sea. And obviously out of the goodness of his heart as every poor merchant in Ancen Medina has no need of money.'

'I gave him the pearl,' Mila muttered, now quaking with fear, 'to pay the merchant for his passage.'

'Oh, Mila,' Billington sighed. 'Whatever have you done?'

Faizan was incandescent with rage. 'Seize him!' he cried, and the two aides burst in pushing Billington aside and dragged Mila out by the arms.

'Billington, help me!' Mila cried as he was dragged through the market.

Billington grabbed his hat and stumbled from the dwelling and quickly followed. 'This is an outrage!' he cried, catching up to Faizan. 'You can't just drag someone away like that without charge. What is he being arrested for? The pearl was his, for heaven's sake! He's a minor as well, what manner of treatment is this for someone barely out of childhood?'

Faizan turned and pushed Billington back. 'Stay out of this Billington, the magistrate is in charge now!'

'Well, it seems that *you* are the one in charge of the *magistrate!*' declared Billington. 'May I also remind you of our contract?'

'Billington, if you wish to build railroads through my land, you must at least respect the laws of my land!' and Faizan stormed off through the market after the others.

All that morning Billington paced the outside of the courthouse of Ancen Medina town. The two silent guards at the high arched entrance had barred him from passing through to the proceedings. And even more worryingly it seemed to Billington that Faizan held so much sway in his land that even the law belonged to him. And now, it seemed, Faizan had called his bluff. Billington's brief upon departing England had been to secure contracts through *all* the land stretching from Ancen Medina right the way through to the Red Sea. And Faizan had guessed that. By now, Mila's fate really was in the hands of God, or at least what he considered to be a thorough scoundrel, deceptive and contemptuous of his own people even.

And Billington despaired at the thought of what might be in store for the poor boy.

Despite his concern for Mila in the hands of Faizan and

his 'lackeys,' as he called them, in the end he left the courthouse in exasperation. He still had much to do in preparing for his onward journey in the pursuit of further contracts and, whatever the outcome of the court, could delay no more than a day or two at most.

But he was resolute of one thing though, that should Mila be freed, he would fulfil his promise to the boy and arrange passage back to his people...wherever that may be. He knew that many of the navigating sea merchants would be familiar with the West African coast and he was determined to find one and pay for his passage.

It was late afternoon by the time Billington made his way back up from the port to the courthouse. There was no movement and it seemed the two morning guards had been replaced. Although he doubted his chances he thought he might try his luck again with the two new men who stood equally as stony-faced as the previous duo. He marched right up to one of them within touching distance and leaned forward pointing a finger in accusation.

'I know exactly what's going on here!' Billington declared. 'You are simply under the treachery of that tyrant Faizan! Too frightened to oblige what must be a legal right even in *this* country and allow me through to see the boy. This country may well be part of an empire as such, but I work for his Majesty King William IV, the most powerful man on Earth, ruling over an empire that would dwarf this barren little piece of Faizan's land, and there are treaties in place giving me, as an ambassador, certain rights. So, I have no fear of that scoundrel Faizan, and if you don't let me through I shall report this miserable treatment to his Majesty himself, and believe me, there will be repercussions, do you understand?'

The guard flinched at Billington's words and blinked several times in his uncertainty. 'It is too late, sir,' he mumbled.

'Eh, what?' said Billington. 'Speak up, man! If you have some news, spill it out!'

'It is too late,' repeated the guard as loud as he dare. 'The justice has been done.'

'What do you mean, man?'

'The boy Mila has been given another chance.'

'Why, that's excellent news!' said Billington, jubilantly.

'You don't understand, sir. The magistrate has decreed the boy must face another challenge…one set by Faizan. Already Faizan prepares his speech to the people in the market.'

'Damn and blast!' Billington cried, swiping his hat from his head into his hand and setting off running up the slope to the market.

A crowd had gathered outside Faizan's marquee as Billington arrived gasping and doubled over in breathlessness. Faizan was just appearing from behind the canvas as Billington pushed his way to the front of the crowd, but Mila was nowhere to be seen.

'My dear people of Ancen Medina,' Faizan began, removing his fez and clutching it to his chest. 'Today is a day of great mourning for me and for you, my people. I, Abram Faizan, your loyal servant is in deep sorrow for a loss so great that I doubt I will ever recover. Last night my giant, the great Andreas went missing.' Faizan bowed his head and seemed to wipe a tear from his eye. 'And it pains me to say this, but it was the boy you have come to praise and respect that was instrumental in Andreas' disappearance.'

There was a murmur of surprise and mumbling between the people as Faizan continued. 'Yes, that's right…the boy Mila has enticed my Andreas away. Can you believe it? But you know this to be the truth. The boy asked for the giant as a prize. And when I asked him to reconsider – a very reasonable request on my part in response to an outlandish request from a boy who was simply too ignorant to know what he wanted –

he decided to steal Andreas instead! What treachery, my people!'

Some of the crowd nodded in agreement with Faizan's sentiment. Others were unsure or doubtful that the giant might actually be missing.

By now Billington had caught his breath. He pointed his finger accusingly at Faizan. 'How the devil can a mere boy steal something as large as the giant? Was the giant so stupid as to have no mind of his own and allow a boy to lead him off? I say Andreas must have left of his own free will. You, Faizan, declared to these very people here that Andreas was not your property, not a slave. Indeed, Andreas said it himself, unless you *made* him say it! It seems to me that you take these people to be fools again!'

Now the crowd seemed to agree with Billington and many muttered their approval.

But Faizan had not finished. 'Of course he was not a slave!' he cried. 'He was a free man, happy and contented with his family here! And this boy has enticed and encouraged him to abandon his dear family with the promise of riches from the beautiful pearl. Oh, but how naive Andreas is. He is not stupid as Billington says, but he was a simple man of simple beliefs and needs, unaware of the dangers and cruelty in the outside world. Indeed, Andreas was like a brother to me.'

Faizan feigned tears once again, clutching his fez tightly as he wrung his hands in mock grief. 'When I think of my poor brother Andreas,' he snivelled. 'Probably lost somewhere in the desert, abandoned by some deviant merchant who has taken the precious pearl for himself, or even drowned Andreas at sea. Yes, the very pearl that should have belonged to you, my beloved people. Indeed, I had planned to put this very pearl in a museum, guarded night and day, for all to see and admire its beauty, and many would have come from far and wide to see this great wonder, bringing their prosperity to

Ancen Medina. Such things belong to you, my people, but now that pearl and my dear brother Andreas are both gone, thanks to the treachery of *this* boy!'

Suddenly Mila appeared from the marquee assisted by Faizan's two aides and the magistrate. Mila stood with his head bowed as Faizan continued.

'No, of course Andreas was not *stolen* as such,' said Faizan. 'He was enticed, deceived in his simplicity, much like a devious man might entice a child away into slavery with the promise of sweet things. And in that sense he *has* been stolen. The boy has ripped the heart out from my family, and Andreas has run away to be a poor lost child in the wilderness somewhere.'

Now some of the crowd seemed to sway Faizan's way and there was much unsettlement, some feeling sorry for Faizan's loss, while others were unsure or unconvinced.

Again, Faizan spoke up. 'But my dear people, despite my great loss and the breaking of my heart, I am a merciful man. Indeed, I have pleaded with the magistrate that the boy must be given one more chance. I now respectfully ask the magistrate to speak.'

The magistrate stepped forward and cleared his throat. 'The accused was given the opportunity to tell the truth of this heartbreaking event, and to his credit he has done so.' The magistrate reached out his hand, lifting Mila's bowed head up to face the crowd. 'How speak you, boy?'

'I am guilty,' Mila sobbed.

It seemed clear to Billington that Mila had been beaten unnecessarily. Mila had never denied enticing Andreas away in the first place, but it seemed obvious that Faizan had wanted him to also appear as a liar in front of the people. Tell-tale bruises and welts on his legs could be detected at close range despite the natural dark colour of Mila's skin. These glistened in the bright sun as though they had been quickly and not too successfully treated with balms as though to cover up what had really gone on inside the courthouse. No, this was just some extra torture for the pleasing of Faizan.

'On that point,' the magistrate continued, 'I have listened to the request for mercy by Abram Faizan, that the accused be given the chance to gain his freedom. The boy will face a challenge, upon the successful completion of which, there will be no punishment. The boy will walk free once again.'

'What challenge?' demanded Billington. 'And as for punishment, I can see with my own eyes that adequate 'punishment' has already been dealt, not that the boy has committed any crime anyway!'

The magistrate scowled and pointed at Billington. 'The boy is guilty!' he cried. 'The charge is enticing a runaway, and the boy has pleaded guilty. And that is why we are being merciful. You, sir, should hold your tongue, lest the court change its mind!'

There was a sudden hush throughout the crowd at the magistrate's outburst and even Billington thought it wiser to say no more.

The magistrate spoke softly now: 'The boy will face the *Cupola*. Take him away.'

There was a massive gasp that ran through the crowd like an ocean wave as Mila was taken by Faizan's aides.

'Cupola?' asked Billington, as Mila was dragged through the crowd. 'What is this Cupola?' He pleaded all around as the people swept past following Mila and the aides. He grabbed an Arab man by the sleeve, spinning him around. 'For heaven's sake will someone tell me, what is this Cupola?' But the Arab man just held up his hands and shook his head in dismay.

The crowd quickly surged towards the eastern outskirts of the town following Mila and his escorts. They suddenly stopped and seemed to gather around in a circle. Billington couldn't figure out what was happening as he struggled to keep up and work his way to the front. The people had encircled a huge concave structure sunk into the desert sands, like a giant soup bowl. Its stone sides were smooth and deep, its makers having defined a surface of near polish, without flaws.

Mila and the aides had stopped poised above the sloping edge along with Faizan and the magistrate. Mila was dangled and lowered over the edge of the *Cupola* as far as the aides could reach before letting him go whereupon he slid to the bottom.

The magistrate held up his hands to silence the crowd, some of whom were openly wailing or sobbing. 'If the boy can escape the Cupola by this time tomorrow, he will be freed. That is all.'

Billington angrily barged his way through to Faizan, grabbing hold of his vest and pulling him face to face. 'What manner of vile torture is this?' he seethed. 'I can see at a glance the boy has no chance of escaping this death trap! By midday tomorrow he'll be cooked!'

Faizan yanked Billington's hand away and pushed him back sharply. 'How do you think I keep the peace in my land, Billington? There is no crime in Ancen Medina because of the justice here. At least not until your 'boy' came along and decided to cross me. Besides, he will be given a sporting chance. There will be a fixture prepared in the morning to aid his escape.'

'A fixture? What sort of fixture?'

'You shall see, Billington,' said Faizan. 'Come the morning you shall see,' and Faizan walked off in the direction of his marquee.

Billington hastened along behind. 'And how many of your previous *criminals* – not that you have any in this *civilised* land – have managed to break this so-called *challenge?*' he demanded.

Faizan turned and smiled wryly. 'None, Billington. And a good night to you,' he added, marching off.

Soon the crowd began to disperse at the shouting and

waving of the magistrate and Faizan's aides, leaving Mila utterly alone at the bottom of a giant bowl with sides so steep he doubted if even a spider could crawl out.

Evening came and Mila was growing colder by the minute. As the sun disappeared and the sky turned cobalt and the first stars appeared above his prison, the silence was broken by the low mumbling of voices.

Billington's face appeared over the edge of the Cupola. 'I haven't got long, Mila,' he whispered. 'In fact, I'm not really allowed to be here at all, but I've managed to bribe the guard with a few of Faizan's dirham I won. Here, I've brought you some food and a blanket. Keep yourself warm tonight; you will need your muscles in the morning.'

Billington lowered a rope tied to a hide bag containing a blanket, some honeyed flatbreads and a gourd of milk and some water. 'Eat well and drink the milk tonight, and finish the rest early tomorrow. The guard will lower a rope and you must give him the blanket and gourds. There must be no sign that anyone has visited tonight.'

'Billington, please help me,' Mila sobbed.

'Oh, dear oh dear, Mila,' Billington sighed. 'I'm afraid this one is out of my hands. I did try to warn you about Faizan, his power here is absolute, and you have crossed him badly, I'm afraid. And whatever were you thinking? Why have you persisted in this obsession with the giant?'

'The giant was alone in a place he was not happy,' said Mila. 'He was away from his family who loved him but could not keep him. I know what it is like to lose my family. And they were beating him like slave. When I saw him last night Faizan's men made him cry like a child and beg for mercy.'

'Oh, Mila, I have no doubt that Faizan is capable of such cruelty, but why ever did you involve yourself in this? Sometimes you have to think of yourself and turn away, no matter how hard it may seem.'

'I have been beaten like a slave, Billington. When I heard Andreas being beaten it made me cry also, like I was being beaten again.'

'I do understand your sentiments, Mila. But we are both so very far from home in a land both strange and savage. Sometimes it is wise to tread so carefully. Sentiments are all very well and fine, but they are useless to a dead man.'

'But, what about your railroad, Billington? Will you tell Faizan that the King will not let him have a railroad?'

'I'm afraid that was merely a bluff, Mila, and Faizan has guessed that. I have to go back to England with Faizan's permission to build across his land, no matter what manner of person he is. If it was up to me alone I would tear up the contract now in order to free you, but that's not the way the world works. The prosperity of the Empire depends upon me and my contracts. But listen to me carefully, Mila. There is a way out of this, believe me. I can see approximately the measurements of this parabola, and it can be done. In the morning they will make sport with you and a device will be presented to enhance that sport.'

At that moment the guard intervened. 'Time is up,' he whispered. 'You must go now before you are seen and we are both thrown into the Cupola along with the boy!'

'For pity's sake!' Billington objected. 'Give me another minute. Mila, listen to me. I understand the nature of this device they will bring. Some of the people have told me of it, whether they were supposed to or not, but they have. And that's another thing, Mila; the people are on your side. They don't like this turn of events at all. I believe Faizan has blundered on this one by trying to make an example of you. And that's a good thing. It will encourage you, come the morning. So, listen to me very carefully now. Try to remember a certain rule of science...'

But the guard, along with another, grabbed Billington and began dragging him away. 'Mila!' Billington called. 'You must watch me carefully in the morning and you will understand!'

'Be silent!' one of the guards hissed as Billington's protesting voice disappeared into the distance leaving Mila alone and crying in the stillness of the night once again.

16.

Billington spent what he considered to be the worst night of his life awake in his hotel room, worrying and trying to work out the chances of Mila escaping from the *Cupola*. He did multiple calculations with pencil, paper, logarithmic scale and slide rule based on varied estimates and assumptions of the diameter and depth of the prison. He spent the darkening hours on a myriad of possibilities from the least likely to the best possibility. He was an engineer with a keen eye for mathematical size and shape, but an engineer works in the precise and he was not hopeful, despite his earlier encouragement to the boy. It was true that the people were largely on his side and that many had furtively described the *fixture* that was designed more for Faizan's entertainment and sport than to actually increase the chances of escaping, and the whereabouts of the *fixture* was unknown to any other than the magistrate's sheriffs or Faizan's aides. But without precise measurements he was still at a loss of a complete formula, and furthermore, he had hoped to measure the exact diameter and depth of the hole but the guards had been too nervous and hasty about his being there at all and the chance to advise Mila on how he should approach the challenge was now gone.

But as long as he had the slightest ray of hope and the possible was still just that, *possible,* he would not abandon the boy to his fate. In the end as the first faint light of day approached he slumped forward at his table into an uneasy sleep surrounded by mounds of scribbled papers and formulas.

He awoke with a start to a commotion from the market.

Quickly he grabbed his hat, stuffed some of his papers into his jacket pocket and followed the crowd who were making their way to the edge of the town. A ring of the magistrate's guards along with Faizan's aides had circled the Cupola allowing no one near.

Billington marched up to one of the guards accusingly. 'So, this is Faizan's idea of sport, is it? Let the poor blighter fry a little before he's given the chance to try?'

Suddenly there was another commotion from behind and the crowd parted as two guards quickly pushed a long wheeled cart through the crowd. It was weighted with large stones at one end and at the front a thick mast with a high jib protruded from which there hung a rope. Billington deliberately stepped in front of the cart forcing the men to pull up sharply and protest at his carelessness.

'Excuse me,' said Billington, casually as he slipped a tape measure from his pocket and quickly measured the rope. Others in the crowd had noticed and quickly gathered round the cart watching Billington as he took more measurements, the height of the mast and length of the jib.

Angrily, the guards tried to push the crowd back but each time some were moved, others crowded around again until Billington had finished.

'Carry on,' Billington said, doffing his hat politely at the men as they heaved and wheeled the cart past with many curses as the crowd parted again.

The cart was set in place with the jib over the side of the Cupola with the rope dangling down tantalisingly near the rim. The crowd was finally let through and quickly surrounded the Cupola cheering and shouting for Mila who had already attempted to reach the dangling rope and slid hopelessly back to the bottom. Billington pushed his way to the edge and frantically waved Mila to stop. Faizan, the magistrate and his two aides stood on the opposite side of the rim, grinning at

Mila's futile attempts.

Billington raised his hands beckoning attention and the crowd hushed. 'Faizan!' he cried, his voice bouncing up in echo from the Cupola against the silence. 'You call this a challenge? You want to see some real sport?'

Faizan shrugged his shoulders casually. 'What are you talking about, Billington? Let the boy jump! What could be more sporting than that?' And Faizan's aides and the guards laughed.

'Well, I'll tell you,' called Billington. 'Push the fixture further out!'

The crowd gasped at the suggestion, and Mila's heart felt as though it had been crushed. There was commotion through the crowd that Billington had somehow taken allegiance with Faizan and Mila slumped to the base of the Cupola in despair as Faizan's aides happily pushed the jib out to a seemingly impossible distance from the rim.

But Billington winked and called out to Mila. 'Chin up, lad. Remember what we learned?'

But Mila didn't understand and desperately tried running up the side of the Cupola, but the rope was even further out of reach. The crowd cheered each time, but again Billington gestured for him to stop.

Billington removed his hat and held it out over the rim slowly making a circular motion with it. The crowd were getting restless and began cheering, egging Mila on to try again. Some thought that the hat gesture was making fun of Mila's plight. Mila tried running the side again and the crowd grew louder as he ran up and groaned in disappointment as he slid once more to the base.

Billington realised the boy didn't understand and in desperation he pushed people aside to give himself room and begged the crowd for silence again. 'Mila!' he cried. 'What did I once ask you? *Have you ever wondered why you can only fall down and never up?*' And Billington removed his jacket which he swung round above his head like a lasso.

And Mila realised, remembering the lesson. He stood up smiling at Billington. He set off jogging round the base of the Cupola and as he gathered pace, he rose slightly up the edge. Another lap and he rose higher. But eventually he got to a place where his weight seemed to shun him and he felt like he might slip back to the base again. The rope was still too high. On each lap he heard Billington cry out above the crowd: 'Down and across, Mila! Down and across!'

Now Mila fully understood. Racing around the bowl had given him the running start over a distance that he needed. On each lap of the Cupola he gained speed. Billington cried out the instruction again and Mila turned down sharply, speeding across the edge of the base in a wide curve. As he ran up the side where the jib overhung, he realised that his body was now almost parallel with the ground above, that the rope was just behind him instead of above and out of reach from his scrambling and sliding attempts, pawing at the impossibly smooth sides. He felt his body hover on the brink of weightlessness, as a spirit about to be called back to Earth, and with one last reflex before he fell, he sprang backwards overhead, twisting as he went. His hands wafted the rope tantalisingly as he missed and tumbled back to the bottom of the Cupola, and the crowd roared in surprise and delight, drowning out Billington's cries.

Faizan's expression dropped like a stone and he cried out in rage at the sudden realisation of Billington's deception. 'Bring the jib back!' he screamed and his aides raced around the rim pushing people aside as they went.

Billington appealed to the crowd. 'Don't let them move it!' he cried. And the people gathered round the fixture, some jumping on top while others climbed the mast and shinnied out onto the jib. The aides took sticks to the people but each time some were moved others crowded in and climbed onto the fixture cheering Mila on.

Billington flinched as Mila had tumbled back down and hoped that the boy had not injured himself. But Mila stood straight back up again and smiled at Billington and swung his hand around above his head in acknowledgement. Billington desperately tried to communicate with Mila above the deafening noise of the crowd. 'Too soon!' he cried, and pointed across the Cupola indicating to where Mila should make the descent on his run. Mila understood and wandered round the base pointing until Billington nodded his head in approval and smiled.

Mila began his run again. Above, the guards and some of the magistrate's sheriffs had joined the chaos, wielding sticks mercilessly against the people as they fought for control of the fixture which now rocked back and forth alarmingly as more climbed on as others were beaten off.

Billington clasped his hands together to his chest and looked skywards. He would have prayed had he been a believer, trusting only his mathematical calculations to be somewhere near correct. It was a risk bringing the jib out; there was a margin of error, but not much. It really depended on a combination of that margin in his calculations and Mila's instinct and a belief that Mila's jump from the correct position would bring him in touch with the rope.

Mila was on his third lap of the Cupola. Even in his race against Adunga he felt that he hadn't run as fast before. Onto his fourth lap and Mila rose to the highest point he could where Billington had indicated. He felt the sun peeping over the heads of the screaming people above, warming the bowl of the Cupola. Soon it would be too hot inside and he doubted whether he would have strength for another attempt, the strain on his upside leg was telling and his muscles felt to be on fire. Faintly, against the roar above, he heard Billington's cry to descend and he turned sharply and sprinted down as hard as he could, once again gaining momentum on the outside curve of the base, he rose up the other side, even higher this time in direct line with the rocking jib. He sprang overhead again as he had before, twisting in his flight. His left hand brushed the rope and evaded his grasp but his right hand caught it, sending him into a wild spin, swinging back and forth as he dangled precariously in mid air.

The crowd erupted in massive cheers. Billington appealed to Mila to calm himself, wait and catch his breath as the spinning subsided. Mila reached up and grasped the rope with both hands; panting and gasping and feeling sick. He waited for the briefest of times, against Billington's appeal and reached one hand over the other, inching his way up the rope that quivered from the tremble of the mobbed fixture. A man clinging onto the jib above reached out his hand, crying out and pleading Mila not to give up. Mila was near to exhaustion, his lungs hurt and his head felt to be bursting with the pump of blood pounding behind his eyes and every fibre in his body told him to let go. One more hand over, another few inches up and Mila cried out in agony about to slip his grip when a hand grasped him firmly around the wrist. He was pulled up and another hand snatched his free arm. Another man on the jib behind gripped onto the legs of the man who held Mila, preventing the both of them slipping into the Cupola. Others held onto the mast reaching out over the rim trying to reach Mila and the jib man began to swing Mila back and forth until the crowd finally grasped him by the legs and hauled him over the rim.

The people mobbed Mila joyously as Billington tried to push through, but his efforts were futile as the people raised Mila above them chanting his name as they carried him away from the Cupola. Many tried to get near to Mila just to touch him as though he were blessed by God.

Faizan was furious, screaming that the challenge was unfair and that for the boy to be aided by the people was cheating, but Billington forced his way through, equally as furious that Faizan was trying to dupe the crowd again. 'Try telling that to these people!' he cried jubilantly. 'Your only hope of salvaging the slightest vestige of respect from them is to acknowledge the challenge as complete and let the boy go!'

Billington finally managed to get through to Mila and hugged him hard. 'Well done my boy!' he said delightedly as Mila collapsed to the ground in exhaustion.

'Billington?' Mila whispered. 'How does it work? You can only fall down but never up?'

'Why, centrifugal force of course! You remembered and you will certainly never forget after this!'

'I will never forget,' Mila answered weakly.

The people parted as Faizan barged his way through. 'Very well, Billington. It seems you have won again.'

'Just as well I didn't have a hundred dirham on it then, eh what?'

'Just as well, Billington, just as well,' Faizan grumbled. 'The boy is free. No doubt it pleases you to know you have a nice houseboy to take back to England with you now, to comfort you in your old age?'

'I will do no such thing!' protested Billington. 'This boy is a man and a free one to do as he pleases in this world.'

'And what might please the *boy?*' Faizan asked sarcastically.

'I want to go home now, Billington,' Mila whispered.

'Then take this...*boy* away and out of my sight, Billington,' Faizan growled as he marched off. 'I never want to see him again!'

Faizan stormed away, bellowing and cursing at his aides as he went and the crowd once again cheered and mobbed Mila with many a backslap, bowing and handshakes for Billington.

17.

It was late in the evening by the time the crowd had dispersed and visitors to widow Amira's dwelling had finally gone home after leaving all manner of gifts of coins, fine oils, cloths and items of copperware. Billington had made the final preparations for his departure east. The stall had been dismantled along with the steam engine and all his engineering instruments had been loaded onto the wagon in the hotel stables before he made his way back to the dwelling.

Amira was astounded at the gifts, enthusing particularly at the beauty of some of the cloths. '*Lamast mmin Allah*, touched by God!' she chattered repeatedly, occasionally bowing to Mila and Billington as she rummaged.

'I've no idea what we're going to do with all these,' said Billington, surveying the array of gifted items cluttering the dwelling. 'I certainly can't drag any with me all across the Middle East. I think the best bet would be for you to give half of them to your wonderful host for taking you in, Mila, then take the rest back to your people.'

'But I can't get home yet,' said Mila. 'You are going on your travels soon and I must wait for Elijah to return for me. And when you are gone I will have nowhere to live until he comes back.'

'Elijah?' said Billington. 'And who is that?'

'He is the merchant sailor who took Andreas home,' explained Mila. 'And he promised to give Andreas all his gold in trade for the pearl so that Andreas' family could keep him and no longer be poor. He promised that he would return for me in some days' time. I promised him I would say nothing about this. He was afraid that Faizan would find out about the promise and would be waiting for him to seek his revenge for the loss of the pearl. He said he would be dressed as a simple beggar merchant selling trinkets from a bag as his disguise.'

'Oh, Mila,' Billington sighed. 'For all your experience in this cruel world you are still so innocent and naive. Do you really expect this man to come back for you?'

'Yes,' said Mila. 'He is an honourable man, someone I know. He will come back.'

'The problem is, Mila, is that these things go to a man's head. The pearl will consume him with greed and selfishness. Once he was away from here he would think only of the power it would bring him. He may well hand over his gold to Andreas, probably a paltry sum weighed in value against the pearl, and he might not have much choice in that, considering the size of the man...but to risk coming all the way back here to transport a young man all the way to wherever you may live without even knowing where he is taking you, when he has absolutely no need to ever step on these shores again? No, Mila. It just won't happen, I'm very sorry to say.'

'But then I can never go home,' said Mila sadly.

'Well, I'll tell you what, Mila. I shall stay for another day or two at the most. Lord knows, I'm behind schedule as it is and I didn't have much luck at the port the other day, but I shall stay and find you someone who knows that coastline and will take you. I can afford it, thanks to you and the money I won from Faizan.'

Billington was true to his word and as soon as the sun was up he made his way down to the port. Mila did not venture out from the dwelling all that day, he still fretted over Faizan's last words that 'he never wanted to see the boy again,' and thought that Faizan might reek some terrible revenge on him if he saw him about in the market.

Billington told him, however, that he need not worry. Faizan had lost the respect of the people of Ancen Medina and to attempt any such revenge would be the final straw for his credibility. Indeed, that same afternoon, the day after the 'Cupola' challenge, Faizan's aides and his entourage could be seen dismantling the marquee and packing up his travelling show. With no one paying to see his oddities and maidens anymore there was nothing left for him in the market town. The people had lost interest and largely ignored him as he had stood on his platform outside the marquee beckoning their attention. With much angry shouting of orders, the odd wheel of stick, loud cursing and none of the festivity of his entry into Ancen Medina some days before, the entourage finally rolled through the market.

As Faizan's lead wagon passed by the people fell silent, not even the shouting of wares to sell or produce to buy could be heard. Billington watched as Faizan approached the entrance to the Oasis Faraj. He tried to act coolly but inside he still wondered and worried about Faizan honouring the rail contract, even though it was binding within the treaties of both countries, and whether Faizan would scupper all his work simply out of spite. It would prove to be a costly act if that's what he decided. Everything depended on whether Faizan had more greed than pride.

Faizan pulled up but didn't dismount, nor did he doff his fez in respect at the greeting. 'Billington?' he simply asked, 'I trust we still have a contract?'

'Of course,' said Billington, remaining impassive. 'I have my duty to his Majesty, and scoundrel that you are, I'm certain that you won't be the last I encounter on my journey.'

'And there will be a railroad all the way to the Red Sea, and

I will be a very rich man in a very rich land, as you have promised?'

'Of course. The wealth of the Far East awaits you, Abram Faizan. And when the engineers arrive you will accommodate them with the grace and courtesy as expected by his Majesty's finest in accordance with the contract and the railroad shall be built.'

'Good. Then the contract shall be honoured. I wish you safe travels and luck in your further contracts. *Ma'a salama*, farewell, Billington,' Faizan bid, shook the reins of his donkeys, and the entourage rolled on leaving the market as the people once again went about their business, selling, calling, laughing and being happy and Mila eventually emerged from Amira's dwelling in the evening to walk through the market thanking the remaining people that were closing their stalls for believing that he was not a thief.

Billington hadn't had any success at the port that day. In fact, he was considerably worried. It was time to move on, there were certain dates and deadlines to meet with other landowners, and Billington was one who always made sure that he was in place ahead of schedule just to be sure or to account for any unknown delays that might occur. He knew he still had time to reach his next client, there were other commercial vessels due in the coming days that he could certainly pay for passage to the next port, but in this part of the world, he thought, to be late was often considered to be an insult, or even a sign of disrespect. Some might simply say, 'what is this railroad, anyway?' and turn away if he was late, dismissive of what little they knew so far, and never understanding its benefits and his opportunity to explain the wonders of engineering would be gone. Despite all that had occurred between himself and Abram Faizan, at least Faizan had seen and understood. And Billington was there for the contracted date and had gained Faizan's respect — albeit in a manner he could never have imagined — and in the end, even though Faizan had guessed Billington's bluff, he believed Faizan would honour the contract, simply out of greed if nothing else.

However, although the future of the railroad was at stake, there was still an undeniable bond between him and the boy which he simply couldn't let go. It was his last chance. He must find passage for Mila or the boy would have to either travel with him, possibly for months, across the entire Middle East, or stay in Ancen Medina. And Billington simply couldn't bring the boy back to England with him, the culture would be far too alien to him, and the members of the Gentlemen's Club would look upon the boy as a house servant, and Billington — against convention — had always vehemently objected to any concept of slavery.

Billington was certain that Amira would take Mila in as her own, but he also knew that either solution would result in Mila being the unhappiest boy in a land unimaginably far from home.

The following day Billington left the hotel early, taking Mila with him to the port this time. All day they watched the various merchant vessels arrive and leave the wharfs and Billington spoke to each and every one as they arrived or departed on their journeys, speaking in several languages to the many merchants from all over the Mediterranean and elsewhere. Mila looked hopeful every time a new vessel came through the jetty and threw ropes onto the wharf, believing that he might catch sight of Elijah returning for him. But Billington told him that even if Elijah had any intention of returning — which he was convinced would not happen — that it was far too early to expect him. By evening time Mila's hopes had been dashed and Billington was seriously concerned. The choice was stark: leave the boy or take him on a frightful journey with a certain miserable ending.

'Best you go back to Amira's for your supper, Mila,' said Billington despondently. 'I'll hang on here a bit longer, just in case, and while there's a little light left.' He handed Mila a few coins. 'Get me a little wine also, before the market shuts and I'll be along shortly.'

The wine vendor refused Mila's money and sent him away with smiles and many blessings. Mila swung the gourd round his head by its leather thong as he walked back to the dwelling mumbling: 'Centrifugal force. The tribe will laugh at me when I tell them about this!'

It was late when Billington arrived at the dwelling but his mood was buoyant. 'Well, Mila, it seems we're in luck!'

'Elijah has returned for me?' said Mila hopefully.

'Elijah? Oh no, I shouldn't think so, Mila, at least he didn't give me any name and I didn't ask. I was just so relieved to find someone who's made port late, as luck would have it just as I was about to give up for the night. But the point is he is familiar with the West African coast and could possibly find your home with a little help from you. He says he has some business elsewhere in the Mediterranean but is willing to delay that to give you passage.'

Mila was excited at the news and was eager to run down to the port to see the merchant, convinced that it would be Elijah. 'That is why he has come into port so late,' insisted Mila. 'Because he doesn't want anyone to see him, in case Faizan should find out. He has come by night, and in the morning he will be dressed as a simple beggar merchant selling trinkets.'

'Mila, please don't get your hopes up,' Billington objected. 'It is so unlikely to be him. Why, he would be such a navigator and have a vessel that would virtually be capable of sailing through the air to be back from Greece in such a short time.'

'Then it must be him!' said Mila excitedly. 'Elijah is the finest navigator in all the world.'

'Well, I don't know how you think you know this man, Mila. I'm sure he has woven you a very fine story indeed, with tales of his seafaring prowess but he was a stranger. And as certain as I am standing here, you will not see this man again. Just be grateful that someone has agreed passage, for a price that is. If this was really your man Elijah he would certainly not have negotiated a fee from me, would he? As you have already explained, this Elijah has promised to return as part of the deal for the pearl.'

'But he is doing that so that no one will realise who he is,' Mila still insisted. 'He is Elijah, and pretending to be a simple merchant. He doesn't want anyone to know who he really is. Tomorrow he will dress as a beggar and come looking for me. We must go to the port now and tell him that Faizan has gone and that it is safe for him to be Elijah.'

'Mila, really, this is so outrageous. And it is very late.'

'Please, Billington,' Mila pleaded.

'No, Mila,' Billington insisted. 'To disturb the man who may be fast asleep by now would be most discourteous, considering that he has agreed passage despite having business elsewhere. Really, it would be unacceptable and the man might change his mind should we annoy him as such. And we risk disturbing the other sailors as well. Leave him to sleep undisturbed.'

'It is Elijah, I am certain,' said Mila. 'We must let him know I am here and where I can be found so that he doesn't have to look for me disguised as a beggar.'

'No, absolutely not, Mila. We shall await the morning and see him then like respectable gentlemen. I suggest you eat supper now and you go to sleep. And if you have any notion of sneaking out in the dead of night again, then I cannot be held responsible for what might happen, Lord knows you've had enough bother as it is. Don't go tempting fate again, Mila.'

Reluctantly, Mila conceded. He ate a little of Amira's spicy soup and flatbread and talked a great deal about returning to see his tribe again, such was his excitement. Billington stayed a while, and having missed his hotel supper, gratefully accepted Amira's invitation to take food. He drank a little wine as he ate and listened to Mila appreciatively as he recounted tales of his past life, dancing in celebrations and costumes decorated with dazzling trinkets and dyed with Trader's colours and fishing adventures with Injua.

'The tribe will not believe me when I tell them of my adventures in the *great civilisation*,' said Mila. 'They will laugh when I tell them that when you run very fast you go up! They will think as I do, that *centrifugal force* is a god. And how will I explain the steam engine to them, Billington?'

'Why, I don't really know, Mila. Without bringing one to your people, I think that would be a very difficult thing to explain indeed.'

'I think I will have to say it is like many of Trader's tools tied together and it eats fire and walks across the ground.'

Billington spluttered on his wine and burst out laughing. 'An absolutely splendid description, Mila! Oh, I do wish I could meet your people!'

'You would be most welcome, Billington, if you ever wish to come. Together we could tell stories enough to last forever. They will not believe any of the stories, but they will love them just the same and the children will laugh and always ask us to tell more stories every night!'

'Perhaps, Mila,' said Billington softly, sad in the knowledge that in the morning they would part, their paths never to cross again.

Eventually, quite late into the night, Billington thanked Amira and left for his hotel. Mila lay down to his bed of cushions, wrapping the blanket tightly around himself, but try as he may, total sleep eluded him and images of the man he once knew as Brahim and was convinced was the same man as

Elijah drifted in and out of his mind.

As the first traces of the sun crept over the rocky hillsides of Ancen Medina touching them into a glowing orange light, Mila could wait no more. He ran to the hotel, disturbing the morning porter who was about to curse and send him on his way until he recognised the boy from the Cupola. He bowed respectfully and directed Mila to Billington's room. Mila gently shook Billington from his sleep, breaking his snore with a splutter and a grumble.

Mila skipped and ran happily along the wharf, jogging back and forth urging Billington to be quicker. But when Billington pointed to the boat he had encountered the evening before, Mila's heart fell. A man could be seen working the riggings of the boat's sail mast, but clearly it was not Elijah. He was neither dressed as Elijah had been the last time Mila had seen him, nor was he as a beggar. His plain burlap pants, white shirt and wide belt even suggested he might be a slaver and Mila stopped dead, pulling at Billington's arm. 'Billington, this is not Elijah,' he whispered fretfully.

'Well, of course it's not. I did tell you to forget the man, didn't I?'

'But he looks like a slaver.'

'Really, Mila, how could you think I would do such a thing after all we've been through?' Billington reassured him. 'It's fine, you shall see, he's a regular merchant in this area.'

But Mila was afraid, and Billington went ahead alone, addressing the man with a polite: 'Good morning to you my good sir. I must say, your vessel looks even more splendid by daylight than it did before.'

The man jumped down from the boat onto the wharf, and shook Billington's hand. Mila could just about hear the two conversing from his position further down the wharf, Billington asking about the seaworthiness of the boat and confirming the agreed price of passage and the time.

'And the lad I was telling you about is just down here,' said Billington pointing. 'He's a little bit uncertain and untrusting after all he's been through, which is quite understandable, I suppose.'

The man looked down the wharf and smiled. And in a familiar gesture, he raised his hat and waved at Mila, revealing his sandy blonde hair.

Mila leapt for joy and raced down the wharf crying out as he ran into Trader's open arms.

'Well, well,' said Trader, laughing, 'if it isn't young Mila. How on earth did you end up here?'

'It's rather a long story,' said Billington, 'but certainly one worth listening to. I'm sure Mila will have ample time to recount his amazing tale before you reach his home.'

'I'm sorry, Trader,' said Mila. 'I tried to find you to return the net. Obi and I ran to the Baja village with it but you were gone. I wanted Injua to have it back to fish, I am so sorry.'

'Shush, Mila,' said Trader. 'It no longer matters. There comes a time in every man's life for forgiveness. Besides, I have something on my boat that might just interest you.'

As Mila stepped out from the sun into the boat's cabin his eyes strained to adjust to the shade inside. Trader pointed to his hammock in the corner and Mila looked at what he perceived to be a bundle of old rope upon it. 'The net!' he cried, as he approached the hammock. 'But how did you find it?' As he got closer he realised that his eyes had deceived him and what he thought was the stolen fishing net was a chequered blanket.

He reached out to touch and the bundle rolled over.

'Hey, stupid child,' whispered Julieta.

Mila burst into tears and leapt onto the hammock, nearly upsetting the two of them onto the cabin floor.

'Hey, hey, Mila,' Julieta protested weakly. 'What you try to do, you try to drown me again?'

'I thought you were dead,' Mila sobbed.

'She very nearly was,' said Trader. 'I almost missed her. At first I thought it was just a piece of ship wreckage, but my eye caught something moving on the surface. She was adrift some way south, barely a day ago, but out of sight of the shore. Any further south and the Atlantic drift would have taken her far out into the ocean away from anywhere.'

'Dear oh dear,' said Billington. 'Rather a stroke of luck that was. The poor girl must have had a hell of an ordeal. She doesn't look at all well.'

'She's still very weak,' said Trader. 'She's just had water mostly and eaten very little. I thought it best to make the nearest port to rest a while until she's well enough, and then find out from where she came.'

'And it's rather a turn up for the books, eh what?' said Billington. 'She seems to know Mila quite well.'

'I meant to tell you last night, Billington,' said Trader. 'But the girl was sleeping so soundly for the first time without fits or nightmares. I thought it best to let her rest until morning. I had to bring the boat round many times before I could reach her, such was the current. She just kept drifting away from me. And when I eventually picked her out of the water she was barely conscious. She was mumbling and repeating Mila's name. I thought it strange, but couldn't think how it could be the same person until I saw you both here this morning. Even then I wasn't certain; it just seemed too much of a coincidence. I honestly expected Mila to ask who she was.'

'It's Julieta, Billington' said Mila, jumping down from the hammock. 'I told you about her.'

'Well, I'll be damned,' said Billington. 'The young Spanish girl? The one you said was blown up at sea. This is indeed an amazing turn of events. It *is* a coincidence, and certainly is a most incredible coincidence. I never would have believed it.'

'It was the Yoonir,' said Mila. 'It was just as Kobina said; that it would bring me great fortune if I parted with it wisely. I *did* part with it wisely. And I knew it was time to part with it when I met Andreas, and now the star of Yoonir has shined on me at last!'

'Oh, well, I don't know about all that,' said Billington. 'I'm afraid I don't subscribe to such folklore. I just think this is a collection of many coincidences and some incredible odds. A bit like your chances of escaping the Cupola without my advice, eh Mila?'

'No, it was the Yoonir looking after me,' insisted Mila.

'Very well then, Mila,' said Billington. 'I accept that you have your beliefs. Personally, I believe in science, but who's to argue? Stranger things have happened in this world. I suppose as an engineer I have to believe in both the probable and the possible. I wouldn't be here trying to achieve a reality from a dream if that wasn't the case. But, the question now is, what happens next?'

'We let her rest a day or two,' said Trader. 'Then if she is well enough we take her back to her family, wherever that may be. Then I take Mila back to his people as agreed before I continue on my way. I have some business on the island of Kerkyra to attend to then.'

'She has no family,' said Mila. 'They were killed by two men of Captain Youssef, before Youssef and Brahim beheaded them. Her only family were the Barbaries.

'Yes, I remember it all now just as you told me, Mila,' said Billington. 'But what is to become of the poor girl now?'

'She must come home to my people,' said Mila. 'They will love her as their own and look after her well. Please, Trader, can you take us to my home? I want to stay with Julieta.'

'I think that would be a reasonable solution,' said Trader. 'Once she's well enough for the journey, that is.'

Mila reached out to touch Julieta, 'Did you hear that,

Julieta?' he whispered. 'You are to come and live with my people. You will have a family again.'

But Julieta had fallen back to sleep and heard nothing.

'Well then,' said Billington. 'I believe some medication might be in order, something to speed the girl's recovery. I noticed there was an apothecary in the town. I should go and see if someone will look at the girl. Perhaps they might have some of the remedies we have back home.'

Billington returned some while later carrying some new clothes for Julieta he'd purchased in the market and accompanied by a Berber man. Mila nearly leapt for joy at the sight of the simply dressed man carrying a cloth bag, until he got closer and Mila realised to his disappointment that the man wasn't Elijah after all.

'This is Yuften,' said Billington. 'Apparently he is most highly esteemed in these parts for his medical skills.'

Yuften smiled broadly and bowed. '*Salaam*, and many greetings my friends,' he said. 'And what an honour it is to be at service for the great Billington and to greet the great runner!'

Mila smiled and looked at Billington. 'Am I great?' he asked.

'Indeed you are, young Mila,' said Billington. 'I think your story is going to be part of folklore here for a long while.'

'But please,' said Yuften, 'if I may see the patient?'

Billington led the man aboard the boat and over to Julieta's hammock where he laid the new clothes on a bench.

It seemed to Mila that Yuften was the happiest and friendliest man he'd ever met in his life. Everything about him seemed to calm away any fears of Julieta's illness with his confidence, cheerfulness and humour.

'She still has a slight fever,' said Yuften, smiling broadly as he felt Julieta's neck and forehead. 'You must make a brew of these things,' he added, producing some jars and herbs from his bag. Trader took the herbs and lit a small fire on his grill on the deck and brought some water to heat in a pan as instructed.

'This one is cayenne,' said Yuften, chuckling as he sprinkled the spice into the water. 'This will put fire and life back into the girl, like your engine, Billington! Before you know it she will be hooting and running through the market!

'And this one is saffron,' added Yuften, lifting the jar of bright orange spice from his bag. 'Very good for the stomach and to stimulate the appetite. Soon she will be eating so well that the markets of Ancen Medina will run out of food! And it will lift her from any sadness that has occurred from her ordeal. And so, we now add a little lemon and honey to the mixture,' he said, chopping the fruit and adding it to the brew along with a good sized spoon of honey.

Yuften produced another jar, this time containing brownish orange strips of what looked like wood. 'But most importantly,' he said, 'this one is *salic*, from Greece. It is the bark of the *helike* tree, most important for reducing fever and calming the sickness. All these things will bring it down and the honey and lemon will make it palatable.'

Julieta still slept as Trader gently stirred the concoction as instructed by Yuften. As it cooled, Mila gently shook Julieta into consciousness. She took small sips, mumbled her disgust at the taste, but Yuften insisted she drink all the cupful before she went back to sleep.

By midday Julieta awoke again and sat up in the hammock and felt well enough to take some milk sweetened with honey.

Yuften prepared another batch of the brew with the instruction: 'She must drink this three times a day until her fever has gone for at least two days. When this has passed you must make this as well. This is *spirulina*, a remedy for energy,' he said, retrieving some other items from the bag. 'It will help her regain her strength. You make a brew of mint tea and add two spoons of spirulina to it.'

Yuften handed Trader the herbs. 'And I noticed she has sores and welts across the neck and shoulders. Her skin is damaged and will not heal properly without this.' Yuften reached into the bag and produced a small stone jar tightly corked. 'This is very precious, I'm afraid. It does not come cheap, but I suggest you use it. This is argan oil. Very rare plant oil and difficult to produce, but guaranteed to heal wounds that have become infected. You must rub this into her neck and face and encourage her to use it on the rest of her body two or three times a day. Soon she will once again have the natural skin of the beautiful maiden she is!'

'Well, that's quite a bundle of medicines,' said Billington. 'I suppose this is going to cost a pretty bundle of cash.'

Yuften clasped his hands together as if about to pray and bowed gently. 'Alas, these items are not cheap and in my travels are very difficult to find. But for the great Billington who will one day bring much wealth to Ancen Medina and for the great runner, I am prepared to charge cost only. The price is ten dirham.'

'Ten dirham?' said Billington. 'Well, I'm sure I can manage that! Bit of a bargain, I reckon, but I suppose it's a tidy sum by your folk's standard. However, as you have been so helpful and the folk here so accommodating, I'm prepared to double your price, or perhaps make it thirty dirham, even. I wouldn't want to see you out of pocket, eh what?'

Yuften bowed deeply this time. '*Billington, huwa majeed,* a most honourable man,' he said smiling broadly.

'I have much travelling to do,' Trader interrupted. 'How soon will she be well enough to sail?'

'So, you are journeying afar?' said Yuften. 'I should let her rest at least tonight plus one more day. And be certain that there is no more fever and that she is capable of taking solid food. That is my diagnosis, thank you.' He bowed gracefully again. 'I wish you safe journeys and I bless you, travellers, for he who does not travel does not know the value of men.'

By mid afternoon Julieta's fever appeared to be easing and convinced that the girl was on the road to recovery, Billington could wait no longer and was eager to depart. He had already missed his ship and the next one due was two days away, which still gave him just enough time for his arranged meeting. However, by luck that morning, a merchant boat bound for Naples was just loading its wares and Billington managed to negotiate a fee for dropping him off in Nador on the way.

Mila accompanied him back to the dwelling, where he helped Amira to sort out which of the gifts from the people of Ancen Medina she wished to keep and which Mila could take home to his people. They wheeled Mila's share back to Trader's boat with a borrowed cart and Billington said his farewells to Trader.

'Well, I believe the agreed price was forty dirham for taking the boy home?' said Billington.

'Really, there is no need, Billington,' said Trader. 'If I had known the boy was one and the same as the girl spoke of I would never have agreed money. I'll be happy to return the boy and have my net back.'

'But I insist,' said Billington. 'I made a fair packet out of that scoundrel Faizan. Besides, we have something of a tradition at the Gentleman's Club. Every year we see who can tell the most outlandish story from our travels and have a little wager overviewed by an independent arbitrator. I shall be telling the tale of a young lad shipwrecked twice, winning a race, betting a pearl worthy of the crown jewels and using engineering science to escape certain death. I believe I have this one all wrapped up when I get back to England, eh what? The trouble is they'll never believe it!'

Billington returned to the hotel where Mila helped him to

feed and water the donkeys and see that all his possessions were secured. 'We don't want the old steam engine rolling off by itself do we, eh what, Mila?' said Billington as he finished lashing the machine down to the wagon floor.

Billington tethered the donkeys to the wagon and led them down to the wharf where, with the help of the merchant, they carefully manoeuvred his equipment along the gangplank onto the Naples bound boat, all the while Billington protesting, fretting and worrying that his beloved steam engine might drop into the sea.

'Well, I suppose this is it then?' he said sadly, holding his hand out to Mila. 'From here I sail to Nador, where I have another contract awaiting. And then there is a charter boat for the next stage of my journey. It's going to be a long job is all this. Anyway, I must say it's been a pleasure to have known you, Mila.'

Mila grabbed onto Billington, hugging him hard. 'And I will never forget you, Billington,' he sobbed.

'Now, now, dear boy, there's no need for tears. Now is a time to rejoice. You found the young lady you thought was dead and now you are going home at last. I'd call that a happy ending indeed.'

Mila released his hug, wiped his tears and shook Billington's hand. 'You must tell the King that one day I will come to your country to meet him.'

'That's more like it, young Mila,' said Billington, trying to maintain his composure. 'Stiff upper lip and all that, eh what? I'm sure his Majesty would love to meet you too, Mila. You never know, after this strange journey, you just never know. And you are but a young man. Despite all that's gone before, the journey is just beginning for you. And of course, you mustn't forget what we learned on this journey?'

Mila swung his hand round over his head. 'Centrifugal force, Billington! Wait until I tell my people!'

'Good lad!' said Billington, boarding the boat. As the merchant threw his lines, withdrew the gangplank and raised sail, Billington doffed his hat to Mila and the vessel slowly floated away. Mila watched sadly as it cleared the jetty where Billington gave a final wave with his hat. When at last Mila was out of sight, Billington allowed himself to shed a few tears of his own.

18.

Trader stayed in port for two more days, administering the herbal brews as Yuften had instructed and each day Julieta grew stronger. By day she was out of the hammock, applying the argan oil and trying the new blouses and pantaloons that Billington had purchased and eating a little more; soups and bread and milk as suggested by Yuften. And each day Mila looked out for Elijah, convinced that he would still return, eager to tell him that Faizan had now gone and that he had passage home. He watched the boats come and go, carefully observing the merchants as they cast their ropes onto the wharf as they docked, and wandering the market in case he'd missed anyone, looking out for the simple beggar man selling trinkets from a bag.

Eventually and reluctantly, he began to realise that Billington must have been right, and Julieta was well again and Trader, having rigged up a third hammock on board was now ready to leave, eager to complete the journey and continue his business on the island of Kerkyra.

On the morning of the third day, Trader set sail and as the boat cleared the jetty, Mila waved goodbye to the port and town of Ancen Medina for the last time of his life. By midday Trader's boat had lost sight of land and as it picked up a fair wind of the Atlantic breeze and skimmed the waves like a gull in flight, Mila was happy and eager to see his land once again.

As the day wore on Mila recounted much of his story he hadn't already told as Trader navigated. He excitedly described his life on the Seyaad and before that how he escaped from the slave ship, much to Trader's amazement and admiration. And proudly he related the tale of the race and the Giant and how he escaped the Cupola, all thanks to Billington the rail engineer to his Majesty the King of the tribe of England, and Trader laughed aloud, complimenting the boy on either his prowess at survival or his story-telling. But Mila insisted it was all true.

'Well, I suppose it must be,' Trader remarked. 'The best story-teller in the world couldn't make up something like that! No wonder Billington thinks he's won his wager.'

But Julieta was unhappy. She ate but spoke little, and wandered the deck alone but without dancing or singing into the breeze as she had done on the Seyaad and often she just lay on the foredeck watching the waves splash over the bow as it rose and dipped with the swell of the racing sea below. Several times Mila asked her if she was still not feeling better but she dismissed him each time saying she was fine. But each time Mila wanted to make conversation or talk about his happiness at returning home, Julieta would just shrug her shoulders or give single word answers and retreat to her hammock or walk away from him silently to lie down by herself on the foredeck.

Eventually Mila asked Trader if he thought he might know what was wrong with Julieta.

'She misses her family, Mila,' said Trader. 'It's only to be expected. And now she goes on a journey somewhere far from her home.'

'But her family died a long time ago, Trader,' said Mila. 'They were killed by some of Youssef's men, who took revenge and kept her with the men of the Barbaries. She was happy on the Seyaad.'

'You don't understand, Mila. The pirates *were* her family.

She was part of something there, she had purpose. She was fed, had duties to perform and was useful, and maybe considered herself to be a part of that family. The Barbary pirates are a scavenging bunch of thieves that will one day be eradicated from the seas, but they were her family. And now she has no purpose or direction in life.'

Mila thought about Trader's words for a long time, and in the evening as Trader looked for a calm beach to anchor for the night, Mila approached Julieta as she lay on her belly, with her elbows propped on the foredeck and her chin in her hands watching the sun go down.

'Julieta,' Mila whispered. 'Why do you not want to talk to me anymore? Do you not like me once again?'

Julieta rolled over to face Mila. 'Course I like you, Mila. But why you think I want to go live with your people? I am Spanish girl from civilised country. I like you very much, Mila, but not enough to live like savage. I no want to walk about in loin cloth like savage, spearing fish and stab pigs in forest and live in grass hut.'

'But you have no one else. Where can you go? You have no family, but my family will take care of you. You will be treated like a princess of the tribe.'

'I don't want to be treated as anything of a *tribe*,' said Julieta. 'My family were grand, noble people, work hard, rich merchants, live like kings in fine house with very fine clothes and servants. I no want to go to any tribe.

'But what will you do?'

'Maybe when we get to your people I just ask Trader to take me back to Andalucia and I find my own way. I am Barbary and have wits and know how to survive. Even with Barbaries I live good, not walk in forest with loincloth. Maybe you come with me to Andalucia, Mila?'

'But I must go home,' said Mila. 'I have fulfilled my task and found Trader. Now I must tell the tribe. My friend Obi will not know what has happened and the tribe will not be able to decide if he is to live or die. That was the decision before I was sent to find Trader.'

'I know you must go home,' said Julieta sadly. 'Mila, all time I think of you and have big dream on raft. I float in sea like you and cry when not dreaming. I dream of place like my family, work hard and live like civilised people. I dream I have family again...real family.'

'But you *will* have family.'

'Maybe, Mila...we see.'

Trader carried on sailing into the twilight and eventually turned ashore onto the quiet beach of an inlet where the surf was gentle, allowing the receding tide to moor the boat. He built a campfire and made a meal of freshly caught grilled fish and vegetables seasoned with spices from the market town which both Mila and Julieta devoured eagerly.

Mila was elated to see Julieta eating well again, but thought it best not to speak of his happiness and said nothing of his returning home or his eagerness to see his people. Instead he spoke long into the evening of the events since he and Julieta had parted, some of which he hadn't yet had chance to relate to Trader.

Julieta was surprised and impressed with Mila's tale. She smiled and laughed and sometimes frowned, unsure if parts were made up, as though it was part of Mila's culture to make up tribal tales of folklore.

In the end, Julieta sighed. 'You have big adventure, Mila. You live even when death come to visit you. But now you be bored when go back to tribe. You like Julieta now, not happy.'

'But I *am* happy,' Mila insisted. 'I would like you to be happy also. I will be unhappy if we part, as you wish, but I will not stop you. Come and see my family, then maybe you will see. It will be good, I promise.'

'We see, Mila. We see.'

Over the coming days, Julieta's spirit seemed to lift and she appeared happier, wandering about the deck, occasionally swinging on the riggings and humming quietly to herself, but stopping short of outright singing or laughing. Trader commented that Yuften's tonics appeared to be working and her energy was returning, but never did she talk about Mila's people or ask how long before they got there, it was as though she was just happy to be sailing again without caring about anything or anyone else. And Mila never asked her. In the evenings she would eat well alongside Mila, tempted by Trader's tasty spiced fish and grilled meat dishes, recounting to Trader about her life as a Barbary. Mila and Trader laughed as Julieta related the accounts of Mila hanging on for dear life in the crow's nest during high sea swells and how he nearly fell out with the telescope, thinking the deck was only a few feet below him.

One night, Trader produced a bottle of wine and set it on the table alongside the meal he'd prepared. Pouring three cups, Julieta snatched Mila's away and taking a sip said, 'Not for small childrens, Mila,' at which Mila frowned but Trader burst out laughing.

And Mila was just happy to see her better again. Happy and secretly hopeful that Julieta would accept her new life with his family.

The following evening Trader anchored the boat in a quiet lagoon where there was no surf at all. Mila had never before imagined a place as beautiful or blue as the sliver of crescent moon reflected perfectly in the still water the colour of azure and the dying sun clipped the shore's treetops like burning emeralds against the cobalt sky. A few stars had made themselves visible in the remaining daylight, and high above them all, Yoonir hung bright as Trader prepared their evening meal.

'One more day should do it,' said Trader as they sat at the cabin table eating.

'Are we nearly there?' Mila asked cautiously.

'We should reach the Baja village in the morning. I will collect my net and then reach your people before evening, Mila.'

'Thank you, Trader,' said Mila. 'My family will be so happy to see you again, and thankful for bringing me safely home.'

Julieta said nothing and carried on eating her meal. When she had finished she retreated to her hammock saying she was tired, but Mila could tell she was unhappy again now that the time had come to stay with his family and she would be off the sea and unable to sail away if she wanted. And Mila was unhappy, fearing the decision that he thought she was about to make.

Mila retired to his hammock and thought about asking Julieta what she was to do, but she had already fallen asleep.

Later in the night Mila was awakened by the sound of a splash in the silent calm water. On deck he found Trader leaning over the side of the boat holding a line. 'What is it, Trader?' he whispered.

'I have been in this lagoon before, Mila. Sometimes the ray fish come in from the ocean and gather here. We must be very quiet; I am hoping to catch one for tomorrow's meal.'

Mila peered over the edge and to his amazement, bright and clear through the crystal blue water there was a glow of green light from the sand at the bottom of the lagoon. 'Why does the seabed shine, Trader?' he asked.

'It is a piece of wood from a dying forest, Mila,' Trader whispered. 'The glow comes from the decay in the wood. The wood has died but there is a new life in it that glows. It is called phosphorous.'

'Nnamdi the wise man of the Baja told me of *new life*,' said Mila. 'He said that everything and everyone changes, but never truly dies. But I never thought that a piece of wood could change and shine like a star. Nnamdi was right. The wood has changed, but it is not dead, it is beautiful like the Yoonir.'

'It *is* beautiful, Mila, and the fish think it so. I drop the line with a weight on the wood to sink, and a hook with bait. The fish are attracted to the light and the bait. But it seems they are not here tonight.'

'No one can see the ray, Trader,' said Mila. 'That is what Injua taught me. And the ray is wise; he does not take bait easily. It is better to spear them.'

'Very difficult, Mila,' said Trader. 'You can't fish for ray with a spear if you can't see them or they don't come.'

'But the rays *are* here. Watch, Trader,' said Mila, picking up a gaff pole. Carefully he dipped the pole over the edge, ruffling the smooth surface water. 'See in the light how the sand rises so faintly like dust? That is the tail of the ray. It has moved away, but he comes back to your light. It is very clever, Trader, this light you have made in the sea. I must tell Injua about the wood that glows. But why does the ray come back to it?'

Trader smiled as he observed the faint telltale sign of the previously invisible fish. 'Something has come into the ray's life that it doesn't understand,' he said. 'The ray is very clever and wise as you say, Mila and it wants to learn more, so it comes back and observes. It wants to know and discover as we do. We are also curious like the ray but never understand life completely, just like the ray doesn't understand the light.'

'And the ray always knows when the bait is too easy and that he must hunt for it himself. But look again, now, Trader,' said Mila pointing into the water. 'Can you see the dusting of the sand again? Now that the ray has swum away and returned to the light, you can tell where its body must be. It is better to hunt the ray than try to fish for him with bait, like the ray knows it must hunt also. Now is the time to spear him.'

'But I have no spear, Mila.'

'Such a pity, Trader. You could have the ray with one thrust now, if you wanted. When we get to my village I will give you a spear, Trader. I have a very fine one in our hut.'

'Thank you, Mila. You have taught me a good lesson. I will be glad to have your spear.'

'Trader, tomorrow you shall have your net back. Does this mean you will do the good trade with the village again and warn us when the slavers are coming?'

'I'm afraid I won't be able to trade again, Mila,' said Trader sadly. 'I have seen some land on the island of Kerkyra that I wish to purchase and settle. Trading is too dangerous for me now. The slavers have changed their tactics and their movements and the voyaging times are obscure and staggered. They know someone has been spying on them and I risk being found out. I am sorry, Mila, this will be my last run.'

'I am very sad, Trader,' said Mila. 'You have been very good for our tribe. I must tell them that it is too dangerous to live by the ocean now or they may be taken as slaves.'

Mila silently contemplated a life without Trader's visits as he stared over the edge at the green glow in the water. After a long while he asked: 'Trader, how is it that you know so much about the slavers?'

Trader stood silent for a while, gently tugging at the line as though he hadn't heard Mila. 'It is time to sleep now, Mila,' he said eventually, pulling the line from the water.

Mila climbed into his hammock, gently falling asleep, expecting Trader to retire at any moment, but Trader stayed out on the deck as Mila fell into his dreams.

It was late into the night when Trader gently shook Mila into consciousness. 'Mila,' he whispered. 'There is something I must tell you.'

'What is it, Trader?'

'Please, we must not disturb Julieta. Come out on deck.'

Mila followed Trader onto the deck, where Trader climbed onto the cabin roof and sat watching the stars.

'Mila,' Trader whispered, 'you have told me that everything and everyone changes, this is what the wise man Nnamdi said to you?'

'Yes, Trader, he said that I will change in my journey in life, as we all must. That was his lesson before I went looking for you.'

'Mila, you asked me something tonight, but I did not give you an answer. I also have changed, and like you, have learned in my journey, learned a valuable lesson. And I have to tell you this because despite how I have changed, I cannot change my past life and my soul will never rest. I know so much about the slavers because...my people were once slavers, Mila.'

'You, Trader?' said Mila feeling confused. 'You were never a slaver, Trader.'

'I am not one now, Mila. But my family were.'

'That is a good thing that you are no longer a slaver. Even though it is said that slavers can be very rich men and live in fine houses and never be hungry.'

'But it was once my own choice, Mila,' said Trader. 'It was once my family's business before the import of slaves was banned, but my father still operated, smuggling to the New World, and many agents there turned a blind eye and took the money that it brought. And it was expected of me and I complied for a while, although I objected to the trade and worried about it since it was outlawed. I was about to be given the captaincy of a ship, a ship with my own name. I have an English name, but that does not matter anymore and I will not speak of it to you. No longer am I that man of my father's, I am Trader. It is true; I could have had much money and lived a comfortable life. But I committed a great crime in the eyes of my father.'

'What did you do, Trader?'

'I turned on my own family, Mila.'

'What do you mean, Trader?'

'I ran away. And from a distance I wrote to the authorities about my father's activities. I believe he was arrested and imprisoned. The day came, Mila when I could see the light of the children's eyes and feel in my own soul the sorrow as they were taken aboard our ships. It was how I imagined the condemned souls of Earth being hoarded into the underworld for their sins. Only these poor souls had not sinned. I knew then, that the slaves were no different than my own people, and what my family were involved in was not just illegal, but beyond wickedness.

'I ventured one day into the hold, although my father had always forbade it, insisting I was to be a captain and that the 'cargo,' as he called it was not my duty. And then I saw. The inhumanity of my own people I could barely believe. I tried to block it from my mind, but I grew ashamed and vowed that once we returned home I would do something. I couldn't go to the authorities myself, I would have been arrested. And my father would have shot me if he knew what I was about to do, but I managed to retrieve all my money from the banks before writing my letters. From there I purchased this boat and left England forever to be the wandering trader I am today. I could never return to my own country, I was a criminal for my part in the illegal trade. I resolved from then that in my travels I would spy, learn their routes and times and do whatever I could to frustrate the slavers by informing your people and the authorities of my own land when they were coming.

'But forever on my mind is the image of those people. I can only pray that one day they will be free men. My conscience will not let me rest for my sins. Mila, I ask something of you, and I would understand if you did not give it to me. I ask for forgiveness from your people. Can I ever be forgiven for what my people have done? I have felt that I was cursed to forever wander these seas until I was forgiven for my sins.'

'But you are a good man, Trader,' said Mila. 'You are not a slaver. You have changed, just like Nnamdi said we all must. Now you have brightness in your soul like the piece of wood that once thought it was dead but was only changing into something more beautiful. And you said to me that there is a time in every man's life for forgiveness. I forgive you, Trader as you have forgiven me for stealing the net.'

'Mila, you are such an innocent and remarkable young man. What my people have done hardly compares to the theft of a simple net, but, I am glad and thank you, Mila. It is important for me. I hope also, that your people can forgive me.'

'I think they will understand, Trader. For so many years you have helped us with your tools from the *great civilisation*. There are so many things that we could not do as well before we met you. The tribe lives well because of your trade. And you have kept watch on the slavers for us. We might all have been slaves without you.'

'Thank you, Mila,' Trader whispered softly. 'You are a simple young man with a soul of kindness and a heart bigger than any man.'

'And I too will not rest, Trader,' said Mila, as he recounted the events of the slave ship and how they drowned because of his releasing them from chains. 'I have fulfilled my promise to Kobina, but I will never understand why it did not bring him luck as he said it would to those that part with the pearl wisely. Did not Kobina part with it wisely, and then his reward was death for himself and his people? I will never know if he forgives me. For a while I forgot when I was on the Seyaad with Julieta and then when I was with Billington helping him in the market. But now that my life is quiet again I see his face and my sadness and guilt are deep.'

'Do not feel that way, Mila,' Trader whispered. 'The pearl

would eventually have been discovered had it not been passed to you and its wealth probably used to perpetuate the slave trade even further. The slaves were probably better off dead. If they knew the reality of their destiny, many would probably have chosen death. The colonies are cruel places and many would not even have survived the crossing of the ocean. You have been in the hold of slavers and seen. Imagine if you also were in chains? I have also seen this. Try to imagine what you would choose, Mila. Would you just lie in your own filth and hope? Kobina not only made a wise decision, he made the *only* decision. He parted with it wisely. It is not your fault that the land was out of reach when you believed it to be close by. That is fate. You had seen land and you killed the tormentor as Kobina asked because you were not in chains. So, as a slave in chains – which you were doomed to be in time – what would you do, given the choice, to swim for freedom or just hope?'

'I would swim, as I did that night,' said Mila. 'Even if I knew the land was out of reach.'

'Then do not feel guilt. It is time to forget. Be happy, we will see your family again soon.'

'And what will you do then, Trader?'

'There is some land on the island I told you of, a piece of the island of Kerkyra so beautiful with groves of trees of apple, figs and orange and a vineyard, Mila. Have you ever seen grapes, Mila? They are the most delicious fruit of all. And there are green pastures with goats and olive trees beneath the mountains so tall there is snow upon them.'

'Billington once told me about snow,' said Mila. 'I would like to see it one day.'

'There is an old couple there,' continued Trader. 'The husband I met in the tavern one evening. They no longer can look after the property and are willing to sell to live out their days in the little village by the sea. The only other is a daughter, whom I met when looking at the place, but she can't manage the land on her own. She is a very beautiful woman and smiles much when I have visited. I think she may be fond of me. I hope so; I would not like to be alone forever. And her father seems favoured towards me; he always hints that any decent woman cannot be alone forever. I am going back there after I see you home, Mila.'

'Are you in love, Trader?' asked Mila.

'Perhaps,' said Trader. 'We shall see. For a long time, since I left my family I thought I was unable to love. But the island is where I am going to stay. There is much to do there and I will not be idle looking after the place. I promised the woman I would return by the second moon. I will need help, I shall hire some of the young islanders, some lads with fine strong hands such as yours, Mila would be a great help.'

Mila and Trader talked a while longer until eventually Mila became tired and said he was going to sleep. But Trader was still wide awake, his mind mulling over the conversation they'd had and anxious about meeting Mila's people again after his confession. He explained to Mila that he would be unable to sleep and would set a course and sail through the night arriving at the Baja village at first light.

Trader worked the riggings setting the sail as Mila slipped into his hammock. As the boat slowly drifted from the lagoon Julieta awoke. 'Mila, what is happening?' she asked.

'Trader is going to sail through the night so that we arrive at the Baja village by daybreak,' Mila whispered. 'Then we will soon be with my people.'

As the boat finally left the lagoon, the sound of the ocean breeze sweeping the waves sent Mila to sleep, smothering the gentle sobs of Julieta quietly crying.

The boat soon picked up the Atlantic swell, gently swaying Mila's hammock as he slept and dreamt of Billington bowing before a man in a fine headdress of gold and feathers and robes of many colours like the Head of his own tribe on ceremony that must have been Billington's king. Then Mila was on the end of a long rope being swung round by Billington and Mila did not want to let go, but Billington was telling him: 'You must defy science, Mila, for your people call you from across the sea.' And as he let go he sailed high into the air to settle on a quiet shore with lush forest in the twilight where the star of Yoonir shone down upon the beach. Kobina stepped from the forest, but his face was no longer full of sadness as in his previous dreams. Kobina smiled upon Mila and the Yoonir reflected his white tattooing as bright as the many stars above him. He reached out his hand to Mila and Mila grabbed it tightly as Kobina said silently with his eyes: *you are forgiven, Mila.*

As Mila awoke in the early light he realised that Trader held his hand and was gently shaking it. 'We are nearly there, Mila,' Trader whispered.

Mila arose as Trader resumed his place at the helm but Julieta was still asleep and he left her undisturbed as he went on deck. As he yawned and stretched he realised they were very close to shore and the blue haze of early morning was defining the trees along the beach into shapes. He rubbed his eyes and in a blink a man stepped from the forest, smiling at him as the boat passed. The first glimpse of sun caught the white of his tattooed face and chest as he waved.

'Kobina!' Mila cried as he ran to Trader. 'Stop, Trader! Stop the boat!'

'What is it, Mila?' Trader asked.

'I have seen Kobina on the beach! Look!' Mila turned and pointed. The man was gone.

'I think you are mistaken, Mila,' said Trader.

'But I saw him. It was the same tattoo design of Kobina. He was there.'

'There are no other tribes on this stretch of the coast, Mila.

We are still some fifteen miles from the Baja village. It is very early; your eyes must be playing tricks upon you.'

'But it must have been,' Mila insisted. 'Kobina was a warrior in warrior's markings. There was no one else like him.'

'Then where is he now, Mila?' said Trader. 'If it was him he would wait, not disappear into the forest again.'

'I don't know,' whispered Mila, watching the shore pass.

19.

The sun had lifted over the horizon as the first trail of smoke from the Baja village came into view. As Trader steered his boat into the cove of the village, a familiar figure awaited him on the shore waving. Nnamdi waded into the water to catch the rope cast by Trader as others of the village helped to drag the boat, grounding it onto the sand in the shallow water. Trader jumped ashore doffing his straw hat and extending his hand in greeting. Mila climbed from the boat and Julieta sat on the rail edge, swinging her feet and watching the greetings, unsure of what she was supposed to do.

Nnamdi's face was cheerful, but his first words were quiet and without the rejoice that Mila had expected would greet him on his return. 'It is good to see you safe, Mila. You have had a successful journey and brought Trader back to us. But it is not all good news.'

'What has happened?' asked Trader. But before Nnamdi could answer two familiar figures appeared and Mila knew instinctively that something was very wrong.

The old man Injua that once had owned Trader's net made his way down to the beach followed by Jaji, the proud warrior of his own tribe. Injua was crying at the sight of Mila as he approached, his arms outstretched as they met. 'Many greetings, Mila,' he struggled to say. 'You have returned from a journey I thought you would never come back from,' and he hugged Mila hard as he wept.

'Why are you here with the Baja's, Injua?' said Mila. 'And

why is Jaji here? What has happened?'

'The tribe journeyed here many days ago, Mila,' said Jaji as he approached and Mila could now see the evidence of a desperate fight etched onto Jaji's face and arms.

'The village was attacked, Mila,' said Injua. 'Some were killed, but most survived as we knew the slavers were coming. So we hid and fought back and would not be taken. Jaji put up the bravest fight when they found him. They tried to net him but Jaji cut loose, killing two of them with his knife as they struggled, until they thought it best not to try with one so angry.'

'My family!' cried Mila.

'They are safe, Mila,' said Injua.

Mila slumped down into the sand and buried his head in his hands, and as he mumbled his thanks to the *Yoonir*, he realised that others had gathered around him. Looking up, his mother, father and sister smiled down on him and Mila leapt to his feet hugging them hard as others from the Mjumbi village danced around them joyfully.

Injua approached Trader and held out his hand. 'Not all the tribe survived,' he said, shaking Trader's hand. 'But without your tools, many more would have died.'

'Come,' said Nnamdi. 'There is food and there is much to talk about. And I see you have another with you,' he said pointing to Julieta.

Mila helped Julieta down from the boat and introduced her to the others. 'It is a very long tale,' he said as he led Julieta by the hand up the beach with the others to Nnamdi's hut.

The party talked long into the day, but Jaji spoke the longest, describing the events of the slaver's attack. 'Obi returned to us to face the tribe's justice as a man,' he said. 'But on his return journey he spotted a ship much like the ones Trader has described to us. We painted ourselves as ghosts and took our weapons and hid in the forest, leaving the village empty. The women and children we hid as deep into the undergrowth as we could. The slavers dared to venture after us. Then it was they who were the hunted. Soon, one of us was spotted as we intended, and they ran into our ambush. We attacked, darting from one tree and bush to another, throwing spear and dropping from the trees with axe. They used guns without seeing us and were terrified of our spirit faces when they could see us.'

'I disguised myself as a tree!' said Obi proudly. 'I painted my body with Trader's green dye and became like the forest, screeching like a bird and confusing the slavers.'

'Then there was a sound like thunder,' Jaji continued 'and we all stopped. But the sky was blue and we couldn't understand. The slavers ran from the forest then and some of us followed. There was another ship like the slaver's ship but further out to sea, sending lightning and more thunder into the sky. Some of the slavers got into their boats and began rowing out to their ship, but others were afraid and scattered in many directions. We hunted these down and speared them as they would have done to us. Then the *lightning ship* joined the slaver's ship for a long time and the slavers were taken aboard before it went out to sea again. But as it departed it sent lightning again, this time across the water and the lightning shattered the slaver's ship. I think the *lightning ship* was sent by the gods to avenge the slavers, taking them away to a spirit land to be punished.'

'It was a ship of the realm,' said Trader. 'It's not a god, but a British naval ship, sent to break the black market in slavery. The slave trade was supposed to have ended many years ago, but unfortunately some have chosen to ignore that.'

Nnamdi looked sceptically at Trader, but only nodded and smiled at his words and made no answer. Instead, he beckoned Injua to speak next.

'So, we came to the Baja village to spread the good news of

our victory and also the bad news of death,' said Injua. 'And here we will stay as Nnamdi has permitted. It is a good partnership, as good as the partnership with Trader. We have learned how to fashion good weapons with Trader's tools of steel. With these and Trader's *news* we have been given a great victory over the slavers. And the partnership with the Baja gives us strength in numbers. The slavers will think twice when word of our victory reaches others.'

'Mila,' said Nnamdi. 'It is your turn now. Tell us of your journey to the *great civilisation.*'

Mila tried to recount some of the events of his strange adventure to the amazement of the others, but his emotions got the better of him. Jaji's story of the loss of some of his people and reliving his memory of the drowning slaves forced him to stop before he could finish and he retreated into the forest behind the village to think where he sat for long hours into the late afternoon, trying to visualise the struggle his tribe had endured. Eventually, Nnamdi's intuition told him where Mila might be and he found him once again by the stream where they had spoken so long ago.

'You have changed,' said Nnamdi. 'As I said you would. You left here as a boy and come back a man. No, more than a man...a wise man who has seen many things and learned from them. Now you are also a *voyager*. And the spirit of *voyage* will always be in you.'

'I do not feel like a man,' Mila muttered. 'I am pleased that my family have survived, but I do not understand the meaning of my journey if it ends also with death.'

'But you *are* a man, Mila, and that is life. It is not to be understood, but it carries on. Life is a journey until death. Then it is still a journey, just like the leaf that falls...it never truly dies. And when you cross that river yourself into the *new life*, you will understand. And tomorrow, when you have mourned those that have gone and feel a little better, you shall tell me more of your journey in *this* life.'

The following day Mila spoke to Nnamdi alone in his hut, in his own tribe's language, retelling his story in detail as Nnamdi recited Mila's words after him. As the only means of recording the tribe's history, Nnamdi would memorize and pass down the generations *the greatest story of the tribe's history*, the story of Mila of the Mjumbi, who saw the *great civilisation* and was not a slave.

As Mila told the story of Billington, Nnamdi was puzzled. The steam engine he found difficult to fathom and couldn't quite form an image of it in his mind other than as a mythical creature created out of the metals that Trader had introduced to the tribe so many years ago. He stopped Mila after the description of Billington's lesson with the wine gourd of *when we run faster we go up;* wondering how he could record this image in words the tribe would understand in future generations. 'So, is *centrifugal force* a god?' he asked.

'I think so,' said Mila. 'Billington said it is a part of *science*. And Brahim also believed in science, and a god called *Allah*. So I think science must be a god.'

'Science?' said Nnamdi. 'Trader once spoke of science but I did not understand, so I believed it to be a god. I thought it must be that, as Trader said it was the answer to all things.'

'That is what Billington told me,' said Mila.

'Ah, I think I understand,' said Nnamdi. 'It must be that science is the mother of centrifugal force.'

Mila shrugged his shoulders. 'I think so. Only a god could have helped me from the Cupola. And Billington explained the workings of the god science.'

'Then we must give thanks to both gods for returning you to us,' said Nnamdi. 'The Baja will worship both of Billington's gods from this day, and we will worship the god Allah, as he must also be the son of science.'

Mila continued his story and next told Nnamdi of the different tongues that were spoken in the *great civilisation*, including Trader's tongue and how the people such as Billington and Julieta could speak many of them. He also spoke about how there was a language for all to understand. 'I believe it was the pearl that helped me,' he said. 'Trader's tongue was a tongue for all the people. It was spoken for me on my journey by the fortune of the Yoonir pearl as Kobina had said.'

When Mila got to the part where he saw Kobina on the shore, Nnamdi smiled broadly. 'It is the Baja belief that the deceased do not manifest themselves in dreams to forgive, but appear as spirit in the waking twilight. Yes, Mila, you saw Kobina, but he was passed and no longer of this Earth. Also, the Yoonir star at its zenith has the power to incur dreams that are to become realities.' And Mila was comforted by this, remembering also his dreams of Billington, Andreas and Elijah.

Finally, Mila told the story of Trader's confession about the slave trade and asked Nnamdi to forgive him, but Nnamdi became silent and distant and dismissed Mila as his story was now finished, saying he needed time to meditate.

Later, Nnamdi emerged from the hut and declared that as Mila had safely returned from his journey, there were to be days of mourning in respect of those lost from his people.

The following day there was a quietness that permeated the village as the people of the Baja remembered their neighbour's losses. But there was also admiration and respectful compliments for Mila's survival and offerings of thanks and food for bringing Trader back to the village. Mila helped Trader unload the gifts that the people of Ancen Medina had given to him and Billington. Many were pleased and astonished at the workmanship of the metal and stone ware and amazed at the brightness of the dyed rolls of cloth, but the exchanges and conversation were subdued. The Baja people offered gifts in return as they would on Trader's visits, but Mila explained that they were gifts from the people of Ancen Medina and the *great civilisation* and they blessed Mila for bringing them with him.

Later that day Nnamdi spoke to Mila. 'Bring Trader to me,' he said. 'You will sit with me and listen to my decision about Trader…and tell me if I am wrong.'

But Trader went alone to Nnamdi's hut, saying to Mila that as a man who accepted his guilt, he wished no one to speak for him and must accept the justice of Nnamdi alone for his family's past and ask forgiveness for once being one of them. Later, Mila sat outside patiently awaiting Nnamdi's response for a long time.

Trader removed his hat and knelt before Nnamdi, saying: 'This is the greeting in my country before a man of greatness such as a king or for a man begging forgiveness.'

Nnamdi replied in Trader's tongue: 'I am no greater or smaller than any man.'

Trader spoke at length of his time involved with his family's *business*. And he retold his story as he had told it to Mila on their voyage home, and the sense of loss and sorrow for the people of Nnamdi's kind. Then he explained as much as he could of the way he tried to amend for his past, but then with much difficulty, he tried to explain to Nnamdi why it was dangerous for him to continue bringing the tribe *news*.

'That is most unfortunate,' said Nnamdi. 'I often wondered how it was that you knew about the slavers. We have come to rely on your *news* for a long time now.'

'But I will continue to help,' said Trader. 'For years I have gathered the information about the slaver's movements, but not just for the tribe. I have written and sent the information to the authorities in my own land. The *lightning ship* was one from my own people. And I will continue to write and remind them of their duty. The day will come when there will be no more slavers.'

Eventually, Nnamdi emerged from the hut with Trader and thanked him for all he had done for them in the past. Then Nnamdi called upon the people to gather round and as he explained Trader's story to them, he asked *them* to decide.

A grandmother stepped forward and looking deep into Trader's eyes she reached out, gently touching Trader's face she stroked his cheek then took his hand. 'It is good that you have come back to us, Trader,' she said.

Nnamdi smiled. 'That was my decision also,' he said and beckoned the people to come forward and touch Trader in his sorrow, that the spirit of their forgiveness might stay with him on his final voyage.

More days passed and Trader, although eager to depart, was grateful and at peace with himself having been forgiven and waited respectfully for the days of mourning to pass. During this time Mila took Julieta and they sheltered themselves away from others in the new hut his family had built in the Baja village. Little was spoken between any of them as Mila spent time meditating over the lost people and Julieta respectfully helped Mila's mother gather and prepare food and wash clothes while Mila's father went out to hunt.

One evening Mila's mother took him outside away from the hut to speak. 'She is very beautiful, Mila,' she said. 'But she is very unhappy, and an unhappy woman will not make a good wife. And *you* are unhappy. You do not have to tell me that you love her. You have the spirit of the girl as a wanderer in you now since you returned.'

On the fourth morning, as Nnamdi declared that there should be *no more sadness*, Julieta was found sitting on the beach silently scribing meaningless pictures in the sand with a twig as Trader prepared his boat for departure.

Mila approached cautiously and sat beside her watching Trader load provisions and check the riggings and sails. 'What have you decided to do, Julieta?' he asked softly.

'I would like to be with you always, Mila,' Julieta replied. 'You boy I could be family with, I like you very much, maybe love.'

Mila's heart lifted momentarily until Julieta continued. 'But I can't live here,' she said. 'Trader going now and maybe never come back. I can't even stay for some time and see. If I stay I never see Andalucia again.'

'Have you asked Trader to take you home?' asked Mila, but Julieta remained silent, continuing her scribbles in the sand.

Nnamdi came and joined them, sitting in the sand. 'Tell me, Mila, what is on your mind?' he asked.

But Mila was reluctant to admit his fear in front of Julieta. 'Slaves,' he said. 'There are so many others like Kobina that have been taken away from their villages. Trader has told us of these, and I still feel for them even though I do not know them, they are still in my mind like Kobina. I still feel that I should do something to honour Kobina's spirit. Maybe we can help, like Trader has done.'

'It is a great tragedy,' said Nnamdi. 'But those that are gone are gone forever.'

'But they may still be alive,' said Mila. 'Maybe we should look for them?'

Julieta looked up from her scribbling. 'Oh, you being real stupid child again,' she said. 'You learn nothing from big adventure, even though you see big ocean.'

'She is right, Mila,' said Nnamdi. 'The ocean is bigger than we can ever imagine, Trader tells us so, and you also know this to be true from the lesson of your journey. There is nothing we can do.'

There was a long silence as Mila reflected on Nnamdi's words and Julieta resumed her scribbling.

Nnamdi spoke again. 'Trader has told me of his new land. He plans to settle and pay people to help him work the land. He does not tell me everything that is on his mind, but my wisdom tells me that Trader would not turn you away if you wished to help him in his new adventure. He needs help in his new life. His duty was to return you to your own people, but now that duty is fulfilled he is unsure of what your heart desires and so will not ask you. He does not want to influence you in your time of grief.'

Mila sat silently watching Julieta with her head bowed quietly scribbling.

'And my wisdom also tells me,' Nnamdi continued, 'that you are not the only one unhappy at having to make a decision you are not certain about.'

Trader jumped down from the boat and waved, signalling that he had done and was about to depart. The villagers came down to the water's edge as Trader cast his lines and anchor up to the deck and climbed back on board as some of the villagers waded out to push his boat to sea.

Julieta dropped her stick and stood up, watching the people push Trader's boat out.

'Now is the time to decide, Mila,' Nnamdi gently whispered.

Mila hesitated as the boat cleared the sand underneath and bobbed in the surf. He jumped up sharply and grabbed Julieta by the hand. 'We go and help Trader?' he asked her. 'He said he wanted help. A fine strong pair of hands. Two pairs of hands!'

Julieta smiled. 'Maybe we be like family?'

Mila looked at the people, including his family, who'd gathered around them on the beach. His mother stepped forward, smiling. 'Be happy, Mila the wanderer,' she whispered, hugging the couple.

And Mila sprinted down the beach followed closely by Julieta who skipped and laughed and sang as she went.

'Trader, wait!' Mila cried as he dashed into the water.

Trader laughed as he jumped down from the boat and lifted the two children aboard.

As Trader winched the riggings and the sail picked up a good warm breeze of the coast winds, Nnamdi waded out into the sea waving. 'Remember, Mila,' he cried. 'Remember what I said about the journey!'

Mila waved and watched until the figure of Nnamdi, still stood in the sea, disappeared around the edge of the cove.

'The journey never ends,' he whispered.

Andreas: a true story

It's strange how a fleeting glimpse of something unusual or a chance meeting can imprint on your soul for a lifetime. I grew up in North America in the 1950s and '60s, a time when circuses and travelling shows were extremely popular. I won't name the particular show where I met 'Andreas,' should any innocent relatives of that family still survive. It is suffice to say that many fairgrounds, with all their usual rides, food stalls and attractions also featured a sideshow, or as they called it then, a 'freak show,' which included some of the 'attractions' you may have heard about from that era: the bearded lady, the two-headed snake, Siamese twins and people of all sizes shapes and deformities.

Some of the attractions were restricted by age limits, considered to be too odd for the eyes of young children. However, as a boy of ten years, strolling through the grounds with my father, I was captivated by a poster outside a marquee and a show master in black suit and top hat bellowing to the crowd to witness the 'star' attraction of his travelling show...the Giant. The poster depicted a huge, fierce looking man, towering above and dwarfing the show master. Fascinated, I begged my father to go in and see him, so out came my father's dollar and in we went.

I don't remember every single detail about the Giant, but suffice to say he was big, and I mean BIG. He was, as I recall, described by the show master as being in excess of eight feet tall. But he was also very broad, not particularly fat but quite muscular. And, just as I have described Andreas in the story, he was bearded with black, curly, shoulder length hair which framed an odd shaped, but kindly looking face with a jaw that was wider than the rest. He was dressed in a leopard skin toga and he was chained by his left foot. This frightened me at first as the show master was also telling the people to stay well back behind the rope line. It wasn't until much later in life that I realised this was part of the show, to enhance the sense of danger in the Giant's presence. But as I passed by, the Giant, sensing my fear, winked and smiled at me and I at once felt at ease.

But above all, the image that sticks in my mind to this day is that he was eating at the time, having his lunch. And each time a few of the crowd walked by, the show master would prompt the Giant with a whispered 'stand, stand!' and a tap with a stick on the Giants huge chair. And the poor man would place his plate of food down and stand up, raise his arms, flex his biceps and pound a fist against his chest. Then, just as in the story, he would pick from a bowl of huge copper rings, place one on his forefinger as the show master would ask the crowd to marvel at the size of the Giant's hands and urge the people to buy a ring (another dollar) as a 'once in a lifetime opportunity' to prove that they had actually seen this wonder of the world. Then the Giant would sit again, for the briefest of time as he ate a little more lunch, before he was prompted once again to repeat his performance.

Now, I remember that this sideshow ran from ten o'clock in the morning until ten at night, so the Giant had to be put through this pitiful performance twelve hours a day without a break. I felt so sorry for the man and the image of him having to have his meals as he was forced to act like a circus elephant has stuck with me throughout my life and I often think about him and wonder what happened to him. I remember from the poster that he had been in a Hollywood B movie playing a giant, of course, but my research has drawn a blank and I don't think he even had a name, that's probably how dismissive his 'keeper' was of the poor man's humanity.

After that, I used to fantasise about releasing the man and taking him to a better life. As in the story, I imagined sneaking into the marquee at night and cutting his chains with my father's hacksaw, and giving him some money to find his way home. I even disclosed this idea to a friend and suggested he help me. But my friend laughed at the notion and said that the giant would simply pick me up and crush me, stamp on my head and even eat parts of my dead body before rampaging through the city destroying everything he could. I got really angry at that and ended up in a fight, resulting in us both having bloody noses.

Of course, I never did attempt to carry out such a plan, but I tried to imagine that eventually the Giant got away, or retired to somewhere nice where he was well off and had friends and family to care for him. But as I grew older, I realised that the truth was probably much harsher, that the man probably received no wages and was likely released into poverty without any backup plan for his future once he was past his usefulness.

By writing Andreas' place in The Ray Hunters, I feel some consolation for not having carried out my fantasy, that I have given the Giant some history. I like to think, and although it's unlikely, that the man found some peace and happiness at last.

He will have been long gone now, and I hope his spirit looks kindly upon me for telling his story, albeit in fiction.

Andy Jarvis

Fact from fiction. Notes from the author.

Ancen Medina: the name of this fictional market is similar to the area of port on the outskirts of Casablanca, Morocco, the 'old medina' quarter of the city nowadays referred to as 'Ancienne Medina,' from the French influence. This particular part of the story is not meant to be representative of the area, and is pure fiction.

Barbary Pirates: These were promoted by a collection of North African states in the Mediterranean and beyond for several centuries. The Barbary pirates were Muslim pirates, however, they would take on others, usually as slaves, from a diversity of backgrounds, converting them to Islam. The operations of the Barbary pirates became such a menace to merchant shipping that some countries, notably the United States would pay financial tribute to the Barbary States.

So long as the American colonies were a part of the British Empire, their commercial vessels were protected from attack by the annual tribute London was paying the Barbary States. However, ratification of the 1783 Treaty of Paris recognizing America brought that protection to an end. In October 1784, the American merchant brig Betsy was seized on the high seas and taken with its crew of eleven to Morocco.

Lacking both a naval force to protect American commerce and the ability to compel the American states to furnish the necessary funds to provide for a navy, the Continental Congress, deciding to follow the European lead, authorized eighty thousand U.S. dollars to "negotiate peace" with Morocco to obtain the release of the prisoners. Not surprisingly, two weeks after a ransom was paid and the crew of Betsy were freed, corsairs from Algiers seized two other American vessels, with twenty-one hostages. More soon followed. The conditions of imprisonment were such that by the time peace was purchased in 1796, only 85 of the 131 American hostages imprisoned in Algiers remained alive.

Thomas Jefferson's success in the election of 1800 gave him the opportunity to try the policy of 'peace through strength' that he had been *advocating throughout his government. His cabinet meeting of 15 May 1801 was devoted to a discussion of whether two-thirds of the new American navy - created by Congress during the Adams administration - should be sent to the Mediterranean to protect American merchant ships. The cabinet unanimously concurred in the desirability of the expedition and also agreed that if, upon arrival at Gibraltar its commander, Captain Richard Dale, learned that war had been declared against the United States, he was to distribute his forces 'so as best to protect our commerce and chastise their insolence - by sinking, burning or destroying their ships and vessels wherever you shall find them.'*

The United States fought two separate wars with Tripoli (1801 – 1805) and Algiers (1815 – 1816) The Barbary States, although they did not capture any more U.S. ships, did resume raids in the Mediterranean until the French conquest of Algeria in 1830.

The Mediterranean Squadron of the U. S. Navy operated up until 1860 to suppress the renegade piracy that still existed after the Barbary Wars.

Berbers: the Berber people were the pre-Arab native inhabitants of much of Northern Africa. Today they live in scattered communities across Morocco, Libya, Algeria, Tunisia, Egypt, Mali, Niger and Mauretania.

Centrifugal Force: In physics, the tendency of an object following a curved path to fly away from the centre of curvature. Centrifugal force is not a true force; it is a form of inertia (the tendency of objects that are moving in a straight line to continue moving in a straight line). Centrifugal force is referred to as a 'force for convenience,' because it balances centripetal force, which is a true force. If a ball is swung on the end of a string, the string exerts centripetal force on the ball and causes it to follow a curved path. The ball is said to exert centrifugal force on the string, tending to break the string and causing it to fly off on a tangent.

Dika: An edible fruit indigenous to West Africa. Resembling a small mango, it is much valued and has a variety of culinary uses.

Helike: The Greek word for 'willow,' from which is derived 'salic,' or salacylic acid, more commonly known as aspirin.

Lingua Franca: A language that is adopted as a common language between speakers whose native languages are different. Formerly a mixture of Italian with French, Greek, Arabic, and Spanish, formerly used in the eastern Mediterranean up until the 18th century. Since the 19th century English, being the most widely spread language in the world, has become the more used lingua franca of the modern age.

Railways: There were no plans in 1830 to build a railway across North Africa to the Red Sea. The railways and locomotive building was a rapidly developing industry in Britain at the height of the Industrial Revolution and contributed to making Britain the richest country in the world. Robert Stephenson and Company set up manufacturing locomotives in 1823 with his father George Stephenson, the inventor of 'Stephenson's Rocket.' The first railway proposal in Egypt came about when the Pasha Mahomet-Ali asked the British engineer T.H. Galloway to design a railway in 1834. However, little progress was made. Progress was really made when in 1849 Muhammad Ali died, and in 1851 his successor Abbas I contracted Robert Stephenson to build Egypt's first standard gauge railway.

Seyaad: An Arabic word meaning 'hunter,' appropriately enough for a ship of the Barbary corsairs.

Slavery: An act prohibiting the importation of slaves to the United States was passed in 1807, although the trade itself did not cease. For many years rogue traders smuggled slaves from West Africa to the colonies, such was the demand for unwaged labour. Slavery itself was not abolished in the U.S. until 1865. In 1808 the British Parliament passed the Slave Trade Act of 1807, which outlawed the slave trade, but again, not slavery itself. Emancipation Day was celebrated in the British Caribbean on

August 1st 1834 following the Slavery Abolition Act of 1833.

Xebec: The xebec was usually a lanteen-rigged (triangular sail on a yard at 45 degrees to the mast) sailing ship with exceptional speed making them historically popular with North African pirates. The later Polacre Xebecs, larger but still very fast and capable of carrying more crew, employed a combination of lanteen and square mast sails. Not quite as well armed as a European frigate, xebecs could carry a formidable arsenal of 12 to 18 pound shot cannons. Their excellent sailing characteristics and manoeuvrability made them particularly suitable for hunting wealthy merchant vessels.

Yoonir star: The 'Star of Yoonir' is part of the cosmos of the Serer people of West Africa. It is very important and sacred and just one of many symbols in Serer religion and cosmology. It is the brightest star in the night sky, known as Sirius or the Dog Star in contemporary astronomy and was well known to many ancient civilisations. The practices of the people in the two villages of 'The Ray Hunters,' are not meant to be an accurate representation of those of the Serer, the second largest ethnic group located in Senegal and the Gambia of West Africa. The Serer represent an African people with an extensive religious history and a wide diversity of practices that follow the pattern of many West African people.

The Author

Andy Jarvis was born in Hertfordshire, England. He grew up in Western Canada where his earliest writing was for a high school newspaper as a teen. He currently resides in the north of England where he took up writing again in 2002, after gaining an Open College of the North West diploma in Advanced Creative Writing.

'The Ray Hunters' is his third novel. His first novel, 'Isabel's Light,' was published in 2008 and his second novel 'Solway Tide' in 2014.